Jesse had been too conscious of Shea McAllister from the moment he'd seen her.

And talking to her had only made it worse.

He should see only a felon standing in front of him, a person who was breaking the law. Instead, _____ woman, one who was clea_____.

He stoo_____ toward the hou_____ the sway of her h_____ matter, he told himself. He didn't car___ ___ was Miss America. Shea McAllister was breaking the law, and she would pay. He'd come to Cameron to stop her, and he was going to do just that.

No matter how good she looked in a pair of jeans.

Dear Reader,

Once again, we're back to offer you six fabulous romantic novels, the kind of book you'll just long to curl up with on a warm spring day. Leading off the month is award-winner Marie Ferrarella, whose *This Heart for Hire* is a reunion romance filled with the sharply drawn characters and witty banter you've come to expect from this talented writer.

Then check out Margaret Watson's *The Fugitive Bride,* the latest installment in her CAMERON, UTAH, miniseries. This FBI agent hero is about to learn all about love at the hands of his prime suspect. *Midnight Cinderella* is Eileen Wilks' second book for the line, and it's our WAY OUT WEST title. After all, there's just nothing like a cowboy! Our FAMILIES ARE FOREVER flash graces Kayla Daniels' *The Daddy Trap,* about a resolutely single hero faced with fatherhood—and love. *The Cop and Calamity Jane* is a suspenseful romp from the pen of talented Elane Osborn; you'll be laughing out loud as you read this one. Finally, welcome Linda Winstead Jones to the line. Already known for her historical romances, this author is about to make a name for herself in contemporary circles with *Bridger's Last Stand.*

Don't miss a single one—and then rejoin us next month, when we bring you six more examples of the best romantic writing around.

Yours,

Leslie J. Wainger
Executive Senior Editor

Please address questions and book requests to:
Silhouette Reader Service
U.S.: 3010 Walden Ave., P.O. Box 1325, Buffalo, NY 14269
Canadian: P.O. Box 609, Fort Erie, Ont. L2A 5X3

THE FUGITIVE BRIDE

MARGARET WATSON

Silhouette®

INTIMATE™ MOMENTS®

Published by Silhouette Books

America's Publisher of Contemporary Romance

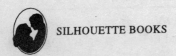

SILHOUETTE BOOKS

ISBN 0-373-07920-6

THE FUGITIVE BRIDE

Copyright © 1999 by Margaret Watson

This edition published by arrangement with Harlequin Books S.A.

Printed in U.S.A.

Books by Margaret Watson

Silhouette Intimate Moments

An Innocent Man #636
An Honorable Man #708
To Save His Child #750
The Dark Side of the Moon #779
†*Rodeo Man* #873
†*For the Children* #886
†*Cowboy with a Badge* #904
†*The Fugitive Bride* #920

† Cameron, Utah

MARGARET WATSON

From the time she learned to read, Margaret could usually be found with her nose in a book. Her lifelong passion for reading led to her interest in writing, and now she's happily writing exactly the kind of stories she likes to read. Margaret is a veterinarian who lives in the Chicago suburbs with her husband and their three daughters. In her spare time she enjoys in-line skating, birdwatching and spending time with her family. Readers can write to Margaret at P.O. Box 2333, Naperville, IL 60567-2333.

For Katy. I am so proud that you're my daughter. Your grace, your laughter and your loving heart fill my life with joy. I love you.

Chapter 1

The steer clearly had a death wish.

Shea McAllister let the rope attached to his halter slide through her hands as she narrowed her eyes and watched the Hereford put on a show. She'd tried four times to get him into the chute, and each time he'd managed to evade it. This time, he shook his head and snorted at her, danced sideways away from the chute, bucked a few times, then turned and ambled across the corral.

Still holding onto the rope, she stalked after him. Becca Farrell, the ranch's veterinarian, would be here soon to sew up the laceration on his flank, and Shea had promised to have the steer in the metal contraption designed to hold him still.

"You're treading on thin ice here, buddy," she called out to the animal. The steer's ears twitched. "You want to make that trip to the stockyards a few months early, that's fine with me."

Reaching the animal's head, she grabbed his halter. "If not, you might want to go into that chute over there." Leaning into the animal's massive side, she pushed until the steer turned around. Then she pulled on the rope again, moving him slowly toward the narrow metal contraption.

They'd only gone a few steps when her dog leapt into the corral, barking happily. The steer's ears twitched again, then he stopped and turned to look at the dog.

Shea wiped the sweat and dust from her forehead with an impatient swipe of her arm. Buster was crouched down behind the steer, rear end up in the air, tail wagging. Clearly he thought this was a wonderful game.

Shaking her head, Shea felt herself grinning. "Buster, you are about the most worthless dog I've ever seen. Get over here."

She snapped her fingers and the shaggy yellow dog scrambled to respond. Scratching his head, she told him, "Go find Maria. Find Maria, Buster."

Buster tilted his head, then with a yip he raced out of the corral in the direction of the house. Still grinning, Shea turned back to the steer.

"Now it's your turn, buddy. You want to go into that chute, or would you rather be on the next truck out of town?"

When the steer showed no interest in moving, Shea applied her shoulder to his side and shoved. He moved a couple of steps, and Shea shoved again. She had managed to edge him halfway to the chute when she heard a truck pull up to the corral and stop.

"See what you've done?" she muttered as she shoved at the animal again. "Here's Becca and you're not even in the chute. It would serve you right if I just shagged your sorry tail back out into the pasture."

But the laceration needed to be sutured, so she braced herself and pushed at the steer again.

"Looks like you could use some help."

The low, slightly raspy masculine voice wrapped around her, strumming across nerves she hadn't even known she had. Despite the heat of the Utah spring sun, a shiver chased down her back.

Spinning around, she dropped the rope attached to the

steer's halter. "Who are you?" she asked the stranger leaning against the corral fence.

Instead of answering, he vaulted across the fence and grabbed the rope from the ground. Jamming his shoulder into the steer's side, he swept off his hat and used it to smack the steer's tail. At the same time he let out a yell.

The startled animal jumped forward, and the stranger merely aimed him at the chute. A minute later, the steer stood secured in the metal apparatus.

"That was slick," Shea said, watching the man dust his hat off against his leg, then replace it on his head.

He shrugged, and his hazel eyes crinkled in a smile. A crease that would have been called a dimple in a prettier man flashed, then disappeared. "It was all in the timing. I surprised him."

"You surprised me, too." Shea let her gaze drift over him once more, then extended her hand. "Thanks for your help. I'm Shea McAllister."

If she hadn't been watching so closely, she would have missed the start of surprise in his eyes. It was gone in a moment, his face smoothly blank as he touched the brim of his hat with one hand and reached for hers with the other. "I'm Jesse Coulton."

His hand was hard and calloused as it closed around hers. He gripped her fingers firmly, and for just a moment a sense of rightness swept over her, a feeling of belonging. But that was ridiculous. Slipping her hand out of his, she flexed her fingers and said, "What can I do for you, Mr. Coulton?"

Again, if she hadn't been watching so closely, she would have missed the flicker in his eyes. An instant later he smiled ruefully. "I don't suppose you'll believe me when I tell you I had no idea who you were?"

She did believe him. The instant of startled shock in his eyes when she'd told him her name hadn't been rehearsed. "Were you looking for me?"

"I was." His gaze touched on the house, the barn and the outbuildings, then lingered on the mountains behind them. "I heard you could use some help."

"You're looking for a job?" He'd surprised her again.

He nodded. "The word in town is that you're short-handed. I need a job." He smiled again, a slow grin that spread across his face and lingered in his eyes. "It sounded like a perfect match to me."

Because her stomach fluttered when he grinned, Shea took a step backward. "We need another hand, but I have no intention of hiring the first person who drives through the gates," she said coolly. "I appreciate your help with the steer, but I'll need to see some references. And I'll check them."

The grin stayed on his face, but his eyes sharpened. "I wouldn't expect anyone to hire me without checking my references. I have a list in my truck that I'll give you."

"I'll take a look at it." She didn't like the way his smile made her insides churn, or the way his voice beckoned to her. "What experience have you had?"

His eyes flickered over the barn again, and when he looked back at her, his grin had faded and there was a hard edge to his gaze. "I grew up in a small town back east, working on farms. I've worked all over, but mostly in Wyoming and Montana for the last several years, running cattle on the range and taking care of whatever needed to be done. I do a good job."

He sounded like one of the drifters who was drawn to ranch work, staying at one place only until he got an urge to move on. It was a common enough story in the west, and no one thought twice about men showing up at a ranch, looking for a job.

But there was something different about Jesse Coulton. Shea studied him, wondering what it was. There was a determination in his eyes that she didn't see in the other drifters who wandered by, looking for work. His eyes glinted with intelligence, and a hardness that wasn't due to years of drifting. There was a dangerous edge to the look in Jesse Coulton's eyes.

She couldn't hire him, she decided abruptly. She would never be comfortable, never feel safe with those knowing eyes of his watching her. There was too much at stake for her, for the ranch.

She had too much to hide.

"Why don't you give me your list of references? I'll check with them and get back to you."

Instead of retrieving the papers from his truck, he stood and studied her. "You have no intention of hiring me, do you?" he said after a moment.

Her hands tightened around the rope that had been attached to the steer's halter, then she threw it to the ground. "I don't hire anyone until I've thoroughly checked their references." She smiled thinly. "That includes cowboys who try to hustle me into making a decision. Let me know where you're staying, and I'll get in touch with you."

Instead of the anger she expected to see, his mouth curved up. His eyes crinkled and his cheek creased again, and her stomach quivered once more.

"I'll bet there aren't too many cowboys who try to hustle you more than once," he said, tossing her a grin over his shoulder as he walked to his truck. "Personally, I like a woman who can stare me down."

"How do you feel about a woman who can knock you on your butt?" she muttered as he rummaged in his truck. She thought she had Jesse Coulton figured out, and he'd surprised her. And intrigued her, although she hated to admit it.

But it would still be too dangerous to hire him.

She couldn't take a chance with Jesse Coulton's knowing eyes, she thought, glancing involuntarily toward the mountains and the small cabin tucked next to a lake up there. Especially right now.

She watched Jesse open the cab of his truck and reach inside. His muscles rippled beneath worn denim and chambray, and she remembered how easily he'd muscled the steer into the chute. His long, lean body would be hard and tough, she thought, honed by physical labor. When he shook her hand, his fingers and palms had been hard, too, calloused and rough. But remembering the way his eyes had softened when he smiled, she suspected that there were times when those rough hands could be very gentle.

Suddenly realizing what she was thinking, she felt her cheeks flood with color. Appalled at herself, she wanted to flee, but instead she straightened her spine and held her ground. She'd look at his references, then say a polite goodbye. And the only other contact she'd have with Jesse Coulton would be via the telephone.

"Here you go," he said, handing her a brown manila envelope.

She told herself to wait until he was gone. It would be easier to dismiss Jesse if he wasn't standing and watching her. But she opened the envelope anyway, suddenly intensely curious about what his former employers had to say about him.

A few minutes later she raised her head to study him. "Your former employers seem to think you walk on water." She kept her voice neutral.

He shrugged. "I believe in giving an honest day's work for what I get in my pay envelope."

"Apparently so." She slid the papers back into the envelope. "Will they say the same things when I call them?"

He shrugged again. "I have no reason not to think so."

"Where are you staying in town, Mr. Coulton?"

"The name's Jesse. And I'm staying at Mrs. Corboy's boardinghouse."

Shea smothered a grin. "Not for long, I'm betting." Melba Corboy's food had driven more than one boarder away. Her sister-in-law, Carly, had been the only person in recent memory who had stayed at Melba's for more than a couple of days. "I'll call you there as soon as I have a chance to contact these people."

"Fine." He watched her carefully, and a look she couldn't interpret flickered over his face. "But in the meantime, you'd suggest I keep looking for a job, right?"

"That's up to you, Mr. Coulton. I won't make a decision before I talk to your references." Shea hated the prim sound of her voice, but suddenly she wanted Jesse Coulton to go away. She didn't like the way her body reacted when he was around, and she didn't like the direction her thoughts took. She was in charge of the Red Rock Ranch, but she suspected that, even if he was working for her, she would never be in charge of Jesse Coulton.

He tipped his hat to the back of his head as he studied her. "From what I heard in town, I didn't figure Shea McAllister for a coward. I thought you'd be a woman who trusted her own instincts to make a decision."

Shea felt her temper rising and tried to grab hold of it with both hands. "I wouldn't be much of a businesswoman if I trusted my instincts," she shot back. "There's a reason people ask for references. I've seen plenty of charming men smile as they slipped a knife between someone's ribs."

"I'm glad to know that you consider me charming."

Was he purposely trying to antagonize her? "I don't care if you've gone to charm school, Coulton. The only thing that matters on this ranch is if you can do the work, and that's what I intend to find out. In the meantime, I suggest you stop pushing. I'll let you know if you have a job when I'm good and ready." She was about to turn and walk away when a familiar truck pulled into the yard.

Becca Farrell eased her way out of the truck, then walked slowly over to where she and Jesse stood. "Hi, Shea. Is that steer all ready for me?"

Shea took a deep breath and tried to block Jesse from her mind. She had work to do today. "He's in the chute," she said, studying the woman in front of her. "Are you sure you should be out here doing this, Becca?"

The veterinarian smiled at her and put one hand on her protruding abdomen. "Cut it out, Shea. You sound just like Grady and I hear enough of that at home. I'm perfectly capable of suturing up a laceration on a steer."

"What can we do to help you?"

Jesse spoke up, and Becca glanced over at him. "Are you the man who was asking about jobs in town?"

Jesse nodded, and Becca turned back to Shea. "Thank

goodness you've finally hired someone to help you, Shea.
It's about time. Dev must have put his foot down.''

"I haven't hired him yet," Shea muttered, feeling the jaws
of a trap tensing to spring shut. "He stopped by to ask about
work, and I haven't had a chance to check his references.''

"Well, let's give him a working audition," Becca said.
Turning to Jesse, she waved in the direction of her truck.
"There's a stool and a leather bag in the back of my truck.
You can put them over next to the chute, then give me a
hand.''

When Jesse disappeared in the direction of Becca's truck,
Shea said in a low voice, "Why'd you do that, Becca? I'm
not going to hire him.''

"Why not?" She watched Jesse set the stool down near
the laceration on the steer's side, then open her bag and set
up what she'd need. "He looks like he knows what he's
doing. And he's not hard on the eyes, either.''

"I have no intention of hiring someone just because he's
easy to look at," Shea snapped. "In fact, that alone would
make me not want to hire him. Kyle Diggett acted like he
knew what he was doing, too.''

Becca turned to look at her. "Not everyone who's looking
for a job is going to be another Kyle, Shea. Do you really
think this guy is like that?''

"No." Shea forced herself to be honest. "His references
all raved about him. I don't think he'd steal from me. But
there's something about him, about his eyes. He looks hard.''

Becca grinned. "The hard ones are the most fun to tame.
Trust me on that.''

Shea's mouth twitched, but she shook her head. "I'm not
interested in taming anyone, especially a man who's working
for me." She turned away from Becca's suddenly sympa-
thetic eyes. "I just don't think he'd work out for us, that's
all.''

"Why don't you give him a chance?" Becca said quietly.
"He could be just what you need. You made a mistake with
Kyle, but that doesn't mean you'd do the same with this guy.
We don't get too many men wandering through Cameron,

looking for work. And Joe, Dusty and Levi aren't getting any younger. They could use some help.''

''I know that.'' Her voice was low as she watched Levi walk slowly out of the barn in the distance. ''They've worked on the Red Rock since I was a baby. I know they need a younger man in here to help them, but they would never admit it. The three of them are more stubborn than a matched set of Missouri mules.''

''Then present them with a done deal.'' Becca spoke briskly as she walked toward the steer and the waiting Jesse. ''Hire this guy, at least on a temporary basis, and make everyone's life a little easier.'' She slanted Shea a look. ''Including your own.''

''My life is exactly how I want it.''

''Sure, Shea, everyone loves working twenty-hour days and having no social life.'' She rolled her eyes. ''Tell me another one, why don't you?''

Shea laughed. ''I thought Grady would have fixed that smart mouth of yours by now.''

Becca grinned. ''Grady is very fond of my smart mouth.''

''I noticed,'' she answered, her voice dry.

Shea hung back and watched as Jesse helped Becca settle herself on the stool, then handed her what she needed to suture up the steer. He seemed to anticipate every move the veterinarian made, handing her the proper instruments and efficiently cleaning everything up after she had finished suturing the laceration. He listened as she gave him instructions for the steer's care, then carried the stool and bag of instruments back to her car.

''He's a gem, Shea,'' Becca said when he was out of earshot. ''Grab him. You'd be a fool to let him get away.''

''I can't, Becca.'' Shea kept her voice low as she watched for Jesse to emerge from behind the truck. ''I don't think he'd take well to having a woman as his boss.''

It was a lame excuse, but it was the only one she could think of quickly. Everything that Becca said was true. Jesse Coulton appeared to be the perfect employee.

Which was exactly why she couldn't hire him.

It would be too dangerous to have someone as smart and perceptive as Jesse around the Red Rock Ranch. But she couldn't tell Becca that, either.

Becca shook her head. "You're nuts, Shea," she said as she walked to her truck. "I'll be back in a few days to check on that steer, although he should be fine. Keep him close by, just in case."

"Thanks, Becca. I will."

Shea watched as Becca drove away, then turned reluctantly to face Jesse again. "Thanks for helping Becca out. She said you did a good job."

He nodded once. "I like working with animals," he said, and Shea saw the sincerity in his eyes. "You generally know what to expect with a steer or a horse." He looked down as Buster raced up next to him, then squatted in the dust in front of him, his rear end wriggling. Jesse smiled, and his eyes gentled as he reached down to pet the dog. "You generally know what to expect from a dog, too."

No, Shea thought as she watched him with Buster, Jesse didn't strike her as a thief. She wasn't afraid that Jesse would steal from her or from Joe, Dusty and Levi the way Kyle Diggett had done. But if she hired him, she'd have a whole lot more to worry about than money missing from her house.

If she hired Jesse, she would put her carefully constructed arrangement in jeopardy. She'd worry constantly about the safety of the refugees hiding in the cabin up by the lake. And the one thing she wouldn't do was endanger those children.

Jesse gave the yellow dog one final pat, then straightened up. Shea's eyes narrowed as she watched him, speculation darkening their bright blue depths. What was she thinking? he wondered.

He wasn't sure, and he reluctantly conceded the first round to her. He would win in the end, he was sure of that, but she had surprised him. He had expected to easily goad her into hiring him. Word at May's, the bar that stood at the edge of Cameron, was that Shea McAllister had a hair-trigger temper and could be pushed into acting rashly if you handled her the right way.

But all the handling so far had been on her part, he ruefully acknowledged. And not only had he been unable to secure a job on the Red Rock Ranch, but he'd managed to alienate her at the same time.

It was time for different tactics. "Thanks for your time, ma'am," he said, touching the brim of his hat. "I'll look forward to hearing from you."

Her eyes narrowed even more. "It's too late to try the polite, subservient routine with me, Coulton. You're good, but I've seen too many of your type. Slick cowboys are a dime a dozen in Utah. So stuff it back in your hat. You're not doing your cause any favors."

Damn, but he was going to enjoy taking her down. It wasn't often that he found an adversary who could match wits with him. "Sorry, Ms. McAllister. I didn't mean to offend you."

He saw her lips twitch and knew she wanted to hide the smile. "Really? That's funny, I had just the opposite impression."

"Now why would I want to offend you when I want you to hire me?"

"That's just what I was wondering." She swiped her arm over her forehead and left behind a smear of red dust. "What's going on, Coulton?"

He was getting sloppy, he thought with disgust. Or maybe he was getting arrogant, which was worse. He'd never had this kind of problem before. No matter what the situation, he always fit right in. He'd never had any trouble getting hired. Shea McAllister was the first suspect who had challenged him.

She was also the first suspect who'd stirred such an immediate, intense physical reaction.

He'd noticed her the moment he'd pulled up in the yard. She was ridiculously slender to be wrestling with a steer that size. But when he'd looked closer, he'd noticed the curves that were only partially hidden by denim and flannel. And although her face wouldn't be considered classically beautiful, the animation and passion that filled her eyes made it certain he wouldn't soon forget her.

He shrugged, trying to ignore his body's reaction to her. "I'm desperate, I guess. I need a job. I'm down to my last fifty bucks. And you were the only place around that sounded promising." It didn't bother him to beg. He'd try anything that worked. He'd gone to a lot of trouble to set up his background and get hired by Shea McAllister.

She didn't change her posture, but deep in her eyes he saw a slight softening. "If I don't hire you, there are other places around Cameron you can try. I'll give you the names."

It would be more difficult, but if he couldn't wrest a job from Shea, he'd settle for another ranch close by. And he would still take her down.

"I appreciate that."

She shrugged and turned away. "No problem. I'd expect my neighbors to do the same."

Before he could answer, an older cowboy came walking slowly out of the barn. When he saw them, he changed directions and headed toward them.

"Hey, Shea." The old cowboy stopped in front of her and pushed his hat to the back of his head. "I have a stall ready for that steer. Thought you might want to keep him close by for a few days." He nodded at the steer, who still stood in the chute in the corral.

"Thanks, Dusty. I'll help you move him in a minute." Her eyes softened as she spoke to the old man, and she touched his shoulder. "Why don't you get some lunch in the meantime? Maria should have it just about ready."

Dusty hesitated, then nodded. "Maybe I will. Don't you move that steer until I help you, hear?"

"I won't," she assured the old man.

She waited until the cowboy had walked toward the house, then turned back to Jesse. "Thanks again, Coulton. I've got a lot of work to do. I'll be in touch."

Her eyes had lost their hard edge, and when she glanced at the old cowboy, he saw real affection. He'd call it love, if he believed in the emotion. And suddenly he realized why she'd been wrestling with the steer herself when he arrived. She was trying to take some of the burden from the old men she had working for her.

"Do you have anyone working for you besides Dusty and the other old cowboy I saw when I got here?"

The softness disappeared from her eyes and her chin lifted. "I have three hands to help me."

"Let me guess. The third one is just as old as the other two."

Her chin lifted even higher. "I prefer to think of it as experience. Not age."

Jesse shook his head, watching Dusty as he reached the house. He gripped the rail tightly as he walked up the stairs. There was no way he could help Shea move that steer. "You're doing most of the work around here yourself." He hoped his voice didn't reflect his shock.

"Joe, Dusty and Levi do a lot." Her voice was cool as she faced him. "My mother is here in the summer, and my brother is available to help whenever I need him. Believe me, Coulton, I'm not desperate enough to hire just anyone."

"This isn't about a job," he said, more roughly than he'd intended. "My God, how do you manage?"

"I manage just fine. I've never been afraid of hard work. I love this ranch, and I'll do whatever it takes to keep it running." Her voice quivered with passion.

Including taking money for smuggling illegal immigrants into the country, men who were wanted criminals in their own country? he thought grimly, and he felt his face harden. He'd needed the reminder. For a moment there, he'd begun to admire Shea McAllister.

Of course she'd have old men working for her. They were probably so grateful to have a job that they looked the other way at her illegal activities. And if she had to work hard herself, she was being well paid for it. With all the money she was collecting for the smuggled criminals, she had to be socking away a small fortune. In a few years she could disappear and never have to work again.

Another old man came walking across the yard, giving Shea a casual wave, and then he, too, disappeared into the house. Shea turned back to Jesse and held out her hand. He only hesitated for a moment before he took it.

He didn't want to feel that connection again, that shock of awareness that had jolted him the first time he'd shaken her hand. He'd been too conscious of Shea McAllister from the moment he'd gotten out of his truck and seen her wrestling with the steer. And talking to her, mentally jousting with her, had only made it worse.

He should see only a felon standing in front of him, a person who was breaking the law. Instead, he saw an attractive woman, one who was clearly unaware of her own beauty. The light that filled her eyes when she spoke animated a striking face. And the passion that made her body quiver only emphasized her slender, graceful strength.

But he shook her hand again, unable to find a reason not to. And the jolt of awareness was worse, this time. It skittered over the edge into attraction.

"Thank you for stopping by, Mr. Coulton," she said firmly. "I'll let you know about the job in a day or two."

He stood and watched as she hurried toward the house, unable to look away from the sway of her hips under the denim. It didn't matter, he told himself.

He didn't care if she was Miss America. Shea McAllister was breaking the law, and she would pay. He'd come to Cameron to stop her, and by God, he was going to do just that.

No matter how good she looked in a pair of jeans.

Chapter 2

Jesse heard the stairs creak and was instantly awake. It took only a moment for him to remember that he was in Melba Corboy's boardinghouse, and relax back into the bed. He didn't have to worry about creaking stairs, at least not yet. As far as anyone knew, he was just a drifter cowboy, looking for a job.

The footsteps stopped at his door. "Mr. Coulton?"

It was his landlady's voice. He scrambled out of bed and dragged his jeans on. "Yes?"

"There's a telephone call for you." She paused. "I think it's urgent."

What could have happened? He'd given his boss the phone number, with the instructions to use it only in a dire emergency. "I'll be right there."

Throwing on a shirt, he wrenched open the door and ran down the stairs, still working on the buttons on his shirt. He grabbed the receiver off the small table that held the phone. "Hello?"

"Mr. Coulton?"

He recognized Shea McAllister's low, husky voice immediately. It was only because she was the reason he was in Cameron, he told himself. "Yes?"

"This is Shea McAllister. Are you still interested in a job at the Red Rock Ranch?" She tried to sound cool and businesslike, but underneath her voice he could hear the panic, tightly controlled.

"Yes," he said, cautious. "Are you offering me one?"

"Yes. When can you start?"

"How about right away?"

"That would be fine." He heard her let out her breath, a small sigh of relief. "Bring your pack with you. We have a bunkhouse you can use."

"I'll be there later this morning."

"I'll be looking for you."

She set the receiver down with a small click, and Jesse stood staring at the phone for a long moment. What had happened to make her change her mind? Because when he'd left the ranch yesterday morning, he'd been sure that she had no intention of hiring him.

He didn't care. Replacing the phone in its cradle, he ran back up the stairs. It only took a few minutes to replace all his belongings in the duffel bag he was using. It took a few more to settle his bill with Mrs. Corboy and throw the bag into his truck. Within a half hour he was driving out of Cameron toward the Red Rock Ranch.

Whatever the reason Shea had changed her mind, he'd been given his opportunity, and he'd make the most of it. He'd find the evidence that Shea was smuggling criminals into the United States, and he'd stop her. Then he'd move on to his next assignment.

It was the way he'd worked for years, and it was the way he wanted it to be. He wasn't interested in entanglements. He had no use for them in his profession, and he had no wish for them in his personal life. He traveled alone and quickly, and he did a good job. All the certificates of commendation he'd received from the FBI over the years said so.

An image of Shea McAllister floated into his mind, but instead of pushing it away, he let it linger there. He was attracted to her. He was willing to admit that, even if only to himself. But she was a suspect, so that was as far as the attraction would go. They'd had good information about her illegal activities, information from what seemed to be an un-impeachable source. And her actions the day before had only confirmed his suspicions.

She needed help desperately. He'd been in town for a few days, talked to a lot of people. It wasn't difficult to steer the conversation around to the largest ranch in the area. And the opinions were unanimous. The McAllisters needed help, big time.

So if she hadn't had something to hide, Shea should have jumped at the chance to hire another hand. Especially one as highly recommended as he had been. His mouth curled up slightly as he negotiated a long curve. He should know. He'd written the recommendations himself.

The Bureau would back him up, if and when she made the phone calls to check on his references. But he suspected that she had no intention of calling.

He pictured Shea again, her long, curly blond hair pulled back in a sloppy ponytail, her hands braced on her slender hips, her eyes flashing blue sparks at him. She was an at-tractive woman, and he'd enjoyed dueling with her. His hor-mones had certainly jumped to attention and noticed her. But as far as he was concerned, she was a suspect. Period.

If some small part of his brain was still thinking about Shea as a potential playmate, he could ignore it. It was his ability to focus on his job and shut out distractions that had set him apart from the rest of the agents at the FBI. And it was his ability to get the job done, alone, that had earned him the name of the Renegade.

His mouth tightened as he turned onto the driveway of the Red Rock Ranch. Shea McAllister would learn, soon enough, that no one was above the law. He was here to prove it to her.

The yard was empty and quiet as he brought his truck to a stop. There was no sign of Shea or any of the old cowboys he'd seen the day before. He waited for the dust to subside, then he stepped out of the truck.

The silence struck him as he slammed the door of the truck. There should be more noise on a working ranch, more activity. Unless Shea and all the cowboys were out in some distant pasture.

Shea walked out of the barn, shielding her eyes from the bright sunlight. Ignoring the small leap in his chest at the sight of her, Jesse headed toward her.

She stopped when she saw him and waited for him to reach her. "Thanks for coming out so quickly," she said, and her low voice sounded strained.

"No problem." He should shake her hand, he told himself. He'd shake the hand of any other potential employer. Reluctantly, he extended his hand, and when she took it, he felt that jolt of recognition again, that tremor of rightness. He pulled his hand back as quickly as he could. He noticed that Shea tucked her own hand behind her back just as quickly.

"You changed your mind," he said, watching her.

"I hadn't made up my mind yet, so how could I change it?"

Heat blazed in her eyes again, and he felt a shimmer of satisfaction. If he could keep her off guard, make her angry, she was more likely to make a mistake.

"I got the distinct impression yesterday that you had no intention of hiring me."

Fire blazed again in her eyes, then she looked out at the pasture behind the house and it quickly died, replaced by a weary resignation. "I didn't think you would work out, no," she admitted. "But there was an accident after you left, and now I don't have any choice."

"What happened?" In spite of his vow to remain detached, he felt his heart speed up. "Were you hurt?"

She shook her head. "I wish it had been me. Joe and Dusty, two of my hands, had an accident. Their truck ran off the road when Joe swerved to avoid a deer, and they hit a rock. Dusty broke his arm and Joe banged up his head.

They're both all right, but neither of them will be able to do much work for a while. So you're hired.''

She looked back at him, and the resignation was replaced by a steely look. ''I'll see how you work out for the next two months. You can consider it a trial period. Once Joe and Dusty are both back at work, we may not need you.''

''I can live with that.'' With any luck at all, two months would be more than enough time to take care of any illegal situation on the Red Rock Ranch.

Shea nodded once. ''Grab your pack and I'll show you to the bunkhouse. You can have your own cabin. Dusty, Joe and Levi have been sharing one for years. Meals are in the house. You're responsible for your own laundry, but you can use the machines in the house. Talk to Maria and she'll tell you the schedule.''

She didn't look back as she talked, hurrying toward three tiny cabins tucked behind the barn. She passed the largest one, saying over her shoulder, ''That one belongs to my men. You can take either of the other two. The doors are unlocked. Pick one and put your stuff inside. Then meet me in the barn.''

She hurried away before he could answer. He watched until she disappeared into the barn, then opened the door to the cabin farthest from the one occupied by her men. There would be times when he wouldn't want to be overheard. And there was always much to be said for distance.

Shea leaned against the stall that held the steer with the laceration, and took a deep breath. She'd done it. She'd hired Jesse Coulton, and he would be working on the Red Rock for at least two months. It would be dangerous and she hadn't wanted to do it, but she'd had no choice.

She had barely managed to get all the work done when all three of the men were helping. Now with two of them incapacitated, even though Joe should be back to work in a week or so, it would be impossible. And there was no one else she could hire.

God knew she'd been looking for long enough. So Jesse

would work for her, and she'd try to hide what she was doing.

Her mind raced over territory she'd been thinking about for the past day. Most of the children hiding in the house by the lake had already been reunited with their families. There were only two left, and they would be gone by the weekend. Miguel, the mysterious man who brought the children, would return to San Rafael. Then she'd have a breather before the next group arrived.

If she allowed it to continue. Dev was due back in town later this month, and it would be harder to hide her activities from her brother. It had been easy, the last few months, because after he and Carly got married, they'd moved to a house in town. And lately Dev had been gone most of the time, helping Carly get moved from New York. But this was their last trip, and soon Devlin would be around all the time.

Dev didn't matter, she told herself. It was the conversation she'd been having with herself for weeks. He would be embarrassed when he found out, and angry, but he'd get over it. She *had* to do this, and she could make Dev understand. A niece and nephew of her housekeeper, Maria, had been the first children to use the house. Maria had asked for her help, and the man named Miguel had brought them to her in the middle of the night. Several more groups of children had followed. She knew what would happen to these children if they didn't escape the war in their country. She was committed to helping them, and Devlin wasn't going to stop her.

And neither was Joe and Dusty's accident. She'd just have to be more careful. She'd gotten sloppy, she acknowledged. Maria knew what she was doing, and so did Joe, Dusty and Levi, although they never discussed it. She would have to change the way she worked, now that Jesse would be around.

A sound at the barn door roused her, and she straightened to see Jesse standing in the doorway. ''Where do I start?'' he asked.

His deep voice rolled over her, stirring the same foreign feelings as it had yesterday. ''We need to treat this steer,'' she said, her voice too abrupt. "I can give him the shot, but I need someone to hold him still for me."

Jesse nodded. "Fine. Where are your halters?"

"He's already haltered. You just need to trap him against the wall so he doesn't move when I stick him."

"I know how to do it." He gave her a mild look, but she saw the flash of irritation in his eyes. "I have done this before, you know."

"I guess you have." She tossed him what she hoped passed for a casual smile. "It's been a while since I broke in a new hand. You're going to have to forgive me if explain too much. And you'll probably get sick of seeing Levi and me. I want to make sure you're trained right, so one of us is going to stick close to you for a while." She intended to keep close tabs on him until both of the remaining children were off the ranch.

Unexpectedly he smiled, and the crease in his cheek flashed again. Her stomach did another slow roll, and she couldn't look away. "That's all right. It'll take me a while to get used to a new boss, so don't worry about it. It won't be a hardship to follow you around."

She couldn't look away from his face. His hazel eyes seemed to glow green in the dim light of the barn, and suddenly she felt breathless. He was standing too close to her, and his subtle, male scent surrounded her. Heat from his body seemed to curl around her, beckoning her closer.

When she realized she was swaying toward him, she yanked open the door of the stall, appalled. Blindly reaching for the syringe full of antibiotic that she'd left on the edge of the wood, she waited while he positioned himself at the steer's head.

"Ready?" she asked, without looking at him.

"All set. Go ahead."

She injected the white liquid quickly into the steer's rump, then stepped away. Jesse unclipped the halter and slipped it off, then stepped out of the stall. By the time she joined him, the steer already had his head stuck in the feed trough.

"It looks like your vet did a nice job," he said.

She nodded. "Becca's great. We're lucky to have her."

They stood at the stall door for a few moments, Shea's heart still racing. Had Jesse noticed that spark, too, or had it all been one-sided? Telling herself not to be a fool, she moved casually away from him. "Ready for the next job?"

"Sure." He stepped back from the stall and watched her. "What do you want me to do?"

"We're going to have to do it together." Shea wished that she hadn't sent Levi out to the far pasture this morning. She'd give anything to avoid sitting in that pickup truck next to Jesse. "We have to go and winch the truck Joe was driving away from the rock."

"Why don't you let me take care of it? It doesn't sound like a two-person job." His voice was casual, and he leaned against the stall. But he watched her carefully.

She shook her head. "No way. It's not a one-person job. And you'd never find that truck without help."

His eyes narrowed, and she saw them harden again. "I'll give it a shot. Tell me where it is, and I'll find it."

"I don't think so. I don't want you to get lost on the Red Rock on your first day on the job."

"I have a good sense of direction. As long as you can tell me where it is, I'll do the job myself."

"No!" She swallowed once and tried to banish her anxiety. Even though he had no way of knowing what she was doing, the last thing she would allow was Jesse Coulton wandering around the ranch by himself. "Believe me, it'll be a lot quicker if I go with you. I don't have the time or the manpower to send out a search party if you get lost."

He shrugged, but the hardness didn't disappear from his eyes. "Suit yourself. I just thought it would be more efficient for one person to do the job."

"Even if it was," she said, "it would hardly be fair to turn you loose on your first day on the job. The Red Rock is a big place."

"A lot of places to get lost. Or to hide," he said, his voice expressionless. "I understand."

She glanced at him sharply, but his face was a blank. "Good. Let's get the truck and we'll take care of that chore."

Neither of them spoke as the truck bounced its way along the rutted road. They would be passing too close to the cabin on the lake, and Shea couldn't allow herself to relax. She'd already been up to the cabin this morning and explained the situation to Miguel. Even though she knew very little about him, she trusted him completely. She'd seen how he loved the children. He'd assured her that the children would stay inside today, but she was still worried.

Her instincts had been right. She shouldn't have hired Jesse Coulton, but she'd had no choice. Every once in a while she glanced over at him. He stared out the windshield of the truck, studying everything with an intensity that was unsettling. It almost felt like he was memorizing every detail of her ranch.

Would he see any evidence of the children she was hiding? No, because there was nothing to see. She'd made sure of that over the past several months. And Jesse was only studying his surroundings because that's what he needed to do, she told herself. He was going to be working here. He needed to know the ranch, become familiar with its roads and trails. There was nothing ominous or sinister about a man trying to do a good job.

"Nice place," he commented after a while.

"Thanks. I love the Red Rock."

"I can tell." She felt his eyes on her, but she didn't look over at him. "There still aren't many women managing ranches these days, especially one so young."

"I'm not that young, Coulton."

"You're young enough. Wasn't there anyone else to manage it?"

"I'm not going to take offense at that." It was no more, after all, than most of her neighbors had said at one time or another. "As it happens, I have a brother, but he wasn't interested. And it's all I've ever wanted to do."

"Then you're fortunate." His voice was quiet. "To be given the chance to do what you've always wanted to do is a gift. Only someone stupid would throw it away." She felt his eyes on her again. "And you're not a stupid woman, Shea McAllister."

His low voice rolled over her, luring her, and she stared out the windshield rather than give into the temptation to look at him. His words were spoken with passion. They almost sounded like a warning, but she had no idea what he could be warning her about. There was no way he could know anything about the children hidden in the cabin. "I know how lucky I am. How about you, Coulton? Are you doing what you always wanted to do?"

She glanced over at him then, and found him staring out the window. His mouth was a narrow line in his face. "I'm doing what I dreamed about doing all my life."

"Then you're lucky, too," she said lightly. She swung the steering wheel to the right and headed down a smaller path. "We're almost there. The truck is just a few hundred feet ahead."

The path became more narrow and the ruts were deeper. The truck bumped over large rocks, and Shea slowed down to the speed of a brisk walk. In a few moments the truck appeared, balanced precariously on the edge of a cliff.

"Your men were lucky," Jesse said, staring at the truck.

"They were. If they'd hit the deer, they might have gone over the edge." She didn't want to think about how lucky Joe and Dusty had been. She suspected she would have nightmares for a long time, remembering her first sight of the truck on the edge of the cliff, only a large boulder stopping it from tumbling to the ground, several hundred feet below.

Stopping the truck, she carefully turned it around, positioning it behind the smaller pickup, then jumped out. Jesse climbed out, then stood next to her. "Quite a view," he finally said.

The cliff overlooked the ranch, the green pastures unfolding in front of them like squares of a bright carpet that contrasted with the red rocks and dirt. Far away, the ranch house and outbuildings were tiny dots of white and red in the distance.

"I love it up here," Shea said, inhaling the dusty scent of pine and heat. "Whenever I get too busy to appreciate the ranch, I come up here to remind myself again how happy I am."

She could feel Jesse look at her, but she didn't turn to meet his eyes. Already she felt vaguely foolish for sharing such a personal thought with him. He was an employee, she reminded herself, and she wasn't trying to talk him into staying at the ranch. Just the opposite. When Joe and Dusty were up to speed, she wanted Jesse gone.

"How far back does your property extend?" he asked. His voice was casual, but she heard an intensity underlying it that made her finally turn and look at him.

"We own most of this mountain. It's not huge, but it goes back quite a ways." She studied his face. "Why do you ask?"

He shrugged. "Just wanted to know how far the territory extended."

"You won't have to come up here much. There are only a few small plots of pasture up here, and we don't keep many head in them. Most of the mountain is unusable for ranching."

"So what *do* you use it for?"

"Recreation, mostly," she said lightly. "There are people from Cameron who like to camp and hike up here. And Dev and I have been known to do some camping ourselves." They were getting too close to her secrets for comfort, and it was time to change the subject. "Ready to pull this truck back onto the road?"

Jesse stepped away from her and nodded, but his eyes lingered on the rough country behind them. She thought she saw speculation in his eyes. What was he thinking?

"Where do you want me to attach the hook to the truck?" he asked, and she pushed the question out of her mind. She had more to worry about than what Jesse Coulton was thinking.

"I'll show you." Unwinding the hook and its attached chain from the bed of her truck, she squatted down in the

dust next to the rear of the stranded truck and peered underneath the bumper. "There's the place where it attaches."

Jesse dropped to the ground next to her and took the hook
from her hands. "I have a longer reach. Let me do it."

Shea watched as he struggled to slip the hook through the
opening in the truck's frame. Even though it was only spring,
the sun's rays were hot, warming the denim jeans and flannel
shirt she wore. Then Jesse moved and his body slid into hers.

The flash of heat was instantaneous. Her thigh burned
where it touched his, blocking out the weaker heat of the sun.
As fire poured through her, she scrambled to move away
from its source.

"No, don't move." Jesse's voice rolled over her from underneath the truck. Even though it was indistinct, it still made
her shiver. "I need to brace myself on something so I can
set the hook."

Shea forced herself to remain motionless, watching as
Jesse's leg almost twined with hers. Sensations she'd never
even imagined before pulsed through her, and her hands
tightened on the rock behind her she was using to brace herself.

Jesse's leg was hard and muscled as he strained against
her. She imagined she could feel each muscle bunching and
releasing, the ripple of each of his movements pressing
against the suddenly supersensitive flesh of her leg.

Shea stared at him helplessly, appalled at the way her body
was betraying her but unable to move away. Jesse pushed
against her one last time, his leg pressed intimately against
hers from thigh to ankle. Sensation quivered its way up her
leg and settled low in her abdomen, pulsing to the beat of
the blood in her veins.

Jesse abruptly untangled his leg from hers and slid out
from under the truck. "It's set. Let's try to pull the truck
back onto the road."

The planes of his cheeks had set into rigid lines, and his
mouth was a narrow slash in his face. But his eyes burned
with fierce need, their hazel depths molten gold. When they

lingered on her face for a moment, Shea saw desire, hot and potent, flicker deep inside.

Then he turned away and stood up, and when he turned back to her, she wondered if she had imagined the expression in his eyes moments ago. Now his face was shuttered and his eyes were cool. When he reached down a hand to help her to her feet, she hesitated only for a moment before she reached out and took it. Surely no one could hide the passion that she imagined had burned in him just moments ago. The need she'd seen must have been her imagination.

But when she was on her feet, he held her hand for a moment longer than necessary before letting her go. A current seemed to flow from his hand to hers, binding them together.

That was ridiculous, Shea told herself as she pulled her hand away from his. There was no connection between her and this drifter she'd been forced to hire. There was no bond, other than that of an employer and her employee, between them.

But her body called her a liar as she turned away from him. ''I'll start the engine,'' she muttered as she hurried to her truck. ''You make sure we're pulling straight.''

She felt the chain tighten on the pickup as she eased her own truck forward. The tires spun for a second, then the truck began moving forward. After a minute, Jesse called to her, ''Hold on. I have to adjust the chain.''

In another moment, he called, ''Okay, just a little farther. There. Stop.''

She turned off the truck and jumped out of the cab. Jesse was back underneath the pickup, detaching the hook. As he slid out from under the truck, Shea forced herself to look away. She didn't want him to catch her staring.

''We're all set.'' Jesse dusted his hands on his denim-covered thighs and looked over the crumpled front of the truck. ''Should I drive this one back to the house?''

''Yes. You can follow me there.'' She threw herself back into her truck, glad to have a few minutes alone, away from Jesse. She needed some time to compose herself.

Jesse watched Shea leap into her truck and head back down the rutted path. She was going too fast for the narrow road, but she didn't slow down. She acted as if the hounds of hell were on her heels.

He couldn't blame her. He felt like doing a little running, himself. The desire that had flared when he'd braced himself against her leg had shocked him. He prided himself on being able to control himself at all times. But he wasn't even close to being able to control his response to Shea.

He wouldn't allow it, damn it.

He wouldn't let his own body betray him. He was here for a reason, and it wasn't to get chummy with Shea McAllister. She was the suspect, for God's sake. She was the last woman he should be playing footsie with.

Even though she had felt awfully good, pressed against him. Her legs were long and firm, toned by the hard work she did all day. He wondered how those long legs of hers would feel if they were wrapped around him, holding him close to her.

Suddenly realizing where his thoughts were heading, he gave a savage curse and forced his attention back to his surroundings. His job was to find out where she was hiding the refugees, he told himself, not speculating about her legs. For the rest of the trip back to the barn, he tried to catalog the landmarks and pay attention to where the roads were. The first chance he had, he'd explore this unused part of the ranch. His money said this was where she was hiding the illegal aliens.

Almost before her truck had come to a complete stop, Shea was out and standing in the yard. Jesse studied her as he brought the damaged pickup rattling to a stop next to her and saw the quick shuffling of her feet, the restless movements of her hands. When she jammed her hands into the pockets of her jeans, he saw her fingers tremble for a moment.

Maybe he hadn't been the only one who'd felt the electricity that flared between them up on the mountain.

"Levi isn't back yet," she said, and he thought she spoke too quickly. "Why don't we go out and check on him?"

She turned and headed for the barn, and he hurried to catch up with her. No wonder she got so much done. Shea had more energy than anyone he'd ever known. "Where are we going?" he asked as they reached the barn.

"One of the far pastures. Levi was supposed to check on the cattle and come right back. He didn't answer his phone, and I want to make sure nothing is wrong."

She pointed out the saddle he could use, then grabbed her own. "It'll be quicker to take horses than the truck." In a few minutes they had saddled two horses and were riding across the first pasture.

"It looks like you could use a foreman to keep track of what your men are doing," he said casually as they rode across the coarse grass.

She glanced over at him. "I can keep track just fine. Everything is in a jumble today because of the accident. Give us a few days and we'll be back to normal."

"You're giving me a lot of credit," he said, enjoying goading her.

"What do you mean?"

"You just as much as said that you expect me to do the work of two men."

"Two men who are almost twice as old as you." She gave him a pointed look. "Yes, I expect you to get a lot more accomplished than Dusty or Joe alone. You're young and strong." Her cheeks colored, as if she just realized what she'd said.

"I aim to please," he said, keeping his voice casual.

"I hope so, Coulton. I'm counting on you to take up the slack."

She recovered quickly, he had to give her that. "I think you'll be amazed at what I can do."

"We'll see."

She kicked her horse into a gallop, and he followed suit. As he watched her ride ahead of him, clinging to the horse,

Chapter 3

When they had passed through one pasture and were almost through the next, he spotted a man standing next to a fence. Shea spotted him at the same time, because she veered her horse around to head in his direction. As they pulled to a stop next to him, the older man was replacing some tools in a toolbox.

"Hey, Shea. What are you doing out here?"

Shea sat on her horse and watched him. "I wanted to make sure you were okay. You didn't answer the phone when I called."

"I heard it. Just couldn't be bothered." He glared at Shea from under bushy eyebrows. "I'm not going to go and get myself hurt like those damn fools Joe and Dusty. I know what I'm doing out here. You didn't have to come looking for me like I was a baby."

"Then you should have answered the phone when I called. That's why they're in the trucks."

"Never needed no phones before now," he muttered. "Ain't right, calling someone on the telephone out here in the middle of nowhere."

"If there hadn't been a phone in Joe and Dusty's truck, what would they have done?" she asked, shifting on her horse. Jesse had the feeling that this was an old argument.

The older man stuck his chin out at them. "They woulda walked back to the house, same as we always did."

Shea looked away from him and dismounted her horse. "Was there something wrong with the fence?"

"It was down, here and in a few other spots." Levi jerked his head in the direction of the cattle, grazing a few hundred feet away. "Some of the steers musta run into it. A few of them have cuts, but nothing that has to be seen to."

As Shea talked with the older man, Jesse watched her with reluctant admiration. She handled the old man so well, he thought. She made sure he knew she was the boss, but she had a delicate touch that showed how much respect she had for him.

And the old man seemed to think pretty highly of her, too. In spite of his grouching about the cell phones, his affection for Shea was obvious.

Her voice interrupted his thoughts. "Levi, this is our new hand, Jesse Coulton. I hired him to help out until Joe and Dusty are back on their feet."

Levi's eyes were shrewd and appraising as they examined him. "You do much ranch work before this?" he asked.

"I've done my share." He listed the ranches and the jobs from his fictional references. "I've never worked in Utah before, though."

Jesse saw Levi's gaze take in his calloused hands and his sun-browned face. He nodded once. "We can use the help."

He turned back to Shea, but Jesse felt like he'd just passed a major test. A few minutes later, Shea said to him, "Levi will meet us back at the house. It's almost time for lunch, and Maria doesn't like it if we're late."

They mounted and headed back the way they'd come. "Your housekeeper runs a pretty tight ship?" he asked casually. Their informant had said that the housekeeper was closely involved in the smuggling.

Shea laughed as she kicked her horse into a canter. "The

tightest. We all live in fear of her. She keeps us in line, but we don't mind because she's the best cook in Cameron.'' She slanted him a grin. ''A fact I'm sure you'll appreciate after a few days at Melba Corboy's.''

Jesse felt himself responding to her vibrant face and laughing eyes. Her zest for life beckoned to him, insinuating itself into his consciousness like a wisp of smoke.

But no woman had ever made him forget his job, and Shea wasn't going to be the first. ''Melba wasn't so bad. At least she was honest about her cooking skills.''

''Before or after she'd gotten her first week's rent?'' Shea tossed the question over her shoulder.

Because his pulse tripped at the sight of her blond hair streaming behind her and the flash of laughter in her eyes, he pulled even with her and said deliberately, ''If we're talking about honesty, what's the real reason you didn't want to hire me?''

The smile disappeared from her face, and she threw him a startled look. But she recovered quickly. Shrugging her shoulders, she said, ''Gut feeling. I don't like arrogant, pushy cowboys. And I didn't want one working for me.''

''But you ended up with me anyway.''

''That I did.'' Now she turned in her saddle and studied him. ''You happened to be in the right place at the right time. I needed someone, badly, and you were here. So I hired you.'' She gave him an appraising glance, then said, ''We'll see if you're here in another two months.''

She kicked her horse and sped ahead of him, but Jesse was content to lag behind. They would indeed see if he was here in another two months, he thought. More to the point, where would Shea be in another two months?

For some reason he didn't want to think about the vibrant Shea sitting in a prison cell. That wasn't his job, he reminded himself. What happened to her in the long run wasn't his decision. His job was to find out what she was doing, and arrest her if necessary.

And he'd start at lunch by checking out Maria, the housekeeper who was supposedly involved.

* * *

He didn't have a chance to talk to Maria. Ben Jackson, one of the deputy sheriffs from Cameron, was waiting for them when they walked into the house. Jesse had taken careful note of Ben during the time he'd spent in Cameron. He was Devlin McAllister's most trusted deputy, and Jesse still hadn't decided if Devlin was involved in the smuggling. Ben was a tall, wiry man with dark hair and eyes and a serious face. It softened into a smile when Shea walked into the room. Shea gave him a hug, and some of the deputy's reserve melted as he returned the embrace.

Jesse tensed, but the expression on Shea's face was one of sisterly welcome. It wasn't the kind of embrace a woman would give a lover. Jesse scowled at the relief that flooded through him.

"Ben! What are you doing here?" She stepped back and took his hand. "Not that I'm not happy to see you. Stay and have lunch with us, or Maria will be insulted."

"I heard some rumors about Joe and Dusty's accident, and I wanted to find out what happened." Ben's dark eyes softened as he watched Shea. "I thought you might need some help."

"As a matter of fact, I hired someone this morning." Shea looked around and spotted Jesse standing near the door. "Coulton, come here and meet one of my friends."

Jesse reluctantly moved forward. He would have preferred to hang back for a while and watch. "Jesse Coulton," he said to Ben Jackson, extending his hand to the deputy.

"Ben Jackson," the other man replied. His gaze was unapologetic as it lingered on Jesse. "I'm a sheriff's deputy in Cameron. Do you have references?"

Jesse allowed himself an instant of admiration for the deputy's strength, then he raised his eyebrows. "Is that the usual procedure in Cameron?" he drawled. "To get the police to interrogate every newcomer?"

Ben didn't back down. "Not at all. Shea's brother is my boss, as well as the other owner of the Red Rock Ranch. If he was here, he'd ask the same thing. I'm merely doing my job.''

Ben Jackson would be a formidable opponent, Jesse realized. Thank God they were on the same side, although the deputy didn't know it. ''Of course I have references.'' He glanced over at Shea. ''I gave them to Ms. McAllister yesterday.''

Ben turned to Shea. ''Have you checked on them yet?''

''You sound exactly like Devlin.'' She scowled at him. ''Don't worry, I'll check them tonight.''

''Why don't you give them to me?'' Ben said as his gaze lingered on Jesse. ''I'll do it for you.''

''I'm perfectly capable of calling a few people,'' Shea snapped at him.

The deputy's serious face creased in a smile. ''Most people don't like to get phone calls at three a.m.,'' he said, a hint of laughter in his voice. ''As close as I can figure, that's about your only free time.''

''You're as bad as Dev,'' Shea muttered, turning and walking out of the room. She reappeared a few moments later and handed Ben several sheets of paper. ''Here are copies of Jesse's references. I'll call them this afternoon, but you're welcome to take a look at them.''

Ben placed the envelope on a small table, and Jesse knew that, in spite of Shea's words, he'd check on the references as soon as he returned to his office. Jesse had done enough research to know that Ben was almost frighteningly efficient. He and Devlin McAllister were outstanding law enforcement officers.

Normally on a case like this he'd go to the sheriff, explain what he was doing and ask for help. But he hadn't done that this time. He'd learned that Devlin was close to his sister. Although there were no indications that the sheriff was involved in the smuggling, Jesse couldn't take any chances. And that applied to his deputies, as well.

A short, heavyset woman appeared in the doorway that appeared to lead to a dining room. Her black hair was pulled back into a severe bun and her dark eyes snapped. "Lunch is ready, if any of you are interested."

Levi walked in the door just then and headed straight for the dining room, as did everyone else. Jesse found himself seated next to Shea at the long table. Maria passed around platters of fried chicken, bowls of green beans and mashed potatoes and baskets of corn bread. For a few minutes there was silence, as everyone concentrated on the meal. Then Ben asked, "What exactly happened with Dusty and Joe?"

Noise erupted as everyone tried to talk at once. Shea and Levi were telling him their version of the story, and Maria appeared in the door to add her opinion of witless cowboys who couldn't drive straight. The worry he saw in her eyes took the bite out of her words. Jesse tried to ask a question, and the result was a jumble of sound that pressed against his ears.

Shea must have seen the shock on his face, because she broke off what she was saying and turned to him. "I take it you're not from a large and vocal family," she said, grinning. "Don't mind us. We all like to talk, and we all want to make sure we get our turn. It'll settle down in a few minutes."

Sure enough, pretty soon the volume decreased and Shea told Ben what had happened with Dusty and Joe. She assured the deputy that both men were fine and would be back on the ranch in a day or two.

"The doctor wanted to keep both of them in the hospital for observation, just to make sure there weren't any other problems. And I knew we didn't have anyone to take care of them during the day, so I made them stay." Her grin flashed again. "I figured you'd stop by to find out what was going on. I was going to ask you to go get them tomorrow. I don't want to listen to them complain all the way home."

Another smile flitted across Ben's face. "That may be pushing friendship a little too far."

Shea gave a deep, theatrical sigh. "I guess I'll just have to do it myself, then." She turned sorrowful eyes to Levi. "You can do everything here on the ranch by yourself, can't you, Levi?"

Ben laughed. "All right, all right, you've made your point. I was going to offer, anyway. Cameron is having a peaceful spell right now. It shouldn't be any problem to get away."

Jesse watched the interplay, knowing that his face wouldn't give away what he was feeling. If he had anything to say about it, things wouldn't be peaceful in Cameron for long.

After making the arrangements to pick up Dusty and Joe the following day, the deputy turned to Jesse. "It was pretty coincidental, you showing up in Cameron just when Shea needed to hire someone."

Jesse leaned back in his chair. "I had already spoken to Ms. McAllister about a job before her two cowboys had their accident. So I'd call it more luck than coincidence. For both of us."

Ben studied him for a moment, then nodded slowly. "I'm going to assume your references will back that up."

Jesse was close enough to Shea to feel her tense. "Knock it off, Ben. I checked the written letters he had, and I'll call his former employers this afternoon. But who else was I going to hire? We needed someone right away, not in the weeks or months it would take if we had to go looking."

"I'm not disagreeing with you, Shea. I'm just going to do some checking for you. I promised Dev I would help you out if you needed anything, and checking Coulton's references is something Dev would have done."

She turned to Jesse. "Excuse us for talking about you as if you weren't here. I'm afraid my brother has an excessive dose of protectiveness. And Ben seems to be taking Devlin's remarks about watching out for me way too seriously."

"Don't worry about it. I understand about brothers and sisters."

But he didn't, not really. He'd never had a sibling, and the only person he'd ever felt protective of was his mother. And she didn't need his protection. He watched the interplay between Shea and her brother's friend with something that felt suspiciously like jealousy.

He'd never wanted to be a part of a family, never felt any

need to put down roots and cultivate ties. Most of the families he'd seen in his line of work were pitiful excuses for loving units. Now, sitting at this table, watching the affection these people had for one another, he wondered fleetingly what he'd missed. Even Levi, who was only an employee, was treated like a member of the family and acted like one. And the bantering they'd done about Joe and Dusty had been a very thin veneer for the concern that was obvious.

When he turned his attention back to Shea, she was giving Ben instructions about picking up Joe and Dusty the next day. Finally she turned to him when Maria brought in cherry pies for dessert.

"We have a lot to do this afternoon." She accepted her pie almost absently and began to eat it. "Levi is going to drive you around the ranch, get you oriented. There's a lot of territory to cover, and you'll be able to jump in and help more quickly if you know where everything is. Then there's more fence down on the other side of the pasture we were at this morning. You and Levi can take care of that. That should take us to dinner. Generally, your time is your own after dinner, unless there's something urgent that needs to be done."

"Fine." He wondered what she was going to do that afternoon, and decided that he'd keep an eye on her. "Do we drive or take horses?"

"You drive whenever you can on this ranch. The horses don't have cell phones."

She shot a look over at Levi, who pretended to ignore her. Why the insistence on keeping in contact? he wondered. Did it have something to do with the men he assumed were hiding somewhere on her ranch? That was another thing he'd find out.

Shea leaned back in her chair and once again he was aware of the energy that seemed to vibrate out of her. Jesse could well believe that Shea could keep a ranch this size running almost single-handedly. He had no doubt that she was able to will herself and her employees to do almost anything.

He didn't want to admire anything about Shea, but it was

impossible not to be impressed with her devotion to the ranch. It was clear she'd sacrifice just about anything for the Red Rock Ranch. So why was she risking it to smuggle illegal aliens into the country? Didn't she know that she could lose the ranch if it was used for illegal purposes? And especially why would she smuggle in criminals? It could only be for the money.

Anyone as passionate about their property as Shea seemed to be probably wouldn't hesitate to do whatever it took to keep it going. She must be paid handsomely for the risks she was taking.

She leaned toward him, and her scent seemed to curl around him. It was surprisingly feminine, a mixture of oranges and some subtle, fragrant flower. It had to be her shampoo or her soap, he decided, trying to distract himself from the effect it was having on his body. She didn't seem like the type to dab on perfume before she went out and wrestled cattle.

"Ready to go?" she said as she pushed away from the table.

"I'm set." He waited for Levi, then walked out of the house with the older man. As they headed toward a truck parked next to the barn, he felt Shea's eyes on his back. When he turned around, she was standing on the porch, watching them leave. She stood gazing after them as the truck bumped down a rutted track next to the pasture. Jesse watched her in the rearview mirror until the truck rounded a corner. She stood still as a statue until they were out of sight.

Shea waited until Levi and Jesse's truck disappeared around a corner, then she took a deep breath. Thank goodness Jesse was going to be gone all afternoon. She'd been too aware of him at lunch, especially after that moment up on the cliff, next to the car. She was being foolish, she knew, but she was glad to have some space. She waved goodbye to Ben as he headed back to Cameron, then let herself relax.

"Maria," she called as she went into the house and the

screen door slammed behind her. "Do you have that food ready?"

"It's here," the housekeeper grumbled. "But I don't know why you have to go up there today. That Miguel, he's shiftless but he's perfectly capable of preparing meals."

"But the children love your fried chicken so much, Maria," she teased. "Even Miguel has complimented you on it. Don't you want to make them happy?"

"Me, I'd be perfectly happy never to see that Miguel around here again," she muttered. "But take the chicken. There are some beans and corn bread, too. Those poor children need some good meals."

Shea put her arm around the housekeeper's shoulders and dropped a kiss on her cheek. "Thanks, Maria."

Maria watched her with concerned eyes. "It's a good thing you're doing, Shea, but you need to be careful. That man you hired, he has knowing eyes. He watches everything. I saw him, today at lunch."

Shea tightened her hold on Maria, then stepped away. "I know. That's why I sent him out with Levi this afternoon. Levi will keep him busy and away from the cabin. And in a couple of days, all the children will be gone. Then there won't be anything to worry about."

"Until the next group comes along. Mark my words, Shea. That one is going to bring trouble."

Shea managed to keep her face carefully blank. She had no intention of telling Maria that Jesse Coulton had already brought trouble to the Red Rock. He'd made her feel things she'd never experienced before. And all he'd done was press his leg up against hers. Even Kyle Diggett had never caused the sensations that fluttered inside her every time she looked at Jesse.

"I can handle trouble, Maria." She winked at the housekeeper and grabbed the baskets of food off the counter, anxious to get away from the older woman's knowing eyes. "Doesn't Mom always say that trouble is my middle name?"

"And she says that someday it will catch up to you, too," Maria called after her as she hurried out to the Bronco.

Loading the food carefully into the back, Shea looked around once to make sure that Levi and Jesse weren't close by, then jumped into the truck and headed back up into the mountains.

By the time Levi and Jesse returned from mending the fence, Shea was mounted on Demon, her huge black gelding. She'd set up the barrels in the corral and was practicing racing around them.

She didn't hear the truck, but she knew the instant that Jesse came into view. Bending closer to Demon's neck, she urged him to go faster, to cut the corners a little closer. And, as usual, he responded, putting on a burst of speed that left her breathless. After the final run, she reined the horse in and dismounted, looping the reins over the top rail of the corral.

"That was impressive," Jesse said as he watched her approach. He leaned against the railings, his chambray shirt pulled taut over his shoulders. He'd discarded his hat, and the sun made his dark hair gleam.

"It was a good workout."

"Do you compete in rodeos?"

Shea ran her hand down Demon's neck. "We have been known to race around a barrel or two."

"You're a woman of many talents, it would appear."

His gaze brushed over her skin with the intensity of a caress. Her skin burned as if he'd actually touched her. "I do what I have to do to keep the ranch going. I race for my own pleasure."

"I'll bet you usually win, too," he murmured. He reached out and absently scratched Demon's nose.

"We win our share of races." A shiver chased itself up her spine as she watched him. For a moment, she imagined that those long, clever fingers of his were caressing her, stroking down her back, fluttering against her skin. When she found herself swaying toward him, she jerked herself away.

"Did you finish the fence?" She needed to remind herself that she was the boss as much as she needed to remind him.

There would be no repeat of the situation that had developed with Kyle Diggett.

"It's finished." He straightened, too, and scowled at her. She wondered if he had noticed the tension that had trembled in the air between them for a moment. "Levi found a few other things to do, too."

"Good. I think I'll have you stick with him for a few more days. He can show you how we do things around here."

"Do you have some usual way of working?" he asked. His voice sounded casual, but there was a tension beneath it she didn't understand.

"What do you mean?"

"Is there a specific way that you divide up the chores? Do you usually work alone, or with the rest of the men?"

"It depends on what's going on. If we're branding or vaccinating or castrating calves, we all work together. We try to schedule those kinds of things when we know there's nothing else pressing or when we know Dev will be around to help. The rest of the time it just depends on what has to be done."

"I work best when I work alone."

She gave him a sharp look. "You can't imagine I'm going to turn you loose on the Red Rock before you know how I like things done."

"Does that mean you'll be training me yourself?"

Shea felt as if she was being maneuvered into a corner. She swung around to face Jesse. "Do you have a problem working with Levi? Because if you do, let's get it on the table right now."

Jesse held up his hands. "I didn't say that. I just like to learn from the source. If there's a way you'd like me to do things, I'd prefer that you teach me yourself."

"Levi knows exactly what I want. He's perfectly capable of training you. And as for working by yourself, I'll see what Levi has to say after he's worked with you for a while. I don't turn anyone loose to work on my ranch before I'm sure what they'll do."

"You're awfully defensive. It sounds as if there's a story there," Jesse said.

Kyle Diggett's face flashed into Shea's mind, and she sighed, her anger dissipating. It wasn't fair to paint Jesse the same color as Kyle. She really didn't think Jesse would steal from the ranch. "Maybe there is. But it's nothing that you need to worry about. Levi will show you what you need to know, and we'll go from there. I can't make any promises about what you'll be doing until I know what kind of a job you do."

Jesse turned the conversation to the work he had done with Levi that afternoon, and after she'd rubbed Demon down and put him away, they headed up to the house for dinner. He again took the chair next to hers, and once more she was far too aware of him as he sat close to her.

"You need to get a life," she muttered to herself after he'd brushed his arm against hers and she'd practically jumped out of her chair.

"I beg your pardon?" he said politely.

"Nothing. I was just clearing my throat." She stared blindly down at the food she was eating, realizing that she hadn't tasted a thing. Pushing abruptly away from the table, she said, "I'll see you all in the morning. I have some paperwork to do."

She hurried into the office and closed the door behind her, then leaned against it. No, she certainly wouldn't be working closely with Jesse Coulton any time soon. She didn't like the way her body reacted when he was close to her, and she didn't like the awareness that seemed to shimmer in the air between them. She needed to look at columns of numbers for a while to get him out of her head.

It seemed like hours later when the phone rang, startling her. She put her finger over the spot she'd been working and answered the phone.

"Red Rock Ranch. McAllister speaking."

She tensed when she heard the voice on the other end, then relaxed. "That's not a problem," she said. "Isobel will be happy that her cousins were able to get here so quickly. I'll meet you in," she glanced at her watch, "an hour or so."

She gave directions quickly to the relatives of one of the

children she was shielding, then hung up the phone. The house was quiet and dark. Only the hall was illuminated, and Shea knew that Maria would have gone to bed long ago. The housekeeper was up very early in the morning.

Grabbing a coat against the chilly spring evening air, she slipped out of the house and headed toward the Bronco. There were lights in both Levi's cabin and the one that Jesse was using. She'd have to be careful.

She slipped into the vehicle and eased it into gear. The house and barn stood on a small hill, so she released the brake, put the truck into neutral and let it coast down the hill. When it had slowed almost to a stop, she started the engine and headed quickly up into the mountains and the cabin where the children were hiding.

Two and a half hours later she returned the same way to the house. There was a little-used road that led out of the mountains and onto the main highway, and she had used it tonight. She hadn't wanted to drive past the house, not with Jesse possibly awake to hear her. She didn't want him wondering where she had been and what she'd been doing so late at night.

She smiled as she let the truck roll to a stop next to the garage. Isobel had recognized her cousins and flown into their arms with tears on her face. The joy shining out of the little girl's eyes when she'd turned to say goodbye to Shea made all the risks she took worthwhile. Only a week before, Isobel had been a frightened, confused child, alone in a strange country and wondering what was going to happen to her. Now she'd been reunited with members of her family, and with a little help would have a safe and happy life in this country.

The smile lingered on her mouth as she slipped out of the truck and quietly closed the door. All the lights were off in both Jesse's cabin and Levi's. Both men had worked hard today, and they were probably sound asleep. She needed to sleep, herself, but she knew from experience that it would take a while for her to wind down.

She headed over toward the pasture. The moon shone

down on the grass, giving it a pearly glow, and the cattle in the distance were shadowy, almost abstract figures. The air had a cool bite to it, but the night was clear and beautiful. She breathed in deeply, inhaling the pine and animal scent, relishing the quiet moment.

She was almost at the pasture fence when she heard a sound behind her. She started to spin around but two hard arms wrapped around her chest and a hand clamped over her mouth. When she began to struggle with her assailant, he roughly wrestled her to the ground.

She landed on her stomach, dazed and winded, the weight of the man pressing her into the dirt. Metal clicked next to her ear, and something cold and hard touched her head.

"Don't move."

Chapter 4

Shea froze, the harshly whispered words echoing in her ear. A stone ground into her cheek and her fingers dug into the cool dirt. Momentary shock held her immobile. Assaults like this weren't supposed to happen in Cameron, Utah.

The cold metal was abruptly removed from her head and the heavy weight on her back shifted. Immediately she tried to turn over, to see her assailant. She drew a deep breath to scream, hoping that it would rouse Levi or Maria or Jesse, but the hand clamped over her mouth again. And the arms that were so frighteningly strong held her in place easily.

"It's all right," the whisper said, and the hands holding her shifted, gentled. "Don't scream. I'm not going to hurt you."

Shea recognized that voice. She struggled harder, finally freeing one of her arms and using it to pry the hand away from her mouth. "Let me up," she managed to pant.

The weight disappeared from her back and Jesse Coulton's strong arms lifted her to her feet. "What in the *hell* do you think you're doing?" she demanded, watching him slide a deadly looking gun into the waistband of his jeans.

"I could ask you the same thing," he said coolly.

"What's that supposed to mean?" She dragged her hands through her tangled hair and tried to quiet her still-pounding heart.

"I heard someone out here, obviously trying not to make any noise. It's late at night, everyone's supposed to be sleeping. I thought you were a prowler of some sort, and I did what anyone would have done."

"No one on my ranch carries a weapon like that." She nodded at the gun protruding from the waistband of his jeans. "Who are you, Coulton, and what's going on?"

The moonlight dappled his face, highlighting the hard planes of his cheeks and shadowing his eyes. It was impossible to read his expression. "I'm a cowboy who takes his job seriously. There are two women and an old man living on this ranch. I'm sure everyone in town knows that. I had no idea who was out here, but I came prepared."

"This isn't a big city, Coulton. We don't have muggings in Cameron. And none of my neighbors would try to hurt me."

Even in the dim light, she saw his face harden. "The way I understand it, Cameron has had its share of big city problems lately."

"Everything that happened in Cameron in the last year was directed at specific individuals. And the criminals, however twisted their thinking, all thought they had good reasons to do what they did. We're not having a crime wave."

"And I intended to make sure nothing happened on your ranch."

Shea sighed, finally noticing that his shirt wasn't completely buttoned and his feet were bare. Clearly he had run out of the cabin only when he'd heard her. "I suppose I should be thanking you instead of snapping your head off, even though you did overreact. But the gun is another matter. I don't want to see it again."

"I have a permit to carry it."

"I don't care if you have a license to carry around a whole arsenal. My hands don't carry weapons."

"You have plenty of guns in the house."

She was surprised he'd noticed the gun case. He'd only been in the dining room, and the case was in the living room. It was just another reminder of his attention to detail, she told herself grimly. And another reason she needed to be careful.

"That gun collection was my father's, not that it's any of your business. It has nothing to do with cowboys packing side arms."

For the first time, his face softened. She almost thought he was trying to hide a smile. "Isn't that a little melodramatic? You're making me sound like some kind of desperado."

Her lips twitched in response, and finally she laughed. "You're a piece of work, Coulton. I guess I'm glad you were paying attention tonight. But please put that gun away and don't let me see it again. You took ten years off my life tonight."

He leaned against the fence and appeared to relax. She wished she could see his eyes, though.

"Where were you tonight, anyway?" he asked. "I thought you had paperwork to do."

It was just a casual remark, she told herself. A conversation. A way to dissipate the tension and get things back to normal again. But the air around them seemed to tighten and swell with unasked questions.

"I went for a ride up into the mountains." She waved her hand in the direction of the cliffs behind them. "I was tense and I needed some fresh air and solitude."

"Kind of dark up there, wasn't it?"

"There was plenty of moonlight. And I didn't go for the scenery."

"I can think of lots better ways to reduce tension than driving up into the mountains in the dark."

Suddenly his voice was different, a low murmur in his throat that rasped against her nerves. Tension flared again, the heat unmistakable. Her heart started to pound and she began to tremble. *Ignore it,* she ordered herself.

"Driving works for me." She tried to make her voice

brisk, but she failed miserably. She hardly recognized the throaty purr as her own voice.

He didn't answer. Instead, he reached out and trailed one finger down her cheek. He lingered at the angle of her jaw, and she felt his finger tremble. "I bruised your cheek. I'm sorry."

"Don't worry about it." She could barely get the words out. Her heart thudded so hard in her chest she was sure he could hear it. And every nerve in her body leapt in response to his touch on her face. When he let his hand drop, she wanted to beg him to touch her again.

Instead of moving away from her, he leaned closer and looked at her cheek. "I think I need to kiss it to make it better," he murmured. Without giving her a chance to think, to protest, he brushed his lips over her cheek.

She tried to inhale, the ragged, unsteady breath catching in her throat. Her heart stuttered, then began to pound out an ancient rhythm that echoed the throbbing inside her. Jesse lifted his face for a moment and stared down at her.

Her heart raced faster when she saw the desire in his eyes. She wasn't the only one who was affected by that simple caress. For a moment his eyes were unguarded, and what she saw was wild, unfettered need.

She swayed closer, the need inside her yearning for him. He hesitated for a moment, desire battling with denial in the depths of his eyes. She saw the instant that desire won.

He wrapped his arms around her, hauling her close. Weaving his fingers into her hair, he tipped her head so the moonlight shone full on her face. "I've wanted to do this since the first moment I saw you, wrestling with that steer."

She couldn't look away. Never before had she seen such desire, such naked need, in a man's face. For her, Shea McAllister. And she blurted out the only thing she could say. "I think I have, too."

He groaned and covered her mouth with his. The kiss wasn't gentle. It wasn't a civilized caress. It was as wild as the need in his eyes, crushing her mouth beneath his, laying a claim and taking possession.

She rose to meet him. Wrapping her arms around his neck, she moved closer, so that her body pressed against his from leg to chest. The hard planes of his body surrounded her, branded her with his touch. And when she slid her hands along his back, she realized he was trembling.

She was trembling, too. His mouth had gentled and now he nibbled at her lower lip, every tiny bite making her tremble more. When his tongue glided along her lips, she groaned.

He slipped into her mouth, tasting, teasing, and she groaned again. He tasted of coffee and hot male, dark and intoxicating. When he slid his hand down her back and cupped her hips, pressing her against his hard length, her voice quivered with wonder as she murmured his name.

The sound seemed to shock him back to reality. He froze, one hand on her hip and the other tangled in her hair. Then, slowly, he stepped away from her.

"I'm sorry," he said in a low voice. "I was out of line. I shouldn't have done that."

His face was still hard and taut with passion, and she had no trouble seeing the evidence of his arousal, even in the dim moonlight. But she saw the anger in his eyes and wondered if it was directed at her or himself.

"I didn't exactly try to discourage you."

"You should have."

"Sorry. I don't do a lot of things I'm supposed to do."

His face softened. "No, you don't, do you? I've never met anyone quite like you. And I'm sorry, Shea. That really was inexcusable. I frightened you half to death, then I took advantage of your vulnerability. I promise you it won't happen again."

She tilted her head and watched the regret on his face. "You're an honorable man, aren't you, Jesse?"

"There are certain rules I live by," he said stiffly. "Kissing your employer is definitely against most of them."

"I imagine that up until now, it wasn't a tough rule to keep."

His face softened again, involuntarily she thought, and he

half smiled. "It's true that all of my other employers have been men. But they all had wives or sisters or daughters."

She stepped away from him, knowing that he was right. The last thing that she or the Red Rock needed was for her to get involved with another drifter cowboy. The few kisses she'd shared with Kyle Diggett had been bland, passionless things compared to what had just happened with Jesse. But they had still blinded her to Kyle's true nature. That wasn't going to happen again.

"You're right, of course. And I don't have time to get involved with anyone right now, let alone someone I work with." She wondered if the regret she saw in Jesse's eyes, even if it was grudging, mirrored her own. "So we'll just chalk it up to fear and nerves and forget about it. Agreed?"

"Agreed." He raised his hand and touched her cheek again, almost as if he couldn't help himself. "Although I am sorry that I bruised your cheek."

She had to fight the temptation to let her fingers linger on the spot where his had been. "Don't worry about it. I've had far worse."

"But not from me."

"It's all right, Jesse," she said, her voice low. "You were trying to protect my ranch. How could I be angry at you, or upset with what you did?"

He tilted his head. "Most women would be screaming about it."

"I'm not most women."

"I'm beginning to see that," he said slowly. He watched her for a few moments, then said, "Do you want me to walk you to the house?"

"No, I'll be fine."

"Good night, then."

"Night."

She walked toward the house, too aware of Jesse standing and watching her. Even though she'd told him not to walk her to the door, he'd make sure she got into the house. When she reached the porch she turned around, and he raised one hand in response. Waving quickly, she slipped inside and locked the door behind her.

Jesse watched Shea's progress through the house. One by one, the lights on the first floor went out. Soon there was only one light burning, and he assumed it was her bedroom. Banishing images of her bed from his mind, he forced himself to stand and wait until that light, too, was out. Only then did he head over to her truck.

He'd managed to screw up royally tonight, he thought grimly. Not only did he break every single rule he'd ever had about the job and getting involved with a suspect, he hadn't even been aware that she was gone from the property.

He hadn't given her enough credit. He'd imagined that she'd play it close to the vest for a while, wary because he was around. He'd taken it easy tonight, secure in the knowledge that Shea was doing paperwork on his first night on the ranch, and she'd slipped past him.

It wouldn't happen again. Running back to his cabin, he grabbed a small flashlight and several small plastic bags. Then he walked over to her truck, training the light on the vehicle.

It was covered with dust. It usually was, but he thought this dust was a different color than the bright red dust of the ranch. Snapping on a pair of latex gloves, he used a piece of paper to scrape a little of the dust into one of the plastic bags. His first piece of evidence against her.

He went over the truck methodically, taking samples of fibers from the seats and carpets and checking every scrap of paper in the car. There was precious little to be found.

But he had a start. The dust could be compared to that on the Red Rock, and if it wasn't from this ranch, Jesse had confidence that the FBI lab could find a match for it. He had some fiber and hair samples, and they, too, could be compared with Shea's clothes and hair. He held one bag up and shined the flashlight on the single strand of hair. He smiled grimly. The coarse black hair hadn't come from anyone on this ranch. But he guessed it would be a perfect match for a refugee from San Rafael.

As he turned off the flashlight and headed back to his cabin, he recognized the irony of what he'd been doing. Not an hour earlier, he'd been locked in a passionate embrace with Shea. He'd forgotten the reason he was at the Red Rock Ranch, his job, everything but the way she felt and tasted. He'd been so aroused, so hot for her, that he probably couldn't have remembered his own name.

Now he was coolly logging in the first of the evidence he hoped to use to convict her of a crime. He was a cold bastard, he acknowledged. But he had to be. He had no feelings. His life was his job. He did what needed to be done to solve a case, and never had any regrets. He was the Renegade.

He thought he would be up before Shea the next morning, but when he stepped out of his cabin into the predawn darkness, he saw that he was wrong. Someone was in the barn, and he knew it wasn't Levi. He could hear the old man's snores coming from the large cabin. Hurrying toward the light coming from the barn door, he told himself he was anxious to get on with his job. Seeing Shea again had nothing to do with it.

His hands had burned during the night, remembering the silky softness of her hair and the satin smoothness of her cheek. Her scent had swirled around him, waking him from restless sleep, tormenting him with memories of her taste. He'd woken too many times, hot and aroused, with visions of Shea slipping just out of his reach.

But that was the nighttime. He had no control over his dreams, but he sure as hell could control what happened during the day. And during the daylight hours, he intended to be all business.

She was measuring out rations of corn for the cattle in the barn. Besides the steer with the laceration, there were a few others. He thought he approached quietly, but she turned around as he got close.

"Good morning," she said, and her voice was too bright.

"Don't you think it's stretching it to call it morning? What are you doing up so early?"

"We have a lot to do today, and I wanted to get started."
She spoke a little too quickly. "We're going to have a long
day, and being shorthanded isn't going to help."

He gave a lazy shrug and leaned against a stall, watching
her. "That's what I'm doing here. I figured there'd be a lot
of catching up to do."

He saw the flash of relief on her face at the businesslike
conversation. He'd bet she was wondering how he was going
to handle the little incident of last night, the little incident
that was the reason he was up so early. Even though the
memories of their kiss had tortured him all night, he'd be
damned if he'd give her the satisfaction of knowing it.

"Great," she said briskly. "Let's go ahead and give the
steer his injection, then you can help me feed the rest of the
cattle in the barn."

They worked together smoothly and with few words, taking care of the steer with the laceration and then tending to
the rest of the cattle. It was still dark by the time the last
stall had been cleaned.

"Thank goodness you were up early." Shea gave him a
weary smile. "This chore usually takes twice as long."

"I guess we make a good team," he said lightly.

"I guess so."

She didn't look at him as they headed toward the house,
but warning signals flashed in Jesse's brain. It had almost felt
as if they didn't need to talk about what to do. He'd known
intuitively what she needed, what she was going to do next.
And he didn't like it. He only wanted that kind of connection
with a suspect if he was going to be able to use it to arrest
her.

"I suppose once you've worked on a couple of ranches,
the chores are the same everywhere." Her voice was too
bright again, as if she, too, was looking for an explanation
for the peculiar connection he'd felt in the barn. As if she,
too, didn't want to acknowledge it.

"Pretty much. Cattle need to be fed, stalls need to be
cleaned, fences need to be mended."

"Right." They'd reached the porch of the house, and he

paused. "Breakfast will be ready in a few minutes," she said. "But the coffee will be hot. Come on in."

He'd noticed a coffeepot in the tiny kitchen of his cabin, and he knew the smart thing would be to go back to his cabin, alone, and make his own coffee. But he went into the house with her anyway.

He had more of a chance to study the house this time. Shea hurried toward the kitchen, and he followed at a slower pace. The living room was furnished with mission-style furniture that looked comfortable and inviting. A massive stone fireplace filled one wall, and above it were several paintings. Shelves filled with books covered one wall, and the gun case stood against another. The room beckoned, but he'd bet that no one spent much time in it. It had the feel of an unused space, waiting for someone to fill it with life.

"Go ahead in and look around." Shea's voice came from behind him, and he turned around.

"Sorry. I didn't mean to pry."

She waved one hand, clutching a coffee cup with the other. "You weren't." She grinned at him. "Being incurably nosy myself, I excuse it in other people."

He wandered into the room, heading for the paintings above the fireplace. "These are very good. Are they scenes from the Red Rock?"

Her face softened as she smiled. "Yes, they are."

"Who painted them?"

"My mother. She's a very talented artist."

"I can see that." Shea was right. The woman who'd painted these pictures had a gift. Her love and passion for the land leapt out of the canvas.

"She's down in Arizona right now, painting. She always takes off in the fall and comes back in late spring. She'll be home in a few weeks." Shea smiled again, her love for her mother shining out of her face. "She says she's faced as many Utah winters as she intends to face."

He didn't want to see that softness in her eyes or listen to her talk about a mother she clearly adored, although he wasn't sure why. It was a well-known fact that even criminals loved their mothers. Heading out of the room, he asked, "Where can I get some of that coffee?"

"In the kitchen. There's always a pot going. Help yourself anytime during the day."

"Thanks."

Levi came in a few minutes later, and Maria put a stack of pancakes on the dining room table. After they finished eating, Shea pushed back from the table.

"Levi, why don't you and Jesse check on the pasture that borders the Hilbert land? See if it's ready to be grazed. The herd on the back pasture is going to need to be moved in a few days."

"Okay." Levi barely stopped eating long enough to answer.

"When you're done with that, take a look at the truck that Joe and Dusty crashed. It's going to need some repair work, but I'd like to avoid a big mechanic's bill." She turned to Jesse. "Do you know anything about fixing cars and trucks?"

"A little. That was never my area of expertise."

"Why don't you leave it for a few days?" Levi spoke up. "That'll give Joe something to do until he's up to working again. And you know how he feels about his trucks." Levi took another gulp of coffee.

Shea stared across the table at the older man, pinning him with a glare of laser intensity. "I need to know what's wrong with the truck so I can plan how much we'll need to spend to fix it," she said deliberately.

"But Joe..." Levi's voice trailed off as he stared at Shea. Suddenly he nodded. "Right. We'll take a look at the truck today."

Jesse watched the interchange, certain that some unspoken message had been sent. He wondered if it had anything to do with keeping him close to the house and away from the mountain. What *had* Shea been doing up there last night? He'd bet his badge it had something to do with her smuggling of the illegal aliens.

He'd find a way to get up that mountain today, one way or another.

A few minutes later he and Levi were in the truck, heading in the exact opposite direction. He wondered if that had been deliberate, too, and suspected that it had. Leaning back against the cushion of the truck, he said casually, "The three of you and Shea do a lot of work around here."

"We manage. Dev used to help out quite a bit, but he moved to town when he got married, and lately he's been gone a lot."

"Shea sure seems to love what she's doing."

The old man's face softened as he glanced at Jesse. "That she does. Even as a little girl she would trail after her pa or one of us, begging to help. All she's ever wanted to do was work the Red Rock." The old cowboy smiled. "She's the one who named me, you know."

"What do you mean?" In spite of his vow to stay uninvolved, Jesse hungered to know everything he could about Shea.

"I was the only cowboy who didn't wear Wrangler jeans. I liked Levi's jeans better. When Shea was a little girl, she found that fascinating, and she started to call me Levi." He shrugged. "The name stuck."

"So you've known her since she was a child."

The old man turned fierce eyes on him. "I've known her since the day she was born. And I'm telling you, there isn't a better boss, or a better woman, for that matter, on either side of the Mississippi. I'd take it powerful bad if anyone was to hurt her."

"From what I've seen, most of Cameron feels the same way," he said smoothly.

Levi watched him for a moment, then turned his attention back to the road. "I've got eyes in my head. You leave that girl alone. She doesn't need anything from the likes of you."

Levi might be getting on in years, but clearly he was still a force to be reckoned with. "I'm just passing through, Levi. I'll remember what you said."

"You do that, and we'll get along just fine." He shifted

gears and pulled the truck over to the side of the road. "Now let's take a look at this pasture."

Shea pushed away from the desk and rubbed her eyes. She'd just finished the bookkeeping that had been interrupted by her trip the night before, and she was ready for a break. Miguel and the one remaining child needed enough food to get them through to the weekend, and now was a good time to take care of that. Levi would keep Jesse busy for at least the rest of the morning, and she could drive up to the cabin without worrying.

It was a beautiful morning, she thought an hour later as she was heading away from the cabin. She'd told Miguel and the young boy about the trip to the rodeo Saturday, and that the boy's cousins would meet them there. Miguel would leave for San Rafael as soon as the boy was gone, and she could stop worrying about Jesse finding out what she was doing.

Or Devlin.

She still felt ashamed and embarrassed that she hadn't told her brother, but she knew she couldn't, at least not yet. Devlin was the sheriff of Cameron, and what she was doing was technically illegal. She didn't want to put her brother in the horrible position of condoning his sister's illegal acts. Or of being forced to arrest her. So for now, Devlin couldn't know.

So far, it had been easy to keep the secret from him. He'd been preoccupied with Carly's problems when the first children arrived, and after he and Carly got married they'd moved into town. Lately he'd been busy helping Carly sell her apartment and move from New York. He hadn't had much time to spend at the ranch in the last few months. Devlin had been apologetic, but Shea had been glad.

But Carly's apartment had been sold, and in a few weeks, or even less, Devlin would be back in town to stay. Shea's hands tightened on the steering wheel. It was going to be hard to hide what she was doing from Dev.

Pulling the truck to the side of the road, she slid out of the cab and wandered over to a small stream that splashed its way down the mountain. The water flashed in the sunlight, turning the rocks a dark, blood red and making the minerals in the stones gleam like diamonds. She sat down on a rock next to the stream and trailed her hand in the fast-running water.

She was being squeezed from both sides, and she didn't know what to do. There were hundreds more orphaned children in San Rafael in desperate circumstances, living on the streets, in constant danger and literally starving to death. They needed the safety and shelter of a loving home, and many of them had relatives in the United States eager to take them in.

She wanted to help them, needed to help them. But soon she would have to worry about Devlin. And now there was Jesse.

Her thoughts skittered away from the enigmatic man she'd hired yesterday. He was only here on a temporary basis, she told herself. Only until Joe and Dusty were back on their feet. Then he'd be gone.

It didn't matter that he made her skin tingle and her hands tremble. She wasn't interested. She had a ranch to run, and children to save. And Jesse was dangerous.

Before she could decide what to do, she heard the sound of a truck straining to get up the road. She jumped to her feet. Something must have happened, because Levi had understood that he was to keep Jesse away from the mountain this morning.

Her heart pounding, she ran over to the road and watched one of the ranch trucks round a corner and come into view. But it wasn't Levi at the wheel. It was Jesse, and he looked as shocked to see her as she was to see him.

Chapter 5

Shea watched while Jesse stopped the truck and got out. Anger and fear coiled inside her. If she hadn't stopped, if she'd continued back to the house, she might not have seen Jesse. And if he continued on this road, he would have come to the cabin.

"What are you doing up here?" she demanded.

"Would you believe I was lost?"

"No, I won't. You and Levi had specific orders about what to do this morning, and none of your work involved coming up here. Why are you here, Coulton?"

"I thought we were on a first-name basis by now," he said, leaning against the truck.

He stood in the sunlight, quirking one eyebrow at her. His arms were crossed in front of his chest and his legs were crossed at the ankle, and all she could remember was how he'd felt the day before. Her skin heated and her heart began to pound, and because that frightened her almost as much as what he might have found, her temper erupted.

"The only thing I'm going to be calling you is unemployed unless I get some answers. When I give an order, I expect it to be obeyed. When I tell you to do some work on the opposite side of the ranch, I don't expect to find you wandering around up here, miles away from where you're supposed to be.''

He shrugged, and the careless gesture only made her more angry. ''You told us to take a look at the truck. That's why I'm up here.''

''The last time I checked, the truck was in the garage.''

''The cap was missing from the radiator. I thought I might be able to find it if I went back to where it had crashed.''

Shea took a step closer to him, too angry to remember to be careful around Jesse. ''First of all, I did not tell you to look for missing radiator caps. I simply wanted to know the extent of the damage. And secondly, if someone had to come up here and look for something, why didn't Levi do it? He knows the mountain a lot better than you do. He wouldn't have gotten lost.''

''I thought Levi could use a break. He's having a cup of coffee.'' He gave her an innocent smile, and she ground her teeth. She was very certain that Jesse hadn't been innocent in a long, long time.

''I'm sure your mother thinks of you as a considerate person, Coulton, but you're barking up the wrong tree if you think I'll fall for that. What were you doing up here?''

Something in his eyes shifted and hardened as they stared at each other. ''I don't care whether you believe me or not. I'm telling you the truth. I came up here looking for the radiator cap and I got lost. I must have taken a wrong turn. End of story.''

Even in the hot sun she could feel the heat from his body, and she was abruptly aware that she was too close to him. Anger vibrated in the small space between them, anger and some other emotion she didn't want to recognize. But taking a step backward would be losing ground, and she knew well that she couldn't do that. Experience had taught her that a woman who was in charge of a ranch couldn't afford any sign of weakness.

"You can take one more turn and go right back where you came from. I'll talk to Levi later."

He shifted and stood up straight, and now he was so close she could almost feel his breath. His hazel eyes burned into her, their green lights sparking. Her heart betrayed her by slowly rolling over in her chest, but she didn't move away. She wouldn't allow herself to do that.

"I thought you would appreciate my taking the initiative," he drawled.

"Are you going to give me that corporate nonsense about being an empowered employee?" She glared at him.

His lips twitched and suddenly most of the tension dissipated. "I wouldn't dream of it, Ms. McAllister. No, ma'am. I know that's not the way you do things. God forbid you should have an employee who's capable of thinking by himself."

She couldn't suppress a smile, although she tried to scowl. "Just remember that, Coulton, and we'll get along fine."

"Don't worry, Shea. I won't forget it again."

Although his lips still curved up, the smile was gone from his eyes. Shea shivered. They held nothing but a cool challenge now. It was almost, she thought, as if he knew her secret. Almost as if he was telling her that he'd find her out, one way or another.

But that was ridiculous. Jesse Coulton was a drifter cowboy, with no more interest in her refugees than the man in the moon. Shaking off the chill that had enveloped her, she said, "You can follow me back to the house. I was on my way home."

"Fine." But he didn't move. He continued to watch her. "What were you doing up here, anyway?"

"This is my ranch. I can go anywhere I want, without explaining myself to you or anyone else," she answered coolly.

He nodded once and moved to get into his truck. But before he turned away, she saw a flash of anger in his eyes. Anger and a hard determination that disturbed her. Was he the kind of man who had to be in charge, who didn't like a woman telling him what to do?

She hoped not. He'd accepted a job on the Red Rock, knowing that she would be his boss. And she hadn't noticed any signs of resentment yesterday. Especially not last night.

She turned abruptly and climbed into her own truck. She wasn't going to think about the kiss they had shared. It had been a mistake, one fueled by nerves and adrenaline. And it wasn't going to happen again.

Jesse followed her down the mountain, keeping his truck close to hers. In spite of her vow not to think about the mistake she'd made the night before, it haunted her memory. Jesse's taste lingered in her mouth, and his scent seemed to cling to her. Every time she caught a glimpse of him, in the truck behind her, she remembered the way his fingers had tangled in her hair, pulled her close to him. By the time they reached the house, her temper had cooled but desire had bloomed into life.

She was a rational adult, she told herself. She could handle this. Climbing out of her truck, she approached Jesse with a smile plastered to her face. "Why don't you get Levi and we'll take a look at that truck?"

He nodded once. "He's probably in the house. We'll be right back."

His eyes were cool and unreadable. Whatever emotion had raged through him up on the mountain was now gone. Or at least well hidden. Shea allowed her gaze to follow Jesse up to the house, then she deliberately turned and went into the garage.

She was staring at the crumpled front end of the truck when Levi and Jesse came into the garage. Levi was pointing out the repairs that the truck would need when she heard the rumble of a vehicle pulling into the yard. She jerked to attention.

"That sounds like Ben's truck."

Jesse watched her run out into the yard. He shot a questioning glance to Levi, who shrugged.

"I think she's been listening for that truck most of the

morning. She's been powerful worried about Joe and Dusty.''
He shook his head and spat into the dust. ''They're a couple
of damn fools. I wouldn't have hit that rock.''

The emotion in the old man's eyes betrayed his words. ''It
looks like everyone around here has been worried about
them,'' Jesse said.

Levi shrugged. ''You get used to the way a fellow works
after you been working with him for a while.'' He glanced
at Jesse out of the corner of his eye. ''I'm not saying there's
anything wrong with you. But Joe, Dusty and I have been
together for a long time.'' He shrugged again. ''I don't want
to have to get used to anyone else.''

Jesse understood it was the most he was going to get from
Levi. The old man wasn't going to reveal his fear for his
friends to a virtual stranger. And Jesse couldn't blame him.
He understood how to hide emotion.

''Might as well see how they're doing,'' Levi muttered,
and hurried out of the barn after Shea.

Jesse followed more slowly, content to watch the reunion
from afar. The missing radiator cap weighed down his shirt
pocket, knocking against his chest as he walked. Every tiny
bump reminded him of his purpose on the Red Rock Ranch.
And it sure as hell wasn't to be a welcoming committee to
Joe and Dusty.

It was bad luck that Shea had caught him this morning.
Levi had bought his excuse of looking for the radiator cap,
and he should have had plenty of time to look around. He
scowled as he watched Shea embrace two more old men,
both of them looking fragile and still shaken.

She'd been one step ahead of him today, too. It was a new
experience for him, and he didn't like it one damn bit. But
it couldn't last forever. Sooner or later he'd get his chance,
and then he'd nail her to the wall.

Just then Shea looked around, spotted him, and gestured
at him to join them. He sauntered over to the group, assessing
the two other cowboys that worked at the ranch. They were
both as old as Levi, but their eyes were sharp and shrewd.

''Jesse, this is Joe and Dusty,'' Shea said, introducing him.

She turned to the men, one of whom had a cast on his arm. The other had a bandage covering a spot on his head. "Joe, Dusty, I hired Jesse Coulton to help out until you get back on your feet. I'm counting on you to help me train him."

Dusty gave him a nod, but Joe examined him with suspicious eyes. "You qualified to work on a ranch the size of the Red Rock?" he barked.

"I think so." Jesse glanced over at Shea. "I gave the boss my references, and she hired me."

"We'll see." Joe's voice was grim, and Jesse knew he'd have to watch his step. It was clear that Joe wouldn't cut him any slack.

"Jesse and Levi were looking at the truck," Shea said, stepping between them and taking Joe's arm. "When you're up to it, could you take a look at it for me? I want your opinion before we do anything about it."

"I'll take a look at it right now," Joe said. "It's about time I got back to work."

"Not right now." Shea steered him gently toward the house. "Maria is going to have lunch ready soon, and you know she'd skin me alive if I made you late for a meal." She grinned at Joe, and Jesse felt his chest constrict. "I'm already number one on her list of troublemakers."

The old man's eyes softened, and Shea linked her arms through Joe's and Dusty's as the group made its way toward the house. The serious expression on Ben Jackson's face lightened as he watched Shea with the old cowboys. Clearly, Ben thought as much of Shea as everyone else.

The next instant the moment disappeared as everyone started talking at once. Joe and Dusty complained about the hospital food and the forced inactivity, Levi railed at them for being stupid enough to need to go to the hospital in the first place, and Shea tried to out-talk all of them. Ben just grinned at the show. Jesse felt as if his head was spinning as he tried to watch Shea and keep track of what everyone was saying.

Shea McAllister had been nothing but a surprise to him from the moment he'd stepped foot on the Red Rock Ranch.

And he didn't like surprises. She'd completely shattered his preconceived ideas about her, and it had taken little more than twenty-four hours.

The three cowboys who worked for her clearly adored her, as did her brother's friend. And if Jesse hadn't known who she was, he might be well on his way to joining them. He scowled and stared down at the food on his plate. He hadn't been prepared for Shea McAllister, and that annoyed him. He prided himself on being prepared for everything.

"You can't frown like that while you're eating, Coulton." Shea's voice was too close to his ear.

Jesse snapped his head up to look at her. "Excuse me?"

Shea grinned at him, making his breath catch in his chest. "Maria takes it real hard if she thinks someone's not enjoying her food. You'd better eat up. You don't want an ugly scene, believe me."

"I wasn't frowning."

"You were doing a darned good imitation, then." Her smile dimmed. "I'm sorry if I came down too hard on you this morning. My temper got the best of me."

Shea thought he was sulking because she'd yelled at him. He leaned back in his chair. "I've noticed that about you."

Instead of taking offense, she grinned at him again. "It's another of my failings. I have a lot of them, I'm afraid."

"You don't seem too concerned about it."

This time she laughed out loud. "I don't have to be. Joe, Dusty and Levi, not to mention my beloved brother, are only too happy to point my faults out to me. So I let them worry about it. I have better things to do."

Her blue eyes were bright with laughter, shining at him, inviting him to join the joke at her expense. She shimmered with vitality. Something painful tugged at his chest, twisted inside him. Suddenly his determination to dim that light in her eyes made him vaguely disgusted with himself.

Appalled with himself, he pushed away from the table, muttering, "I have a lot of things to do before we get back to work. I'll be out in the barn."

The radiator cap slapped against him as he hurried out of

the room, one small deception among many. A necessary one, he reminded himself harshly. When someone broke the law, sneered at it, you couldn't always play fair. And playing dirty against the criminals had never bothered him before now.

As he strode out of the house, he tried to close his ears to the sounds of laughter and love that he left behind. So what if Shea seemed to be universally adored? So what if he found her attractive and disturbing? It didn't matter. The only thing that mattered was justice, and he was going to have it. No matter the cost.

Two days later Shea jumped out of bed and hurried to the window. A clear, sunny day, perfect for a rodeo. She dressed carefully, then hurried downstairs to grab a quick breakfast.

Jesse was already sitting at the dining room table, finishing a stack of pancakes. His eyebrows rose as he spotted her.

"Pretty fancy clothes," he said.

She grinned at him as she poured herself a cup of coffee. Even her disturbing attraction to him couldn't dim her enthusiasm today. Not only was she excited about the rodeo, but the last child would be picked up today. "Demon and I are competing in a rodeo today. My clothes are all part of the show."

Jesse's eyebrows rose. "You're racing today?"

"Yep." She waited for the toast to pop up. "We're leaving as soon as I have enough to eat to satisfy Maria."

Jesse watched her as he took a swallow of coffee, then said, "Mind if I tag along?"

She stared at him, appalled, as her happy mood vanished. "You want to come with me to the rodeo?"

"I'd love to. I'd like to see you race."

Her mind struggled with all the excuses she could give him, discarding one after another. She had given him and the other three cowboys the day off, and there was really no reason to refuse his request.

Except for one.

One small child. She was going to meet Paolo's family at

the rodeo today, and turn the boy over to them. How could she do that with Jesse trailing along with her?

"You've already seen the show, remember?" Her answer was weak, but she was stalling for time to think of a better excuse.

He leaned back in his chair. "That was only a few practice rounds. I have a feeling you're a different person when you're actually competing."

How could he know so much about her when he'd been working for her for less than a week? And she'd done her best to avoid him the last couple of days, too. "I'm sure you've been to more rodeos than you'd want to count. You don't really want to waste your day at another one, do you?"

He smiled at her, a slow smile that was full of promise. "I've never been to a rodeo where you've competed. Believe me, I'd remember that."

She shrugged helplessly. "I can't stop you, I guess. But I think you're going to be bored."

His smile turned enigmatic. "Believe me, Shea, that's the last thing I'm worried about."

"I'm leaving in a half hour," she said abruptly, reaching for the coffeepot. "If you're ready, you can follow me there. The town is a little over an hour's drive away."

"Is someone else going?" His sharp words made her turn around to face him again. But his eyes were merely questioning. She didn't see a trace of the hardness that had filled his voice.

"I'm going alone. Why?"

He quirked an eyebrow at her. "Why don't I just go in your truck? It seems silly to take two vehicles."

"If you drive there yourself, you can leave when you like," she pointed out, ignoring the panic that was beginning to swell inside her. "You won't be tied down to my schedule."

"I don't mind. It's my day off, remember?" His smile was open and guileless.

It would be all right, she told herself, trying to calm her panic. Paolo was already safely stowed in the hidden compartment in the horse trailer. She usually had the children ride in the cab of the truck with her, but because of Jesse's presence on the ranch, she'd told Miguel to hide Paolo. She'd planned on stopping, once they were away from Cameron, to let the boy ride in the truck with her.

But he would be safe and comfortable in the small compartment. He even had a tiny window, concealed among the metal grill work on the side of the trailer. Paolo would be fine. And once they got to the rodeo, she could think of a way to get rid of Jesse temporarily while she reunited Paolo with his family.

She shrugged. "Suit yourself." She set the coffee cup down on the table, disturbed to find that it rattled. "If you're not in the truck when I'm ready to go, I'm leaving without you."

"I'll be there."

He was, too. By the time she brought Demon out of the barn and loaded him into the trailer hitched to the pickup, Jesse was lounging in the cab of the truck. As she was securing Demon in the trailer, she took a chance and opened the door that hid Paolo. His anxious eyes smiled when he saw her. She whispered a few words of reassurance, then closed the door again.

Paolo would be fine, she thought sadly. He was only eight, but already he'd seen far too much in his short life. Riding in a hidden compartment in a truck would hold no fears for the boy. On the contrary, it would seem like a luxury to him, after what he'd been through in San Rafael.

She slammed the door of the truck harder than necessary as she slid into the seat next to Jesse. He sat up in the seat and nodded toward the mug of coffee steaming in her cupholder.

"I thought you might need more of that."

"Thank you," she said, looking at him for the first time, feeling her anger dissipate like the clouds in a Utah sky. "How did you know?"

His mouth quirked up in a half smile, the same one that regularly made her heart do back flips. "I'm a fast learner.

It didn't take long to realize that your attitude toward life depended on how much coffee you had in the morning. And you didn't have much today.''

She couldn't stop the smile that curved her lips. ''I'm always nervous the morning of a rodeo.'' Lately, it had been for reasons other than her race. ''I usually try to sneak out of the house before Maria can yell at me for not eating enough.''

''You mean I should have smuggled out some pancakes, too?'' His voice was light and teasing, and when she glanced over at him, she saw that his face was alight with laughter.

It softened the hard planes of his cheeks and made his hazel eyes devastating pools of green. A relaxed and laughing Jesse was a dangerous man, she realized, as the impact hit her square in the chest. He was hazardous to her good intentions.

''The coffee was perfect,'' she reassured him.

They talked the rest of the way to Panguitch, and she had to admit that she enjoyed Jesse's company. The disturbing intensity that seemed so much a part of Jesse on the Red Rock was gone, replaced by a relaxed and comfortable attitude. By the time they reached the outskirts of the small town and began to slow down in the rodeo traffic, Shea was almost sorry the comfortable intimacy was going to end.

''Is all this traffic headed for the rodeo?'' he asked, incredulous.

''Of course.'' She glanced at him out of the corner of her eye. ''You've been to rodeos before, haven't you?''

He was silent for a moment. ''All right, I'll confess. This is my first one.''

''You've never been to a rodeo before?'' She heard the astonishment in her voice, and didn't bother to hide it. ''I thought you'd been working on ranches for several years.''

''I have been. But I never saw the point in watching a rodeo on my day off. Why pay good money to go and watch cowboys get bucked off a horse when it happened to me all week long?''

Shea's lips quivered. "I've never thought about it quite that way before."

He grinned at her. "I found more interesting things to do on my days off. And none of them involved flying through the air to land on my backside."

"Don't let anyone hear that kind of heresy. You'll be hounded out of Utah by an angry mob."

"I'll have to trust you to keep my secret, then."

They were stopped in a line of traffic waiting to get into the fairgrounds, and she turned to look at him. That was a mistake, she realized immediately. His laughing eyes held her mesmerized, and she couldn't look away. For a moment, the Jesse she saw was a tender man, one who could care about her and make her laugh. He was also a man who could make her forget her obligations, she realized with a jerk of guilt.

She'd given barely a thought to Paolo, hidden in the horse trailer. Guiltily she looked back out the windshield, willing herself to forget about Jesse and the way she was drowning in his eyes. She had to think of a way to get rid of Jesse long enough to connect Paolo with his family.

Jesse noticed the change in Shea immediately. One moment she was laughing, open, her eyes inviting him to share the joke. The next moment she sat straight and tense in the truck, her hands clenching the steering wheel, her mouth a taut line in her face.

What had happened? Had she seen someone outside the truck? He scanned the crowds of people, but couldn't tell if anyone was paying attention to them. He had almost convinced himself that her trip to the rodeo today was innocent, made strictly for her own pleasure. But something or someone had just reminded her otherwise.

"Something wrong?" he asked casually.

She shook her head, jerkily. "No. I'm just anxious to get inside and get settled. I don't like to keep Demon in the trailer for too long. He gets antsy."

And now she was antsy, too. He wondered why. "It looks like the traffic is moving again."

"It won't be long," she muttered.

He wondered if she was reminding him or herself. "How long before you race?"

"A couple of hours. The barrel racers generally go first, and I always allow extra time. But we'll have to keep moving once we get inside."

After another few minutes they were past the gate. The attendant gave them a stall assignment and directed them toward the unloading area. Shea pulled the truck to a stop, slid out, and hurried to open the door to the trailer.

"Could you do me a favor?" she asked in a low voice.

"What's that?"

"Take Demon out and walk him over to his stall. After you find out where it is, walk him around for a few minutes. I need to hand in my registration form to the rodeo officials, and..." A red flush colored her cheeks. "I drank a lot of coffee, but I don't want to make Demon wait. Would you mind?"

She'd managed to back him into a very tidy corner, he thought with angry admiration. How could he refuse to take care of her horse while she saw to the necessities of nature? All of his suspicions came swarming back. He pushed the camaraderie of the trip to the rodeo out of his mind. Clearly, there was more on Shea's agenda today than a barrel race in a rodeo.

"I'll take care of him for you."

She backed Demon out of the trailer, and murmured a few words to him. The huge black horse snorted once and tossed his head, almost, Jesse thought, as if he understood every word she said and was answering her. Shea ran her hand down the horse's back, then handed him the lead rope.

"I'll meet you at the stall in a few minutes."

"We'll be there."

He looked back over his shoulder as he led the horse away, but Shea had disappeared into the trailer again. He lingered as long as possible, but she didn't come out of the trailer. Once he was out of sight, he trotted along as fast as he could without drawing attention.

"Sorry, fella," he said when he reached Demon's assigned

stall. "She'll walk you around a little later. Right now I have to find out what she's up to."

He raced back to the trailer, but Shea was gone. She'd left the gate open, but the trailer itself was empty. Spinning around, he scanned the crowd for her bright blond head, but he couldn't pick her out of the masses of people. The sun blazed down at him, forcing him to squint, making it harder to distinguish one person from another.

Jesse began to push through the people, murmuring, "Excuse me. Pardon me," as he hurried through the crowd. He lingered by the rest rooms for a while, but Shea didn't appear. She wasn't near the registration booth, either.

Jesse's frustration churned as he searched for her. She could have gone anywhere, done anything by now. He had no idea what she could be up to at a rodeo, but she was up to something. He was sure of that.

Shea was going to have to come up with a different profession, he thought savagely. He was able to read her much too easily. Then he thought uneasily of his first few days on the ranch. He hadn't been able to read her so easily then. What had happened in the last few days to make it possible for him to read her like a book?

That was something he didn't want to think about. Not now, not ever. All he wanted to do was find Shea and catch her in some illegal act. Then he could arrest her and get out of Cameron. He needed to get away from Shea. He'd enjoyed himself too much this morning on the ride to the rodeo. He'd allowed himself to let down too many barriers. And that was dangerous.

Just then he spotted Shea. She was crouched on the ground, in front of a little boy and his parents. She held a stick of cotton candy behind her back with one hand, and with the other she was giving the child a hug. When she leaned back and presented the boy with the bright pink cotton candy, his face lit with awe and excitement.

She stood up, embraced the two adults, then bent to kiss

the boy again. As she turned away, he saw tears on her face. Jesse's heart stopped in his chest, then it began to thunder again.

What the hell was going on?

Chapter 6

"Are you all right?"

The words seemed to tumble out of his mouth on their own as he hurried toward Shea. The couple standing behind her gave him a wary look and drew the child closer to them. Ignoring them, he saw nothing but the tears swimming in Shea's eyes.

She gave him a blinding smile and nodded. "I'm fine. I just got some dust in my eyes."

Turning back to the couple behind her, she said something in a low voice. He saw the woman smile, the man nod, then the family walked away. She watched them go for a moment, then turned back to him.

"Did you get Demon settled into his stall?"

Her voice was steady and even, but he felt the strain quivering through it. And as she started toward him, he saw her glance at the family one more time as they disappeared into the crowds.

"He's fine." Jesse watched the emotions play across her face and wondered who the family was. And what they had done to make her cry.

"I have to hand in my registration form," she said, walking in the opposite direction from the family. "Do you want to come with me, or wait with Demon?"

"I'll come with you." He paused and glanced over at her. "Were you on your way there when you ran into your friends?"

"Mmm," she murmured. She didn't look at him, but he felt her stiffen. Even her hair seemed to vibrate with the tension. "Little Paul had never had cotton candy before. That seemed more important than a registration form."

He narrowed his eyes as he watched her, but he didn't say anything more. He suspected that the tears in her eyes were inspired by something more important than giving a kid his first taste of cotton candy, but he wasn't about to probe.

Shea McAllister's personal life was none of his business, he reminded himself emphatically. Not what she did at the rodeo, not how many kids she cried over. The only thing he was concerned about was her illegal activities. And as long as he stuck to her like a burr today, she wouldn't have a chance to conduct any of those.

After she handed her registration form to the woman at the makeshift booth, they strolled back toward the stall area and Demon. The closer they got, the more she relaxed. By the time they reached the stall and Demon stuck his head out, demanding attention, all the tension he'd felt when he'd found her with the boy and his family had disappeared.

"Did you walk him?" she said, glancing over at him. The only emotion in her face now was curiosity.

He shook his head. "I wasn't sure what you wanted me to do with him. And I wasn't sure how he'd react to a stranger in the middle of these crowds."

"Demon knows what the crowds mean," she murmured, scratching the big horse's nose. "Don't you, fella?"

The horse tossed his head as if he was answering her, and she snapped a lead rope onto his halter. "Come on, let's start our warm-up."

Shea led Demon out of the stall and began walking him, murmuring to him in a low voice. All her attention was focused on the horse. It was as if the peculiar scene with the family had never happened. And as he leaned back against a stall and watched her with her horse, it was as if he didn't exist, either.

It wasn't personal, he realized. Shea was simply getting herself and Demon ready to race. As he watched, he could almost see her close in on herself, narrowing her focus to exclude anything but the race from her mind. She vibrated with intensity and determination, with the will to do her best. Her passion for what she was doing was etched in every line of her face.

Once again he felt a surge of admiration for her, an admiration he tried to erase from his mind. It would be easier, and far more efficient, if he could think of her as nothing more than a criminal. But Shea was turning out to be the most complicated criminal he had ever pursued.

She had managed to hide her tracks well. If they hadn't been given information by an informant who knew her well, no one would ever have known about her smuggling. She managed to convey an air of innocence which was completely at odds with what she was doing.

And he seriously doubted if anyone he'd arrested had ever cried because they'd been able to give a child his first taste of cotton candy.

"Sorry," she called over to him, interrupting his thoughts. "I didn't mean to ignore you. Demon and I have a ritual we go through before each race."

"It's okay," he said, watching her as he leaned back against the stall. "I invited myself along, so you're not responsible for entertaining me."

"I didn't think I was." She gave him a grin that made his heart roll in his chest. "I just wanted to explain what we were doing. Demon and I are going to head to the ring now. I like to warm up for a while before the race."

"Good luck."

She gave him another grin as she tucked a hat onto her head. "Luck has nothing to do with it, Coulton."

Her jeans hugged her slender hips, and the fringe on the

shirt she wore brushed the curve of her breasts every time she moved. Heat flashed through him suddenly, and he wanted to taste her again, to savor the curve of her mouth clinging to his. He wanted to feel the firmness of her breasts pressed against his chest, and the long length of her legs twined with his.

Instead he crossed his arms over his chest to hide the trembling of his hands, and said, "Then break a leg."

She laughed, a low, throaty chuckle that made his blood surge. "Thanks, Jesse." She raised one hand in a casual salute, then she turned and led the huge black horse away.

He had a serious problem.

For a moment he considered letting another agent take over the case, but he knew he couldn't do that. He was trapped. He'd gone to too much trouble to get this job, to make his background realistic. If he disappeared now and someone else showed up looking for a job, Shea would be suspicious. No, he was stuck with the case. So he'd better get his hormones under control and concentrate on what he had to do.

When he thought he could walk out in public without embarrassing himself, he strolled to the stands. Swinging up into the bleachers, he spotted Shea immediately. She and a number of other women were trotting their horses around the ring, slowly circling the course.

Shea was easy to find. Her bright blue shirt stood out in the ring, but it wasn't her shirt that made her so visible. She was a picture of intensity. The grin was gone from her mouth and her eyes. Instead, she studied everything from the dust on the ground to the placement of the barrels to the distance between the barrels and the boundaries of the ring. Some of the other riders were talking and laughing together, but Shea didn't look at any of her competitors. She sat ramrod straight in her saddle, her competitiveness a fierce flame burning inside her.

Jesse shifted uneasily on the hard wooden seat in the bleachers as he watched her. Why was he able to read her so effortlessly? What gave him the power to figure out what she was thinking?

It had to be because Shea was so open. She didn't try to hide what was on her mind. He allowed himself a slight smile as he watched her circle the ring. Shea never hesitated to tell him or anyone else just what she was thinking.

But the connection he felt went deeper than that. It far exceeded his usual approach. Whenever he was on a case, he made it a point to bore into his target's mind, to think like the criminal he wanted to apprehend. To know them, as completely as possible.

Abruptly he tore his gaze away from Shea and looked blindly down at the program he held clenched in one hand. He wanted to know Shea, all right, but arresting her had nothing to do with it. And it had to stop.

Smoothing out the program, he looked at the schedule of events. He spotted Shea's name in the program, but made himself ignore it. The barrel racers were first, then the bronc riders. There was something for kids called mutton busting next, then the ropers and the bull riders. He suspected that he'd learn far more about rodeos today than he ever intended to know.

When the loudspeaker above him crackled to life and a tinny voice announced the beginning of the barrel racing, he looked up with a start. The ring had been cleared and an aura of expectancy hovered over the crowds in the stands. Suddenly a buzzer sounded and a horse and rider exploded into the ring.

The young woman clinging to the back of the horse guided the animal around a barrel in front of the stands, then across the ring to the next barrel. After circling perilously close, they headed for the barrel at the far end of the ring. The horse brushed the barrel but quickly recovered, then they dashed at full speed the length of the ring and out the gate.

A time flashed on the screen. It was just a little over eighteen seconds, and Jesse had no idea if that was good or bad. The voice on the loudspeaker said, "That was Mandy Powell, with a time of eighteen point two three seconds. Let's give Mandy a big hand."

Several more riders competed, some doing better than

Mandy, some worse. There was no sign of Shea. Jesse stared at the area near the gate, looking for a glimpse of her blue shirt. Just as he began to wonder if the rodeo had been a ruse and she had cleverly managed to ditch him, he saw her burst into the ring.

She leaned far over Demon's neck, her face a blur in the horse's mane. She flew around the first two barrels almost effortlessly, cutting the angles so close that she just missed brushing the barrels. When she raced for the last barrel, she crouched even lower over Demon's neck.

The horse didn't even break stride as he turned around the far barrel. And when they headed for the gate, Shea clinging to his back, the horse put his ears back and ran even faster.

When they were more than halfway to the gate, Shea sat up in the saddle and pulled up sharply on the reins. Demon flattened his ears, but he slowed down. As they left the ring, Jesse saw that the horse was limping slightly.

There was a disappointed groan from the crowd. The announcer said, "That was Shea McAllister, folks. I don't know what happened, but she was on track for the fastest time so far. That's too bad."

Ignoring the murmur of the crowd around him, Jesse jumped up and edged his way out of the stands. Once he was on the ground, he ran around the ring to the area where the contestants entered.

Shea and Demon were off to the side. Shea was crouched down in front of her horse, examining his left front leg. Jesse shoved his way through the crowd until he was standing next to her.

"What happened?"

She looked up at him, her face pinched with worry. "I don't know. I felt him alter his gait during the last dash. I can't feel anything wrong in his leg, though."

Several curious bystanders crowded around them, watching Shea. Seeing the fear and worry on her face, he grabbed the reins that dangled from Demon's bridle and slung one arm over Shea's shoulders.

"Let's get him back to his stall. It'll be easier to examine him there."

She nodded mutely and allowed him to lead her away. For just a moment he thought she leaned into him, pressing herself closer. Then she straightened, but she didn't move away from his arm.

By the time they reached his stall, he knew she'd regained her composure. Working quickly, she removed the saddle and bridle from Demon and snapped a lead rope into place on his halter.

"Let me hold that," Jesse said gruffly.

She handed it to him without a word, then bent over the horse's leg again. Her fingers probed and stroked over Demon's joints, and finally she picked up his foot and stared at the bottom.

Slowly she replaced his foot on the ground, then stood up.

"Did you find anything?" Jesse asked.

She nodded. "It looks like his foot is bruised."

"It wasn't bruised before you started racing." Jesse knew Shea would have checked.

"There must have been a stone under the dirt in the ring." She ran her hand down Demon's back. "They're supposed to rake the dirt to get rid of all the stones. I guess they missed one."

"You would have won, you know."

"Probably."

He watched her scratch the horse's nose. "You don't seem too concerned."

She turned to him. "You think I would have been happy winning if it had hurt Demon even more?"

"Some people want to win no matter what." He watched her carefully.

"I'm not some people." Her voice was biting. "I like to win as much as the next person. Probably more. But a blue ribbon isn't worth risking Demon."

"You would only have had to let him go a few more feet," he said.

"It doesn't matter," she said fiercely. "A few feet or a

few inches, the end result could have been the same. Demon is worth more than one winning run. There'll be other races.''

"It wouldn't have done any permanent damage to let him race on a bruised foot." He wasn't sure why he was pushing her, but he sensed that her attitude about the race and her horse was important to understanding Shea.

"I didn't know it was just a bruised foot. I'm not one of those winning is everything people," she said, and he cringed at the scorn in her voice. "Maybe you are, Jesse. And if you are, then I guess you wouldn't understand."

"I do understand," he said, grabbing her hand when she would have stormed out of the stall. "I would have done the same thing."

She stared down at their hands, still joined together, but didn't pull away. "Then why are you faulting me for doing just that?"

He shifted her hand in his, pressed their palms together. The ridges of her callouses rubbed against his skin, reminding him of her strength.

"I just want to understand you, Shea," he said quietly, and he was appalled to find that it was the truth. And that it had nothing to do with the case. "I saw how determined you were to win, how much you loved what you were doing. And I saw how good you were. You were head and shoulders above the rest of the barrel racers. You should have won."

"I'm older than most of them," she said automatically. "There were a lot of teenagers here today, and I've been competing longer than most of those girls." She looked up at him. "Yes, I want to win, Jesse. I'll confess to being very competitive. But I couldn't hurt Demon just to win. Some things are more important than winning."

His heart turned over in his chest as he watched her in the dim light of the stall. Her hair was disheveled and the blue shirt showed smudges of dirt from Demon's legs. The worry had mostly disappeared from her eyes, but he saw the disappointment, deep in their blue depths.

"I was proud of you," he murmured, and a flush of pleasure filled her face. "I wanted to stand up and cheer for you when you pulled up. It doesn't matter what the scoreboard says, Shea. You were the winner here today.''

Her blue eyes softened as she stared at him. ''Thank you, Jesse,'' she whispered. ''I'm glad you understand.''

He understood far more than she realized, he thought with a jolt. And none of what he saw pointed toward Shea being a criminal. For the first time, he allowed himself to wonder if their informant had been wrong. If he had made a mistake. Because, for the first time, Jesse couldn't think of Shea as a criminal. He could think of her only as a woman.

He swayed toward her, unable to take his eyes off her face. Her mouth softened and trembled, and her eyes began to drift closed. He needed to kiss her, needed to feel her in his arms. But just as he gripped her shoulders and moved closer, there was a noise outside the stall.

''I hope I'm not interrupting.''

Jesse jerked back and looked at the man standing on the other side of the stall door. His twinkling eyes said that he knew exactly what he'd been interrupting.

Shea looked over at Pat O'Connor and felt hot color flood her cheeks. What would the veterinarian from Cameron think? ''Hi, Pat,'' she said, her voice too bright. ''I didn't know you were the vet for this rodeo.''

''The regular guy was sick, and they called to ask if one of us could take over. Becca passed the job onto me.''

Shea could just imagine what Pat would tell his partner, Becca Farrell, when he returned to Cameron. ''I'm glad you're here,'' she said, determined to act as businesslike as possible. ''I think Demon just has a bruised foot, but I was going to call Becca when we got home. Now you can take a look at it.''

Pat eased into the stall and bent down next to the horse. Before looking at his foot, the vet examined Demon's whole leg. Finally he lifted the foot and probed at it carefully.

After a while he stood up. ''I think you're right, Shea. It looks like a stone bruise. I can't find anything wrong with his leg otherwise. Give him a few days, and he should be as good as new." Pat glanced over at Jesse, his curiosity evident.

"This is Jesse Coulton," Shea said. "He's the new hand on the Red Rock."

"That so? Nice to meet you, Coulton." Pat reached over and shook Jesse's hand, his eyes full of speculation. "I'd heard that Shea hired someone."

"I was lucky enough to be in the right place at the right time," Jesse said coolly. Shea saw the shuttered look in his eyes and wondered what he was thinking. Was he mortified that he'd been caught almost kissing his boss? Was he angry at Pat for interrupting them? She couldn't tell.

Pat turned back to her. "I'll tell Becca what happened. She can stop by and take another look at him in a few days."

"Thanks, Pat." Shea felt Jesse's tension behind her, and she willed Pat O'Connor to leave. He must have heard her unspoken words, because he turned to her and smiled.

"Take it easy, Shea." He glanced over at Jesse. "Glad to meet you, Coulton. Maybe I'll see you around town."

"Never can tell." Jesse's voice was noncommittal.

After Pat walked away, Shea fiddled with Demon's halter. She wasn't sure why she didn't want to face Jesse.

"I'm sorry," he said after a moment.

"What do you mean?" She turned to look at him.

"For putting you in a compromising situation."

Warmth bloomed inside her. "Isn't that a bit old-fashioned?"

"I'm your employee," he said stiffly. "You were about to kiss me, for God's sake. What's O'Connor going to think?"

"I don't care. I'm an adult, and so are you. What we do on our own time is nobody's business except ours."

"That's naive, Shea. I work for you. Cameron is a small town. You know damn well that you'll be the talk of the town."

She lifted her chin. "It won't be the first time, and I'm sure it won't be the last. I don't care what people say."

Jesse stared at her for a moment, then shook his head.

''Why aren't I surprised? I should have figured that's what you'd say.'' A teasing smile played around his mouth. ''Maybe I don't want my reputation tarnished. Did you ever think of that?''

She tilted her head and studied him, then slowly smiled. ''I'd guess that your reputation was the last thing you worried about. I think you care even less than me if people are talking about you.''

A startled look flew across his face, as if she had surprised him. He recovered quickly. ''If I want another job, I have to worry about my reputation.''

''Are you telling me that you're quitting?'' She was shocked at the bitter disappointment that swept through her.

''Of course not,'' he said quietly. ''Do you think I'd leave you in the lurch?''

''You have no contract with me or the Red Rock,'' she countered. ''There's nothing stopping you from looking for a better job.''

''I'm not going anywhere, Shea.'' For a moment, his eyes hardened and he reminded her of the stranger who'd come to her ranch looking for a job, tough and faintly dangerous. Then he smiled and the fleeting impression was gone. ''You took a chance on me, and I'll stay as long as you need me.''

He looked over at Demon, then back at her. ''Will he be all right alone? Do you want to look around the rodeo?''

The subject had been firmly changed, but that was fine with her. She had no desire right now to examine her feelings for Jesse. So she grinned at him and said, ''I'd love to walk around the rodeo. Demon will be fine. I'll give him some food, and he'll be as happy as a mouse in a cheese factory.''

A few minutes later they emerged from the barn into the bright light of the spring day. Shea glanced up at Jesse, walking beside her, and wondered what he was thinking. Why had he wanted to come to the rodeo with her? The only explanation was that he wanted to spend time with her, get to know her.

She wouldn't allow herself to think about that. She wasn't ready for a relationship, especially not with a man who worked for her. Memories of Kyle Diggett and what he had done flashed through her mind, and she moved a step away from Jesse.

He turned to her, as if he sensed her withdrawal, and said, "What do you like to do at a rodeo?"

His eyes were friendly and his smile casual. There was no trace of the dangerous man she'd glimpsed just minutes ago. Forcing herself to smile, to act as casual as Jesse, she said, "I like to compete in the barrel racing. I don't usually spend much time with the rest of the rodeo."

His smile turned into a grin, genuine and pleased. "Then we can discover it together. What do you want to do first?"

They spent the rest of the morning and most of the afternoon wandering through the rodeo grounds, stopping occasionally to watch the events going on in the ring. Jesse stayed close, but he didn't touch her again. It didn't matter.

Awareness of him hummed through her, magnified every time they laughed at the same moment or looked at each other in perfect agreement. Every time his hand accidentally brushed hers, heat flooded her. When he put his hand at the small of her back to guide her, she began to tremble.

Letting Jesse come to the rodeo with her had definitely not been a good idea. She'd spent the day painfully aware of him, her body betraying her every time he'd so much as looked at her.

It was approaching time for dinner when she turned to him and said, "Ready to call it a day?"

"I'm ready whenever you are."

"Let's get going, then. I need to get back to the ranch."

"There was nothing going on today, was there?" he asked.

"No, but I'm not usually gone this long."

"Can't bear to be away?" His voice was teasing, but she shook her head.

"No, I can't. I'm afraid that Levi will try to do too much, or that Joe and Dusty will be doing work they have no business doing."

"You need to get someone else to help you out, Shea."

She shot him a look as they reached Demon's stall. "That was supposed to be your job."

"Are you sorry I came with you today?" The air was suddenly filled with tension.

"Of course not." Tension ratcheted higher. "I had a wonderful time." She hesitated. "I don't remember when I had so much fun at a rodeo."

"But now you need to get back."

"Now I need to get back," she echoed. "Would you grab the tack while I take Demon?"

She led the horse out of the stall, and watched as Jesse carried the saddle and bridle. In a few minutes, Demon was loaded into the horse trailer, the tack was properly stowed, and they were driving slowly out of the rodeo grounds.

"Are you sorry you came with me today? You wasted one of your days off." She glanced at him as she spoke.

His eyes were full of heat. "I'm not sorry at all. And I wouldn't say my day was wasted." His gaze held hers, and she felt herself responding to the need in his eyes. "I learned a lot today."

Chapter 7

His voice was deep in the silence of the truck, and heavy with meaning. Swallowing once, she dared a glance over at him. His gaze was full of unmistakable desire.

Blindly she turned her gaze to the road. She wasn't ready for this, she thought wildly. She wasn't ready for the need that churned inside her, the wanting. She wasn't ready for the way Jesse made her feel.

The ride home seemed far longer than the trip to the rodeo. Silence swirled around them, a silence charged with rising tension. Jesse was sitting too close, his leg only inches away from hers. His arm rested on the seat behind her, his fingers a mere whisper away from her neck. Her skin jumped every time he shifted on the seat.

Finally, after what seemed like an eternity, she saw the driveway to the Red Rock ahead. She took the turn too fast and skidded on the gravel driveway. Relief trembled through her when she pulled the truck to a stop outside the barn.

"Thanks for coming with me, Jesse. I hope you had a good time." She held onto the steering wheel to hide the shaking of her hands.

"I'll help you get Demon settled in for the night," he said, ignoring her silent plea to disappear.

He jumped out of the truck, but she sat behind the steering wheel for another moment, gathering herself.

It wasn't a problem, she told herself. She could walk into the barn with Demon, settle him for the night, and then casually say good-night to Jesse. She could do this.

Sliding out of the truck, she went around to the trailer and saw that Jesse had already removed the saddle and the bridle. She clipped a lead rope onto Demon's halter and backed him out of the truck, then led him to the barn.

The ranch was silent in the soft darkness of dusk, and the barn was dim and quiet. Everyone would be in the house, eating dinner. A horse whickered softly, but otherwise she and Jesse were alone.

"Where do you want the tack?" he said, breaking the silence.

Thankful for the mundane question, she gestured to her left. "In the tack room. You'll see the pegs where they belong."

Demon grunted and tossed his head when she turned him loose into his stall, and immediately looked in his feed trough. Snorting with disgust when he found it empty, the horse turned and stared at her accusingly.

"All right," she said, sliding her hand down the horse's head, grateful for the routine chore that might dissipate the tension. "I'll get it."

As she poured grain in Demon's feed trough, she noticed Jesse slip out of the tack room and lean against the stall across from Demon's, watching her. Her smile faded and she felt tension creep up her back again.

"Okay, you're set for the night," she said to the horse. Her voice sounded unnaturally loud in the quiet of the barn.

She turned to Jesse. "Are you interested in dinner?" she said brightly. "I'm sure Maria saved some for us."

"Sounds good." He didn't move. He just watched her as she stepped out of the stall and latched the door behind her.

Shea rubbed her suddenly sweaty palms down the legs of her jeans. "Ready to go?"

"Do you want to check the tack room first and make sure I put your things back where they belong?" he said, standing up straight.

"All right."

She stepped into the dimly lit room. The smell of leather filled the air, along with a hint of Jesse's fragrance. His subtle, musky scent swirled around her, sharpening her desire. "Everything's fine." Need shot through her again, and she turned blindly to leave.

Jesse had come into the tack room behind her, and she crashed into him. He grabbed her arms to steady her, and her heart gave a painful lurch.

Staring up at him, she saw the hot flare of need in his eyes. His hand gentled on her arm until his fingers were skimming over her skin. His eyes burned with a green fire, and she couldn't force herself to step away.

She told herself to move, to go into the house where it was safe, but her feet wouldn't obey her. Didn't want to obey her. Instead, she stared up at him, her heart thudding against her chest and blood roaring in her ears. Her gaze locked with his, and heat pooled deep inside her. Fingers of need clawed at her, sharper and more fierce than anything she'd ever felt.

She saw the hesitation in Jesse's eyes, the attempt to draw back. But then, with a muttered curse, he tightened his hands on her arms and yanked her against him.

He took her mouth in a blaze of heat and possession. There was nothing gentle about his kiss, nothing soft. He tasted of desperation and a passion so intense, so all-consuming, that he couldn't control it.

She felt him struggling for that control, reaching for it, and shuddered with the desire that swept through her. There was no hesitation, no room for thought. Curling her arms around his neck, she pressed herself against him and opened her mouth to him.

He groaned as he speared his hands into her hair, holding her mouth to his. She felt the tremble of his fingers as he skimmed one hand over her cheek, down her throat. Every inch of her throbbed, and when he pulled her into the vee of his legs, the hard length of his arousal burned into her.

She moaned into his mouth, clutching at his arms, moving against him. He dragged his mouth away from hers and said, ''Shea.''

She could barely manage to open her eyes. His face was hard and taut, his eyes glittering with passion, his skin pulled tight over his cheekbones. ''What?'' she whispered, hardly able to get the word out. Her mouth was swollen and her tongue wouldn't work.

His eyes darkened. ''Nothing.''

He kissed her again, pushing her backward until she was pressed against the wooden wall. He touched her face, and then his hands were everywhere. He skimmed down her sides, measuring the curve of her waist, then he slid around and cupped her hips. When he pulled her closer, fitting her against the swollen ridge of his jeans, a flash of lightning shot through her.

His hands flexed on her hips, sending shudders of desire streaking through her. When he let his hand slip lower and trailed his fingers over the heavy seam of her jeans, she whimpered with need.

He tensed even more, his whole body quivering as he stayed absolutely still against her. Finally, slowly, he pulled his hand away. When he curled his fingers around her neck, she could feel him shaking.

She felt him take a deep breath, his body trembling, his breath catching. Finally he settled his hands against her shoulders and leaned away from her. ''Shea,'' he began, but his voice trailed away. She followed his gaze and saw him staring at her blouse.

''This shirt,'' he said hoarsely. ''It's been driving me crazy all day. Why did you wear this?''

Through the haze of passion and need that still throbbed inside her, she struggled to understand what he meant. ''What's wrong with my shirt?''

''This fringe.'' With one finger he teased the fringe on her shirt that brushed against her breast. "All I've been able to think about today was this damn fringe, swinging back and forth. Touching you, the way I wanted to touch you."

He touched the fringe on her blouse again, his finger brushing the edge of her breast. She caught her breath, the sound echoing through the quiet barn. Jesse's eyes darkened again. Slowly, his finger trembling, he traced the black fringe down her breast. When he stopped, his finger was touching her nipple.

A shock jolted through her, even through the layers of clothing. Her legs trembled, and if Jesse hadn't been holding her up, she would have collapsed in a heap on the ground. "Jesse," she whispered, her voice breaking.

His eyes fluttered closed, and he bent to kiss her again. Lost in sensation, trembling with her need for him, she was startled when she felt cool air on her chest. Breaking away from his mouth, she looked down to see that he'd unbuttoned her blouse and snapped open the front clasp of her bra.

Jesse brushed her shirt to the side and stared down at her bare breasts. Suddenly self-conscious, she tried to pull her shirt together. He grabbed her hands and held them lightly.

"You're beautiful," he said, his voice hoarse. "More beautiful than I could have imagined." Bending down, he took the tip of one breast in his mouth. When he tugged at it gently, her knees buckled and she slid to the floor.

He followed her down, his lips and tongue playing with one breast while his hand caressed the other. Desire throbbed and built inside her, until she could think of nothing but Jesse, nothing but her need for him. He rocked against her, his heat and hardness pressing against the juncture of her thighs. Mindless with wanting him, a desperate need spiraling inside her, she fumbled with the button of his jeans.

He groaned and surged against her, then stilled. Wrapping his arms around her, he pulled her against him and held her tightly. But he had already retreated. Shea felt him distancing himself from her.

Struggling to free herself, she propped herself on her elbows and looked at him. "What's wrong?" she said quietly.

Rather than looking at her, he pulled her shirt together and began to button it. "We're in the barn, Shea." His voice was tight and controlled, but she heard the remnants of desire trembling in it, and she relaxed just a little. "Anyone could walk in on us. Do you want Levi or Joe or Dusty to find us like this?"

"Of course not. But is that why you stopped?"

His hands stilled on her buttons. "No, not completely. I was too close to losing control, too close to making love with you right here." Now he did look at her, and there was a fierceness to his eyes that she hadn't seen before. "When I do make love with you, Shea, it won't be on the floor of a barn. It won't be when someone could walk in on us. When I make love with you, it's going to take all night. And I won't be working for you when it happens."

She reached out to grasp his shoulders, to keep him from moving away from her. "Why does that have anything to do with it? If it doesn't bother me, why should it bother you?"

"I came here to do a job. And that's what I intend to do."

His face was closed and remote, and for a moment he looked like a stranger. Like the dangerous, forbidden stranger who'd appeared in her yard, looking for a job. Then she shook him. "I wouldn't have met you if you hadn't come here looking for a job. Why should that make a difference?"

He struggled to his feet, then reached down and pulled her up next to him. "I keep my business separate from my pleasure." His voice was harsh in the echoing silence of the barn. "And right now, you're business."

His words were implacable, dropping into the space between them. But she felt the tension that shimmered from him, and she saw the need, deep in his eyes. And she saw how hard he tried to fight both of them.

Her heart soared. Giving him a careless smile, she dusted off the seat of her jeans and the back of her shirt. "I'm sure you're right," she said cheerfully. "It would probably be bad for the morale of the rest of the men working here if we were involved. I don't want jealousy to affect the business of the ranch."

He scowled. "You think I'm worried that Joe or Dusty or Levi are going to be jealous? You think that's why I don't want to touch you?"

She tilted her head and studied him. "Isn't it?"

"Hell, no, I'm not worried about that, and you know it."

"Then what are you worried about, Jesse?"

"I need to be able to do my job. And I can't do it if I'm involved with you."

"Why not?"

He let loose a string of curses and narrowed his eyes at her. She stood her ground, waiting for him to finish. When he took a breath, she said, "That's very interesting, but I didn't hear any reasons for not getting involved in your creative monologue. All I heard were a lot of words that made me blush."

He scowled at her, but she saw the reluctant smile in his eyes. "You are one mouthy piece of work, Shea. I don't think you know how to blush."

He would be surprised at how often she'd blushed since he arrived at the Red Rock. It was something she had no intention of telling him, at least not right now. "I just want to make sure I understand what you want." Turning to switch off the light in the tack room, she grabbed for her composure. When she could face him with a calm smile, she turned around.

"Shall we go get some dinner? I'm starved."

Jesse watched her walk down the barn aisle ahead of him and tried to keep his eyes off the sway of her hips in the tight denim. And he'd be damned if he'd look at that fringe on her shirt one more time today. When she reached the door, she turned around and waited for him. He felt himself tightening all over again when the fringe on her shirt swayed gently against her breast, and swore silently to himself.

Once again, Shea had managed to surprise him. He was sure his blunt words would embarrass her enough to make her back away, but instead she'd coolly issued him a challenge. A challenge that his body ached to answer. A challenge he'd have to be a damned fool to even consider. And no one had ever called Jesse Coulton a fool.

Jamming his hands into his pockets, scowling at the sight of the fringe on her shirt bouncing gently against her back, he hurried to catch up with her. When he reached her side, she turned to him with an easy smile.

"You'll have to be properly contrite to Maria about being late for dinner."

"You mean she doesn't consider fooling around in the barn an acceptable excuse?"

Instead of flinching from his bluntness, she grinned at him. "She'd be shocked speechless. It would almost be worth telling her that was why we were late just to see that. But I think we'd better stick with the rodeo."

"Fine," he muttered. "You can handle the excuses."

She grinned again. "Don't worry. I'm a pro at them. Maria's heard plenty of excuses from me over the years."

For a moment, jealously descended over him like a suffocating curtain of black rage. How many other men had she dallied with in the barn? How many other men had she teased and kissed and caressed? How many other men had touched her?

Then he remembered the tentative way she'd kissed him at first, her instinctive shyness when he'd bared her breasts. He thought about the shocked pleasure on her face when he'd touched her, and the stunned expression in her eyes when she'd looked at him.

Shea might have a smart mouth, and she might be very good at hiding her feelings, but she didn't have a lot of experience when it came to men. He'd be willing to bet the ranch on that.

Suddenly more cheerful, he slung one arm over her shoulder. When he felt her tense, he smiled to himself. "I'm looking forward to this."

"To dinner?" she asked.

"To watching Maria make you squirm," he said.

Her shoulder relaxed just a bit beneath his hand. "She's

had enough practice,'' she said lightly. ''But I can handle Maria.''

She could. Jesse watched a few moments later as the housekeeper frowned at Shea, her dark eyes flashing. Shea kissed her cheek, gave her a hug, and sat down at the table. As Jesse slid into another chair he saw the older woman's eyes soften as she watched Shea.

''I saved you some stew,'' Maria muttered as she hurried off to the kitchen. ''I know what riding that monster of a horse does to your appetite.''

As soon as Maria left the room, Joe, Dusty and Levi all began talking. In the jumble of voices, Jesse heard questions about the rodeo and bits of news about what had happened on the ranch that day. After a moment, Shea, laughing, held up her hand.

''One at a time,'' she said.

Levi asked, ''How did you do at the rodeo? Take first, as usual?''

The smile faded from Shea's face. ''Demon came up lame at the end of my run. So I pulled him back, wouldn't let him finish.'' She looked down at the plate of stew that Maria had put in front of her. Jesse saw the anguish in her eyes. ''Doc O'Connor was there. He took a look at Demon, thought it was just a bruised foot. He should be fine. And there'll be other races.''

She was still upset, Jesse realized. Not about losing the race, but about the injury to her horse. Even after the vet had told her that it wasn't serious.

''I'll help you soak his foot after dinner,'' he heard himself say.

She glanced up at him, and he saw the sudden warmth in her eyes. ''Thank you, Jesse. But I'm sure I can handle it myself. You probably have things to do after being gone all day.''

''Nothing that can't wait,'' he said casually. It was only an excuse to spend more time with her, he told himself. An excuse to get to know her better, so he could do the job he'd come here for. There was nothing personal about his offer.

And pigs were going to come flying over the mountains any day now, he added grimly. What was the matter with him? After that scene in the barn just minutes earlier, he should be tripping over himself in his hurry to get away from her. The last thing he needed to do was spend more time alone with Shea. But he would be in that barn with her tonight. He'd just make sure he kept lots of space between them.

Conversation turned to the ranch, and the three hands told Shea what they'd done that day. When Dusty casually mentioned that he'd given the injection to the steer with the laceration, Shea shot around in her chair.

"What do you mean, you gave that steer his injection? You know you're not supposed to be doing any work."

Jesse watched as Joe edged forward, a belligerent expression on his face. "As long as we're talking about working, I started in on the truck today."

Shea crossed her arms and sat back in her chair. "I didn't realize I should have tied you both down before I left this morning."

In spite of her teasing words, Jesse saw the concern on her face as she looked at her two employees. Clearly, she cared about the two men who had been injured. And just as clearly, she was determined that they not start working again before they were ready, even if it meant she had to do twice the work herself.

Shea was a complicated woman, and Jesse shifted on the wooden seat of the chair. He should be a lot farther along in his investigation by now. He should at least have found the place where the illegal aliens were staying, and with any luck should have caught Shea with them. Instead of going to the rodeo with her today, he should have stayed on the ranch and searched for the hiding place.

He'd start looking tomorrow, he told himself. He'd wasted today at the rodeo, thinking that something was going to happen there, but he'd get to work tomorrow.

His traitorous body told him that not a thing about the day had been wasted, but he refused to listen. Instead, he paid close attention to Shea, wondering if something had happened at the ranch while she was gone.

But the rest of the conversation was mundane, with Levi recounting exactly what he'd done that day. Jesse was ready to leave when Maria came into the dining room, holding a cake.

Shea turned to smile at her. "How did your day go, Maria?"

"Just like every other day." She looked at Shea, and a warning flashed. "I got lots of cleaning done."

"That's great," Shea answered, and the answering flicker in her eyes told Jesse she'd understood Maria's unspoken message. "But you could have waited until tomorrow and I would have helped you."

The housekeeper snorted. "When? In your spare time?"

"I would have made time, Maria."

"It was nothing," the housekeeper muttered. "You know I don't mind."

For a moment, Jesse thought Shea was going to argue with Maria, then she must have remembered his presence. With a strained smile, she said to him, "I'm going to work on the books for a while. I'll see you tomorrow, Jesse."

He'd been dismissed and he knew it. Nodding, he pushed away from the table and walked out of the house. But instead of heading back to his cabin, he circled silently around until he was crouched outside of one of the dining room windows.

Shea's voice was an urgent hum, but she was speaking too softly for him to hear what she was saying. Maria said something occasionally, as did one of the hands. But all of them were being careful, speaking in low tones. When he heard chairs scraping away from the table, he hurried to his cabin, closing the door softly when he saw Joe emerge onto the porch of the house.

Something had happened while they were gone today. Had Shea only been a decoy, luring him away from the house? For a moment he cursed, thinking he'd been fooled, but then he remembered her face when he'd asked to go to the rodeo with her.

She had been shocked and frightened, and had fumbled for a reason to tell him no. When she'd agreed to let him accompany her, it had been with great reluctance.

Jesse didn't want to consider how easy it was to read her expressions. He didn't want to think about what that meant. The only thing he was interested in was whether or not Shea was hiding illegal aliens on her ranch. This morning, when nothing had happened at the rodeo, he'd begun to have doubts. But now those doubts were disappearing. Something was happening on this ranch, something Shea wanted to hide.

There was a reason he was known around the Bureau as the Renegade. He did his best work alone, when the odds were against him. And this job would be no different, he vowed. It didn't matter that he was attracted to his suspect. Justice was the only thing that mattered. And justice would be served.

He paced the small living room of the cabin, too edgy to relax. No sounds escaped from the house or the barn. Finally, needing action, he eased out of the cabin and headed for the barn. He'd make sure that Shea hadn't managed to slip past him.

There was no sign of her in the barn. Only the soft sounds of animals settling in for the night greeted him when he opened the door. Stopping in front of Demon's stall, he watched the big horse shift on his front legs. Jesse thought he put the left one down more carefully, as if it hurt.

The horse watched him warily for a moment, but when Jesse murmured to him in a low voice, he ambled over to the stall door. While Jesse scratched his ears, the horse butted his head on Jesse's chest.

"She brings you treats, does she?" he crooned. "Sorry, I don't have any handouts for you. I'll snag a couple of carrots from Maria."

"Don't let her catch you in her kitchen."

He spun around to find Shea leaning up against a stall. Backing away from Demon, he shoved his hands in his pockets, feeling foolish for being caught talking to an animal. "I just wanted to make sure he was all right."

"I guess you're not as tough as you want everyone to think, are you?" She grinned at him, but he saw the warmth bloom in her eyes. "Thanks, Jesse." Demon nuzzled at her shirt, and she held out a piece of apple for him. "I couldn't go to sleep without checking on him myself."

"He seems to be all right, although I think that foot still hurts."

The smile disappeared from her face, and she leaned down to study the horse as he moved toward the other end of the stall. "You're right. He's favoring it, just a little."

"My offer still stands."

She turned to look at him, wariness in her face. "Which offer was that?"

"I said I'd help you soak his foot." He wanted to ask her which offer she thought he'd meant, but instead looked down at Demon's foot. He couldn't afford to lose control of himself twice in one evening. "Do you have some epsom salts?"

"I'll get it."

She turned and hurried away, and he wondered if she was as reluctant as he was to repeat the scene in the tack room earlier. She had to be, especially if there was something illegal going on at the Red Rock Ranch. Shea was a woman who had her priorities firmly in place.

She returned a few minutes later, carrying a bucket full of warm liquid that steamed gently in the cool evening air. "If you'll hold him, I'll soak his foot," she said.

"Fine by me." He grabbed Demon's halter and snapped on a lead rope that hung outside the stall. Shea slipped through the door and set the bucket down, then spoke softly to the horse. He snorted once and tossed his head back, but he didn't move.

She knelt on the floor beside him, lifting his leg and putting his foot in the bucket. Demon flattened his ears, snorted and tried to dance away, but Jesse held onto his halter and murmured nonsense words to him. After a moment, the horse settled down. He shook his head once, then stood calmly as Jesse held him.

Shea glanced up. "You're doing a great job of keeping him still."

"He's an easy horse to handle."

She gave him an unbelieving stare. "You're definitely in the minority with that opinion. Even Becca has a hard time with him."

He shrugged, her words giving him a vague sense of unease. Now he not only understood Shea, but he understood her horse, too. "I haven't had any problems with him."

She grinned at him once, her eyes twinkling. "Watch him. He's tricky. He sneaks up on you when you least expect it."

Kind of like his owner, he thought to himself. Shea had certainly taken him by surprise. He had expected to feel only contempt for his latest suspect, but from the very beginning his feelings were a lot more complicated than that. Now he wondered uneasily just what he felt for Shea.

It didn't matter, he told himself. And when he realized there was a touch of desperation in his mind, he deliberately shut it out. Nothing mattered except the job. Nothing mattered except ensuring that the law was upheld.

Nothing mattered besides justice. Because that was the only thing that mattered in the long run. Love wasn't real and relationships didn't last. Justice was the most anyone could hope for.

Chapter 8

Jesse held Demon securely for twenty minutes while Shea soaked his foot. As she worked, Jesse realized that she'd forgotten his presence in the barn.

She crooned to Demon when he got restless, feeding him slices of apple that she pulled out of her shirt pocket. And when he shook his head and flattened his ears, she chided him in a sharp voice that made the huge horse settle down immediately.

Jesse watched her, amazed. Apparently Shea handled her horse with as much ease as she handled the men who worked for her. When she finally stood up, arching her back to work out the kinks, he looked at her with something approaching awe.

As she moved out of the stall, he unsnapped the rope from Demon's halter and followed her out. Taking the bucket away from her, he headed to the feed room and dumped it down the drain. After rinsing it and stacking it with the other buckets, he turned to find Shea standing in the door of the feed room.

Had she deliberately chosen not to come in, remembering

what had happened in the tack room earlier? While his rational mind hoped so, the rest of him silently urged her closer. His hands burned, remembering how she felt. And his mouth hungered for another taste of her.

"Ready to go?" he asked, shoving his hands into his pockets.

She nodded. "It's been a long day."

"You can say that again," he muttered.

Slipping past her in the doorway to the feed room, being careful not to touch her, he started for the door to the barn. She snapped off the lights, leaving only a small night-light burning, then followed him out into the night.

The night was clear and cool, with a snap in the air that reminded him it was still early spring. Stars blanketed the sky, their number and brilliance still awe-inspiring. "You don't get views like this in the city," he said, staring at the dark sky above him.

"We have a lot of things in Cameron that you don't get in the city," she answered. "The view is just a bonus."

"Have you spent much time in the city?" He glanced over at her as she stared up at the sky show. Needing to move closer to her, he took a step away.

She shook her head. "I've gone for visits occasionally. Once I even went as far as Los Angeles, when my brother was in the service there. But I'm always glad to get back to the ranch."

"You're lucky you have a place like this to call home." He almost didn't recognize the wistful voice as his own.

"Where do you call home, Jesse?"

He shrugged. "Wherever I am at the time."

"Don't you have a family somewhere?"

"My mother is back east, in a small town in upstate New York. Otherwise, no."

"Then isn't that home?"

"It's as good as any, I suppose."

"Are you close to your mother?"

"Yeah. She worked her rear end off for me when I was growing up. I owe her, big time."

"What about your father?"

He compressed his lips, the familiar remnants of anger and grief washing over him. It had never gone away, not even after twenty-two years. "My father was killed when I was nine years old."

He heard her small gasp in the darkness. "I'm sorry, Jesse. That's horrible."

"He was a newspaper reporter in New York City. He'd been writing a series about the mob, and he'd exposed some secrets that made them unhappy. When he didn't stop after they warned him to, they shot him."

"Did they catch the person who did it?"

"Of course not. This is the mob we're talking about, and New York. The paper he worked for sure got some good publicity, though."

"You sound very bitter."

He shrugged, aware he'd revealed more about himself than he should have. "I've gotten over it. It was a long time ago, after all. And my mother and I survived."

He felt her gaze on him. "I'm surprised that you didn't become a reporter yourself and fight for justice, like your father."

He shifted uneasily. She was too damned perceptive. How had they gotten onto the subject of his choice of work? "I can't write worth a damn. And I didn't feel like becoming a martyr, anyway."

"I don't think you're as much of a cynic as you want everyone to believe," she murmured.

"Don't kid yourself, Shea," he said harshly. "I'm the most cynical man you know."

"I doubt that. I know quite a few people."

Her voice was light, but there was an undertone of understanding that made him squirm. He was getting into quicksand here, and it was time to back off. "I'm out of your league, Shea. Why don't we leave it at that?"

To his surprise, she tucked one hand through his arm. "Sorry, Jesse, if you expect me to believe that you're a big, bad man, you're going to have to do better than that." She turned to look at him in the moonlight, and the gentle smile in her eyes made his heart jolt in his chest. "But you can start tomorrow. I'm kind of tired tonight."

She stood on her toes and pressed a kiss to his mouth. Before he could reach for her, she'd slipped away from him and run up the porch stairs. Stopping in front of the door, she raised her hand, then disappeared into the house.

He stood in the yard for a long time, his heart pounding, watching as the light in her room flickered on, then went off again a few minutes later. He would have to be careful. Shea was a complicated woman, far more complicated than the simple criminal he'd thought her to be. She was finding a way under his defenses, and he didn't like it one damn bit. It was time to concentrate on why he'd come here. It was time to find out what was going on, and then get the hell out of Cameron.

When Shea came down early for breakfast the next morning, Maria informed her that Jesse had already eaten. "He's in the barn," the housekeeper said, her voice tinged with grudging approval. "He doesn't mind work, I'll give him that."

"Jesse's been a real find for the Red Rock," Shea said, pouring herself a cup of coffee. "He does a good job, and he's smart. He knows what has to be done without being told."

"Too smart, if you want my opinion."

Shea smothered a grin. She was going to get Maria's opinion, whether she wanted it or not.

"He's going to find out what you're doing," the housekeeper warned. "Then what will happen?"

"Jesse is a good man," she answered slowly. "A man who believes in justice. I'm sure he'll help me."

"You're not going to tell him, are you?" The housekeeper was appalled. "You can't trust him! You know nothing about him."

"I know enough."

"Please promise you won't say anything," Maria said.

Shea shrugged. "It doesn't matter right now, anyway. There aren't any more children coming for at least a week."

"A lot can happen in a week," Maria muttered as she walked into the kitchen.

For a moment, anticipation hummed in Shea's veins. Quite a bit could happen in a week. Every time she thought about Jesse, her body tingled. And she'd thought about Jesse a lot since yesterday evening. He'd made her yearn for something that she'd never imagined, feel things she'd never felt before. And she wanted to feel them again.

She wanted to know more about Jesse. He'd opened up a little last night, but she knew there were large parts of himself he was hiding. As she ate her breakfast, she smiled to herself. He would be on the Red Rock for at least another couple of months. There was plenty of time to get to know him.

When she strode out to the barn after breakfast, she found him cleaning out stalls. "Good morning," she said, and he grunted a reply.

Fighting the need to stand and look at him, she grabbed a pitchfork and started on the next stall. "You should have waited for me. There wasn't any reason to start so early."

"No reason to wait, either. It had to be done, and I was up early."

For a moment she was tempted to ask him if he'd had trouble sleeping, too. But one look at his grim face told her that she wouldn't get much of an answer. Apparently Jesse wasn't in a talkative mood this morning.

Tension swirled through the barn as they worked in silence. Shea glanced over at him occasionally, but Jesse refused to look at her. He shoveled straw and manure with grim determination, as if he were cleansing the demons from his soul along with the debris from the stalls. As the silence stretched between them, taut and heavy, Shea became more and more aware of the man who worked beside her.

"Are you interested in doing some riding later today?" she finally asked, breaking the charged silence.

He glanced over at her. "What do you mean?"

"We usually do only essential work on Sunday." She

waved her hand around the barn. "Like cleaning out stalls. But I was going to ride up into the mountains today and check on our summer pastures. I want to make sure they're ready, since we're going to move some of the herd higher into the mountains next week. You've wanted to see more of the ranch, so I thought you might like to join me."

His hands stilled on the shovel, then he looked over at her. She couldn't read the expression on his face. "What brought about your change of heart?"

"What do you mean?"

"You've been trying to keep me away from the mountains."

Fear fluttered in her chest for a moment, then she suppressed it. There was no way Jesse could know why she didn't want him exploring. "I've been trying to make sure you knew what you were doing before I turned you loose on the ranch. There's a big difference."

For a moment, his hazel eyes bored into her, then he shrugged. The atmosphere lightened. "I'd love to join you. I don't have anything better to do today." He raised his eyebrows. "But why not wait until tomorrow? Don't you ever take a day off?"

"What do you think I did yesterday?" She scowled at him. "I don't work banker's hours, Jesse. You've worked on enough ranches to know there is no such thing as free time on a ranch. There's always something that needs to be done. If I check out the pastures today, there'll be time tomorrow to handle the emergency that's sure to show up."

He studied her for a moment, and she felt like a specimen on a dissecting board. Then he resumed shoveling. "You work hard, Shea."

There was no inflection in his voice, no hint of what he thought. Shrugging, she picked up the pitchfork and attacked the next stall. "It doesn't feel like I'm working hard. It feels like I'm doing what I love to do."

They worked in silence for a while, but the tension in the atmosphere had eased. Finally Jesse said, "When do you want to leave?"

"When we finish in the barn, I guess. That way, you'll have some time this afternoon to yourself."

"What do Joe, Dusty and Levi do on their days off?" he asked.

"Sometimes they go into Cameron, sometimes they just take it easy. They're not getting any younger. Nightlife doesn't seem to have much of an appeal for them anymore."

"And you have so much nightlife in Cameron."

When she glanced over at him, she saw the twinkle in his eyes. "We're known far and wide for the wildness of our parties," she said, trying to keep her face solemn. "People come from all over Utah to go to May's."

He nodded. "That's what I'd heard. It's why I came to Cameron in the first place."

Grinning, she cleaned her pitchfork and replaced it in the feed room. "Let's take the malarkey on the road, Coulton. Saddle up Joey, over there." She nodded at a bay horse that stood quietly in one stall. "He'll give you a good ride."

The sun was only inches above the horizon as they headed across the pasture closest to the house. Shea breathed in deeply, savoring the smell and taste of early morning on the Red Rock. "This might be my favorite part of the day," she said to Jesse. "I love riding out into the stillness of early morning. Everything is alive with possibilities."

Beside her, Jesse looked around. "There's something special about your ranch at this time of the day," he said. "It makes me want to see more of it."

"You'll see plenty of it today," she said lightly, urging her horse into a canter.

He'd been too curious about the ranch. So she'd let him see it, now, when there was nothing for him to find. Maria was right. She might think Jesse was worthy of her trust, she might think he'd be willing to help her, but until she knew him better, she couldn't take a chance on trusting him.

A couple of hours later they stopped in the last pasture. They were high in the mountains and the air was still cool. The tiny lake and the cabin were on the other side of the cliffs, but she'd make it a point to stay away from them. She hoped Jesse had seen enough of the ranch to satisfy him.

"This is the last pasture," she said. "Let's ride the perimeter and make sure all the fencing is intact. We had a lot of snow this winter."

Jesse nodded and headed over to the fence. They'd almost finished circling the pasture when he stopped abruptly.

"What's wrong?" she asked.

He nodded at a small bush. "Do you hear that bird?"

A furious chattering filled the air, and she edged closer. "What is it?"

"It's a scrub jay, related to the blue jay. And it's letting us get awfully close."

Sliding off his horse, he held onto Joey's reins as he walked toward the bird. The jay held his ground, but his chattering became a shrill screech.

"There's the problem," Jesse said in a quiet voice. "Come here and hold my reins, would you?"

Shea jumped off her horse and grabbed the reins from Jesse's hand. He eased over the barbed wire fence and stooped down below the bush. The jay flew away, but landed in another juniper only a few feet away, screeching continually.

"What is it?"

Jesse stood up, cradling something in his hand. "One of its babies fell out of its nest. If I can find the nest, I'll put it back."

He stood scanning the juniper for a few moments, then reached into it and replaced the baby bird in a nest. Then he stepped back over the barbed wire fence.

"How did you notice that?" Shea demanded.

Jesse swung himself up onto his horse, then shrugged. "I heard the bird. It was obvious something was wrong." He gestured to the rocks above the small clump of juniper. "Since we were about done anyway, why don't we sit on the rocks for a while and see what happens?"

They secured the horses to the branch of a scrubby pine, then scrambled up onto the rocks. The sun had already warmed them, and Shea settled back to watch the bird below them.

"Well, who would have thought it?" she said after a few moments.

"Who would have thought what?"

"That tough, hard Jesse Coulton would be a bird-watcher."

She thought she saw a faint stain of pink in his cheeks. "I'm outside a lot. Once I started noticing the birds, it became a game to find out more about them. Then I got interested." He shrugged. "I like to be aware of what's going on around me. Knowing about an area's wildlife is part of that."

She studied him for a moment. "Why do I think there's more to it than that?" she finally asked.

He didn't look at her. "Maybe because you have a nasty, suspicious mind. You thought all kinds of bad things about me before you hired me, didn't you?"

She'd thought he'd be bad for her, and she'd been right. Out loud, she said, "I was merely being cautious. I'd had problems with my last employee, and I wanted to make sure it didn't happen again."

He swiveled to face her. "What kind of problems?"

Tension quivered in the air again, and she wondered why. "The kinds of problems that employers always have," she said lightly. "He didn't work out, and I had to let him go. It was nothing earth-shattering, believe me."

"But he hurt you, didn't he?" Jesse's voice was quiet.

He was too perceptive, and she shifted on the suddenly hard rock. "Let's just say I didn't like facing the proof of my bad judgment. And he's gone now, so it doesn't matter anymore."

Jesse looked like he wanted to ask her more, and there was nothing more she wanted to say about Kyle Diggett. To distract him, she pointed to the bird on the juniper bush, who was still shrieking. "Is she going to go back to the nest?"

Jesse turned and looked, reluctantly, she thought. "Probably. She doesn't like the fact that we're here."

"Should we leave?"

''Not yet. I want to make sure she accepts the chick back. Once she goes back to the nest, we can go.''

They sat quietly for what seemed like a long time. The jay eventually stopped screeching, and suddenly hopped into the juniper that held her nest. When she disappeared into the foliage, Shea saw Jesse smile.

''Bingo. We're golden.''

''Is she on the nest? I can't see.''

''Yeah, she's there. Don't you hear those noises?''

Shea strained to listen, and finally heard a low buzzing noise. ''What is that?''

''She's feeding the chicks.''

They could leave now. But instead, Shea leaned against the sun-warmed rocks and looked at Jesse. ''You're really a sham. You know that, don't you?''

He looked wary. ''What do you mean?''

''You told me last night you were the biggest cynic I'd ever met. But you're nothing but a big softy.''

''Just because I put a baby bird back in its nest?''

''Because you even thought to do it. Because you cared enough to bother. Most people would have ridden by that bird and not given it a second thought.''

''So I'm a bird-watcher. That doesn't make me a saint.''

Clasping her hands around her knees, she leaned forward to study him. ''What I want to know is, why are you so determined to make me think you're a tough guy?''

''Maybe because I *am* a tough guy. I'm trying to be a gentleman, Shea, and you're not making it very easy. You need to stay away from me. The last thing you want is to get involved with me. You don't need to be involved with some-one who's working for you.''

''That's what I thought, too. That's what I've always thought.'' She felt herself softening, yearning for his touch, and had to force herself not to move. ''Now I'm not so sure.''

''I'm sure,'' he said, and his voice was harsh. ''Getting involved in a relationship with an employee is never a good idea.''

"But you're not going to be an employee for long, are you?"

His eyes narrowed. "How do you know that?"

"You're a drifter, Jesse. You told me you were, but you didn't have to. I can see it in your eyes. I heard it last night, when you were talking about your lack of a home. In a few months you'll get itchy and decide it's time to move on."

"Then why in the hell would you want to get involved with me?" he demanded.

"Why would you want to get involved with me?" she countered.

"I don't," he muttered.

"And neither do I."

"I guess we understand each other, then."

"I guess we do."

They stared at one another for a few moments, desire swirling in the air between them. She could see the hunger in Jesse's eyes. Suddenly he pulled her close and covered her mouth with his. Heat and need speared through her as quickly as a flash fire. She opened her mouth to him, desperate to taste him once more.

He groaned and shifted his hands on her, gentling his touch. She'd lied, she thought to herself as her body molded itself to him. She'd told him she didn't want to get involved, but it wasn't the truth.

Her body hungered for Jesse, even as her heart yearned to know more of him. She felt a connection with him, and her body had recognized it long before she'd been willing to admit it, even to herself. Twining herself around him, she lost herself in his embrace.

She felt him tense as he recognized her surrender. Then his mouth and hands were everywhere, as if he couldn't get enough of her taste, of the way she felt. It was as if his hands were trying to memorize her, to learn every curve, every intimate detail of her body.

She shuddered and reached for him, needing to touch him, too. He eased her back onto the rock, pillowing her head with his arm. When he leaned over her, kissing her again, she slid her hands beneath his shirt and let her fingers trace the hard muscle of his chest.

He grew still and tense above her. She opened her eyes to find him staring down at her, his face taut with passion and raw hunger. ''Do you know what you're doing to me?'' he asked, his voice scraping over her nerves.

Slowly she shook her head. He grabbed her hand and held it against his chest, and she felt his heart thundering against her palm. His muscles trembled with his effort at control, then suddenly he moved over her.

Settling into the vee of her legs, he took her mouth again in a storm of desire. The hard ridge of his arousal burned into her abdomen, making her throb with need. But his body was rigid with control, and when she tried to pull him closer, he eased away from her.

''I want you, Shea. I can't deny that.'' He bent down and kissed her, gently this time. ''And I think you want me.''

When he reached up to push a strand of hair out of her face, she saw that his fingers were trembling. ''But it's not a good idea.''

''Why not?'' she asked.

His smile softened his face, took away the harsh lines and hard planes. It was the smile of a different man, a man who wasn't hard and tough. It was the smile of a man who could be persuaded to stop drifting, to settle down in one place. It was the smile of a man who wasn't Jesse Coulton.

''Do I have to tell you all the reasons?'' he said, and she thought there was sadness in his voice. ''I think you know them as well as me.''

''Tell me anyway,'' she demanded.

''You're my boss,'' he said, holding her gaze. ''And that's just for starters. There's a reason why relationships between employees and employers don't work.''

''So you can quit and go work for someone else. Give me another reason.''

This time his gaze shifted away from her. ''I can't quit, Shea, and you know it. What would you do if I wasn't here to help you?''

"Dusty and Joe are getting better. They'll be back to full speed before long."

"Even when they are at full speed, you need help. They're getting old, Shea. They can't do what they used to be able to do."

"So I'll hire someone else." She fixed a fierce gaze on him. "Tell me another reason we can't get involved."

He stared at her for a long time. "I'm leaving," he finally said, his voice flat. "I'm not going to be here for more than a few months."

"You don't have to go."

"I do. You don't understand."

"So explain it to me."

He stared at her for a long time, then rolled over and sat up. "You've always had this place, this home. You've had the town of Cameron. You've lived here your whole life. I don't have roots. I don't know what it's like to have roots."

"You can find out." She sat up and turned to face him. "Cameron is a good place. You'll be welcome here. You can put down roots of your own."

"Give it up, Shea. It won't work. I'm not like you. And you're going to find that out, sooner or later."

She watched him for a moment, wondering at the flash of guilt in his eyes. Wondering why he looked so sad. Then he looked over at the juniper bush that held the jay's nest.

"It looks like it's time to go," he said, and it was clear the subject was closed. "That bird is getting upset that we're still here."

The scrub jay was chattering at them again, sitting on a branch of the juniper. Jesse surged to his feet, then reached down and pulled her up. "Let's climb these rocks and see what's at the top."

She wanted to protest, to tell him no. She knew what was at the top of the rocks. But it was too late. He was already scrambling up the hill, edging around the boulders and grabbing hold of the scrub bushes that struggled to survive in the rock crevices.

She followed him, rehearsing what she would say. They

might as well get it over with now, she told herself. If he had to discover it, and eventually he would, it was best that it happen today.

She saw the instant he spotted it. He froze, staring down into the valley on the other side of the cliffs. Then he slowly turned around to face her.

All the softness, all the gentleness was gone from his face. Once again, he was the hard, dangerous stranger who had approached her for a job. Once again, Jesse was a man she didn't know.

"There's a cabin on the other side of this cliff."

Chapter 9

Jesse watched Shea as she climbed up the hill behind him. All his suspicions had come roaring back as soon as he'd seen the tiny cabin nestled next to the lake. She'd never told him there was a cabin up here.

Finally she stood next to him, staring down at the small valley. "That's been here for years," she said, her voice light.

"You never mentioned it."

"There was no reason to mention it." She looked at the cabin rather than him. "We hardly ever use it."

"What's it there for, then?"

She shrugged. "Emergencies. It's here in case someone gets stuck up on the mountain in severe weather. And Dev and I occasionally use it if we want to get away and spend some time alone. Some of our friends in Cameron have stayed in it, too."

"Why don't we head back to the ranch that way?" His voice was hard with suspicion, but Shea still didn't look at him.

"Sure, if you'd like to see the cabin." She shrugged, but

he thought her shoulders were a little tight. "It'll take a while longer, though."

"I have plenty of time."

They remounted their horses and rode back toward a break in the cliffs. Shea's knuckles were white on her reins, and her back was ramrod straight. And instead of the easy camaraderie of earlier in the morning, tension quivered in the air between them.

Neither of them spoke. When they reached the tiny cabin, perched on the edge of a clear blue lake, Shea finally turned to him.

"Did you want to take a look inside?"

Jesse forced himself to shrug carelessly. "Sure. You never know when I might get caught in bad weather and need to use the cabin."

"That's probably a good idea. The weather in the mountains is unpredictable." Shea's voice was expressionless as she swung herself off the horse's back and looped the reins around a tree branch. "Come on in."

The door wasn't locked, he noticed. "Why do you leave the door open?" he asked, watching her carefully. "Aren't you afraid of vandals?"

Instead of the guilt he'd expected to see on her face, she gave him an exasperated look. "If we kept the door locked, it sure wouldn't help anyone in an emergency, would it? I'm beginning to wonder just how much time you've spent on ranches, Jesse. This isn't the city. The only people who would need this place are Red Rock Ranch people and our neighbors. And all the neighbors know they can use the cabin if they need to."

"You mean anyone could walk in and stay here?"

"Of course." She gave him a look that said a small child would have grasped the concept more quickly. "That's the whole point."

Maybe it wasn't Shea who was doing the smuggling, he thought with a desperate leap of hope. Maybe it was one of her neighbors, using her cabin. Maybe he was focusing on the wrong person.

She disappeared inside the cabin, and he followed her eagerly. Maybe the former employee had lied. Maybe Shea wasn't involved at all.

The cabin was empty, and from the look of it, had been for a long time. He inhaled the slightly musty air and looked around at the shabby furniture, the bare counters, the beds stripped to the mattress. "It doesn't look like anyone's used the place in a while."

She didn't answer him directly. Instead, she disappeared into one of the bedrooms. "Maria is personally offended if it isn't clean. She checks on it regularly to dust and make sure that the bedding is usable and the cabinets are stocked with food."

There wasn't any dust on any of the surfaces, he noticed. He opened up a cabinet and found cans of beans and soup, boxed dinners and bags of pasta. There were jars of spaghetti sauce and what looked like breakfast cereal in plastic containers. Nothing, he concluded, that shouldn't be there if the cabin were really for emergency use, as Shea had said.

He was too ready to exonerate Shea, he realized uneasily. He was too ready to accept what she said at face value, to absolve her completely. He couldn't afford to assume anything.

Letting his eyes wander around the room, he spotted a small edge of brightly colored material sticking out from under one of the couches. Bending down, he pulled a soft rag doll out from underneath.

"You have a lot of kids staying here?" he asked Shea as she emerged from the bedroom.

Color drained from her face. Staring at the doll, she slowly reached out and took it from him. Holding it for a moment, gazing down at it, she didn't say anything. He thought she was trying to regain her composure. Finally she looked up at him. And although she tried to hide it, he saw fear in her eyes.

"Two of our friends stayed up here last fall, and they had two little girls with them. One of the girls must have lost this doll. I'll have to find out."

She set the doll on the couch, carefully arranging it, then stepped back. When she looked up at him, he thought her brightness was forced. "Seen enough here? Ready to go?"

Watching her, he said, "Are you going to show me how to get here from the ranch? In case I ever have to use it."

She nodded once without meeting his gaze. "We'll go back that way."

The ride back to the ranch was silent and tense. When they reached the barn, Shea closed herself in her horse's stall, rubbing him down, then hurried away before he'd finished with Joey. "Sunday we try to take it easy," she said abruptly. "Dinner is at six. I'll see you then."

She practically ran out of the barn into the house. Jesse watched her go, wondering at her reaction. Was she that upset because a friend's child had left her doll at the cabin? Or was there more to it than that? Watching the door to the house slam behind her, he felt his suspicions return in a rush.

He deliberately walked into the house late for dinner that night, hoping to overhear Shea talking about the cabin. Ignoring the unfamiliar shame that tried to distract him, he closed the front door as silently as possible and paused before entering the dining room. But all he heard was Levi's voice, talking about what he'd done that day.

All conversation stopped for a moment when he walked into the dining room, then Shea said lightly, "You should be thankful that Maria's in a good mood tonight. She doesn't take kindly to people who stroll in late for dinner."

Just then Maria came through the kitchen door with two steaming bowls in her hands. Plopping them on the table, she propped her hands on her hips and glared at him.

"Do you own a watch, mister?"

"Yes, ma'am," Jesse answered meekly.

"Then you'd better use it. I don't cook so shiftless hands can waltz into my dining room any time they please. This isn't a restaurant, cowboy."

"No, ma'am."

With one final glare, Maria turned and stalked back into

the kitchen. Jesse heard chuckles from the men at the table behind him, and when he turned around, he saw that even Shea was grinning.

"I told you she was in a good mood," Shea said, her eyes twinkling.

Jesse pulled out the chair next to Shea. Apparently it had become his place at the table. "I'd hate to catch her in a bad mood, then."

Levi chortled. "On a bad day, you'd be wearing your dinner instead of eating it. We don't mess with Maria."

"I'll remember that."

Shea looked over at him, her eyes still smiling. "You'd better watch your step. Maria already gave you conditional approval. Another infraction and you'll have to start over."

"That's hard to believe. Most of the time, I don't think she even approves of you," he said, his voice light.

Shea laughed. "Most of the time she doesn't. But she loves me anyway."

He understood why, he thought with a sudden rush of heat and need. It seemed like everyone he'd met adored Shea. And he was too damned close to feeling the same way about her.

He had to step back, he told himself, and figure out what was going on. Nothing was adding up the way it was supposed to. He hadn't expected to find a doll in the cabin. Their informant had told them Shea was smuggling hardened criminals into the country. They sure as hell wouldn't have any dolls with them. Judging by Shea's reaction, there was something going on at the cabin, but he was beginning to wonder if it was the smuggling of illegal aliens.

Maybe Shea was using the cabin for personal reasons. He scowled, engulfed by a black wave of jealousy, thinking about what those personal reasons could be. And maybe it was perfectly innocent. Maybe she'd been telling the complete truth when she said that a friend's child had left the doll behind.

If so, he was wasting his time here. If no evidence showed up soon, he'd have to leave and call it quits. There were other places he was needed, other jobs waiting for him.

But for the first time since joining the Bureau, he wasn't eager to move on to the next job. He didn't look forward to matching wits with the next criminal, playing the game, plotting all the moves. For the first time, he wasn't looking forward to leaving a place behind.

Scowling again, he attacked his mashed potatoes and thought about the woman sitting next to him. He knew why he didn't want to leave, and it scared him spitless. He didn't want to say goodbye to Shea.

"...and it looks like we got us a real expert here in Jesse," he heard Joe say.

Jesse jerked his head up to find that Shea and the three older men were all watching him. "What are you talking about?"

"I was just telling them how you helped me get that truck's engine purring today."

Jesse saw the approval in Joe's eyes and shrugged. "I mostly just held the wrenches for Joe while he tuned it up. He's the one who's a genius with engines."

"Don't be modest, now, Jesse," Joe said, and Jesse squirmed in his seat. He'd never intended for Joe to tell anyone else how he'd helped him.

Joe described in detail what Jesse had done to fine-tune the engine of the truck, and when he'd finished, Shea turned to him.

"Thanks, Jesse," she said, and the warmth was back in her eyes. "I appreciate that."

"I didn't do anything," he protested. "Joe is the one who did all the work."

"I know exactly what you did." Her eyes glowed at him, and he couldn't look away. For a moment, there was no one else in the room. There was only Shea, looking at him like he hung the moon, and his treacherous heart, which wanted nothing more than to sweep her into his arms and hold on tight.

But he wasn't on the Red Rock Ranch to get soft in the head over Shea, so he forced himself to look away and shrug. "It was no big deal."

For a moment, no one spoke, then the typical dinner chaos broke out again. Finally, Maria served dessert and everyone but he and Shea eventually wandered out of the room.

"Thank you for Joe," she said quietly when everyone had gone.

"I don't mind helping him," he replied.

"That's not what I meant. I know his head is still bothering him, and he's not able to do what he wants to do. You did a lot more than hold the wrenches for him this afternoon, and you somehow managed to convince him he'd done most of the work."

"He had," Jesse said, uncomfortable again. "He figured out what needed to be done. I just supplied the muscle."

"But you made him feel like he could contribute to the ranch. Before today, I hadn't seen him smile since Ben Jackson brought him home from the hospital."

"He's getting older," Jesse said. "It's going to take longer to get back in shape."

"No one wants to admit that," Shea said. "Especially a man who's always been proud of the work he does. You were wonderful with him."

"It was no big deal," Jesse muttered.

"That's why it's a big deal." Shea pushed away from the table. "I have more bookkeeping to do. I'll see you tomorrow."

Her voice was light and easy again, and the fear and tension he'd seen in her face at the cabin were gone. There were no shadows in her eyes, and once more Jesse wondered if he'd imagined them earlier. Had he seen them because that's what he wanted to see? Had he allowed his preconceived ideas about her guilt to color his observations? Had their informant been wrong?

"Could you take a few minutes to talk to me before you do your bookkeeping?" he asked abruptly.

The light in her eyes dimmed fractionally, and he thought she looked wary. "Sure. What's up?"

"I just have a few questions about the ranch."

The wariness eased, and she grabbed a jacket from the

stand by the front door. "Why don't we go outside, then? It's a shame to waste any of this beautiful day indoors. It could turn ugly again any time."

He followed her out of the house, and they both headed for the pasture behind the house. The trees and the barn would allow them some privacy, and Jesse didn't want to be overheard.

They leaned on the fence, watching the cattle in the distance for a moment. The sun was slipping below the horizon, and the first faint streaks of red were appearing in the sky. The trees on the mountains behind them were dark silhouettes against the red and purple of the rocks.

"Tell me about the employee you fired recently," Jesse said abruptly.

He felt her tense beside him. "Do you mean Kyle?"

"How many people have you fired in the past year?"

"Only Kyle," she said, and he heard the reluctance in her voice.

"You needed help pretty badly. Why did you let him go?"

"Why do you need to know?" she countered.

He didn't answer right away. He'd have to be careful, or he wouldn't get the information he needed. Finally he said, "I'm curious. No one wants to talk much about him." He'd stick as close to the truth as possible. Shea was too perceptive.

She didn't answer for so long that he thought she was going to refuse. Finally she sighed. "I had to fire Kyle because he was stealing from me. And worse, he was stealing from Joe, Dusty and Levi. That was the last straw. I couldn't allow that."

"Why didn't you have him arrested?" he demanded.

"Dev tried to arrest him. But he disappeared before Dev could get out here and we didn't hear from Kyle again. He was smart enough not to write and ask for his last paycheck."

"Do you have any idea where he's gone?"

"No, and I don't care." She turned to look at him. "What difference does it make, anyway? He's gone, I split his last check between Joe, Dusty and Levi, and he won't steal anything else from us. As far as I'm concerned, it was a case of bad judgment that I've already paid for. End of story.''

"I see why you were reluctant to hire me,'' he said softly. "You were smart to be careful after an experience like that.''

This time she turned to face him. "You're nothing like Kyle, Jesse. I think I knew that from the very beginning. I wasn't afraid that you'd steal from me.''

"Then why didn't you want to hire me?''

She turned away and stared into the growing darkness. "It was complicated,'' she finally said.

"I'm told I have a good grasp of the complicated,'' he said, trying to keep his voice light. "Tell me about it.''

"I was attracted to Kyle,'' she said after a while, her voice very low. "And after I found out what he was doing, I questioned my judgment. I didn't want to make the same mistake twice. It was easier just not to hire you.''

"Are you saying you didn't want to hire me because you were attracted to me?'' Desire, never far from the surface when Shea was around, roared to life.

She whirled on him. "In a word, yes. How would you have felt in my position?''

"If you'd shown up at my ranch, I would have hired you in a minute.'' Need crashed over him in a wave of heat, and he gripped the top rail of the fence to keep from reaching for her.

"Not if you were serious about running your ranch, you wouldn't.'' She leaned against the top rail of the fence, staring out over the pasture. "I didn't think I had the time or energy to deal with an attraction to an employee.''

"And now you do?''

"Now I don't know what to think.'' She finally looked over at him. "You make me forget my plans, forget what I need to do. I can't think of anything else when you're around.''

The need to touch her, to pull her close and refuse to let go, was a physical ache inside him. But he had to think about the reason he was standing here with Shea, had to think about why he had come to the Red Rock. "Are you always this painfully honest?"

She finally smiled. "It's one of my worst failings. It's gotten me in trouble more times than I can remember."

"It'll get you into trouble tonight, too," he muttered.

She looked back out over the pasture and slowly shook her head. "I don't think so. If you can't be honest with someone, you have no future together, anyway."

Jesse felt a curl of fear in his gut, a fear he tried to ignore. His whole relationship with Shea was based on a lie. But they didn't have a future to worry about, he told himself harshly.

"A little mystery never hurt anything," he said lightly.

When she turned to look at him, her eyes were serious. "I'm not talking about the kinds of games lovers play. I'm talking about telling someone how you feel, making sure they know who you are, sharing yourself with them. I'm talking about fundamental stuff here, Jesse."

"You don't pull any punches, do you?"

Slowly her mouth curled up into a smile. "I don't know how to," she said. "And I'm betting that you're pretty straightforward, too."

"I can be pretty devious when I want to be," he said.

She grinned. "Like when you tried to goad me into hiring you that first day? Telling me that I didn't have the guts to go for it?"

He shrugged. "So that didn't work. It was worth a try."

"You were pathetically obvious. Here's a tip—don't quit your day job and try to get into undercover work. You'd be a miserable failure."

"I'll keep that in mind." His voice was expressionless, and he didn't dare look at her.

Leaning back on the rail of the fence, looking out into the night, she said, "What do you want out of life, Jesse? Are you going to be a drifter forever? Are you going to find a place you like and end up like Joe and Dusty and Levi? Do you have aspirations to buy a place of your own?"

Just a few weeks ago he would have had a swift answer

for her. Now he looked out over the dark pasture and hesitated. He wasn't sure what he wanted anymore. He still believed justice was important, but his job at the Bureau seemed somehow unreal, part of another life. "I don't know," he said slowly. "I'm not sure what I want."

He felt her gaze on him, but he didn't turn his head. "I like what I do. It's important to me. But I've enjoyed my time on the Red Rock more than I imagined I would."

"You have a job here as long as you want one."

Now he did look at her. "I thought I was on probation until Dusty and Joe were recovered."

"You've done a good job. You're reliable and trustworthy, and you work hard. Your probation is over."

"If this is because of what's happened between you and me," he began, but she cut him off.

"This has nothing to do with you and me," she said, her eyes blazing. "And you don't know me very well if you could think it did. The Red Rock is more important to me than anything else. I would never jeopardize the ranch by keeping an employee who wasn't pulling his weight."

"Is that why you're not married? Because you put the Red Rock before everything else?" He couldn't stop himself from asking the question.

She didn't answer for a long time. Finally, she said, "I guess I'm not the only one who says what they think."

He shrugged. "It seems pretty obvious."

"I don't know, Jesse," she said, her voice low as she stared into the night. "I guess it's never been a priority of mine. And mostly I've been too busy to think about it."

"Then obviously you've never met the right man."

"Maybe not. But I'm not sure I'd know him if I did meet him." She turned to look at him. "What about you?"

No one had ever asked him that question before. Even his mother never asked him when he was getting married. Certainly none of his colleagues at the Bureau would ever have the nerve to ask him about his personal life. But somehow, Shea's question hadn't felt intrusive or nosy. And he realized he wanted to answer her.

"I've never thought about it," he said, his voice quiet in the dark. "I've never been in one place long enough to get involved. And even if I had, I was always focused only on my job."

"We sound like a pair," she said lightly. "A couple of workaholics."

"Is your ranch going to be a comfort to you when you're old and alone?" he asked.

"More than your job." Her answer was swift. "At least I'll have my land, my friends, my town. What will you have but memories of all the ranches where you worked?"

"Maybe that's all I'll need."

"Then I feel sorry for you, Jesse." Her voice was steady and sure. "A job, even one you do well, is cold comfort at best. And it's no comfort at all when you're too old to do it well."

"Is that why you keep Joe and Dusty and Levi around?"

"They're family," she said, her voice fierce. "They'll be here until the day they die. Then they'll be buried in the family plot."

He had never met anyone like her. All her passions ran deep and true. Would she love the same way? An ache rose inside him, a need to know. He wanted to feel that passion of Shea's, directed at him. He wanted to know if she gave herself as freely to the man she loved as she did to her ranch and her friends and family.

But he would never know. Because anything she gave him would be given to a facade, a lie who wasn't the real Jesse Coulton. Anything she gave him would be given to a man who was lying to her. And he suspected that was the one thing Shea would not forgive.

"You need to get back to your bookkeeping," he said abruptly.

She nodded slowly, but he didn't miss the sadness in her eyes. Or the regret. And he knew it was for him. "You're right. I do." She moved toward the house. "I'll see you in the morning," she said.

Jesse stood by the fence and listened to her footsteps fade, then heard the door gently close. He was alone. He'd done the right thing and sent Shea into the house, away from him.

Maybe he'd been a fool, he told himself slowly. He had found no proof of any smuggling in the time he'd been on the ranch. And what he'd learned tonight about Kyle Diggett, their informant, had made him wonder about his story. The man had to hold a grudge against Shea. She'd caught him stealing, and fired him. Maybe his story had been nothing more than an attempt to cause trouble for his former boss. And a woman who had spurned him.

He thought about Shea sitting in her office, alone, going over her accounts, and he wanted to run to her, to gather her against him and never let go. He wanted her warmth, her loyalty, and her passion.

When he found himself walking toward the house, he stopped abruptly. He wanted to jump her bones, he told himself harshly. That was all there was to it. He lusted after her, and the rest was all camouflage.

He could resist lust. He'd resisted it before, and no doubt would resist it again. If Shea was innocent of the charges against her, and it looked like she was, he'd tell his bosses at the Bureau that they'd made a mistake, then move on to the next job.

It didn't matter that, for the first time, the next job held no appeal. For the first time, he wasn't excited about dispensing justice and balancing the scales. He'd do it anyway, because that's who he was. He was the Renegade, and once this job was finished, Shea McAllister wasn't going to be any more than a memory.

Shea watched Jesse start toward the house, then stop and scowl. A few minutes later, he turned and stalked off to his cabin. When the door shut firmly behind him, she stared down at the columns of figures again.

She wanted him. It was as simple as that, and as complicated. Jesse touched her in a way no one else ever had. His tough exterior, his inherent kindness, the way he tried to do the right thing, all intrigued her and beckoned to her.

She couldn't have fallen for some nice, easy man from Cameron, a man she'd known most of her life, a man she knew everything about. No, she had to go and tumble into lust with a man she didn't know, a dark stranger who kept most of himself hidden from her. Tonight, she'd practically thrown herself at him. But he'd stepped away, refusing to catch her.

That was probably a good thing, she told herself. She didn't have time to deal with a broken heart. Because Jesse would undoubtedly leave, and if she let him, he'd take her heart with him.

But she had never done the smart thing. She'd never done what she was supposed to do. And she suspected that she wouldn't do the smart thing with Jesse, either.

Her heart wasn't going to let her.

Chapter 10

By the time Shea finished with the books, the house was dark and silent. Maria had gone to bed much earlier, and even Buster had curled up on his bed in the kitchen. She stood up and stretched, then turned off the lights.

She was just about to head upstairs when she heard Demon in the barn. He snorted twice, and Shea tensed. She knew him too well. There was someone in the barn with him.

Without bothering with a coat, she dashed out of the house and ran across the yard into the barn. She skidded to an abrupt stop when she saw Jesse standing at the door of Demon's stall, crooning to him.

"What's wrong? What happened?" she demanded, her heart racing with fear.

He didn't look at her, but she saw his hand tense on the top board of Demon's stall. "Nothing's wrong. I'm just checking on him."

"Why? Did you hear something?"

He shook his head. "I didn't hear a thing. There's nothing wrong. I just wanted to take another look at his foot."

She moved into the barn, finally stopping in front of Demon's stall, too close to Jesse. Demon looked fine. As she studied him, she could feel the heat from Jesse's body wrapping around her, warming her from the inside. The scent of the outdoors clung to him, the fragrance of the wind that sighed through the trees late at night. She needed to think about Demon, but she was aware of only Jesse.

"Why are you here?" she asked in a low voice.

For a while she didn't think he was going to answer. Finally he said, "It's part of my job, Shea. That's all."

"You couldn't sleep, could you?"

He turned to face her. She couldn't move. She felt the tension and the need that poured out of him, and she wanted to step closer to Jesse. But she didn't move.

"Don't ask me that, Shea. You don't want to hear the answer. Demon is fine, and let's leave it at that. Go back to bed."

"Maybe I couldn't sleep, either."

"That's not true and you know it. You've been working on the books. I saw you..." He stopped abruptly and thinned his lips. "Get out of here, Shea."

It was decision time. If she backed off now, if she turned and left him alone in the barn, everything would change. Oh, he'd still work for her. He'd still do more than his share of work, but nothing else would be the same. If she walked away from him now, she would be telling him that he was right. She'd be telling him that he had no future with her, no reason to want to stay.

So she grabbed for her courage and took a step toward him. "I'm not going anywhere, Jesse. Not until you tell me why you couldn't sleep tonight."

"Why would you think that has anything to do with you?"

"How do you know I've been working on the books all this time?" she countered.

He scowled. "A man would have to be blind if he didn't see the light in your study."

"You can't see my study from your cabin." She crossed her arms over her chest and waited for his answer.

To her surprise, he grinned. "You're a piece of work, Shea. You know that, don't you?"

"You're changing the subject. We weren't talking about me."

Just as quickly, the grin was gone. "Why not? That's what this is all about, isn't it? You want me to say I couldn't sleep because I was thinking about you. Isn't that where this is going?"

"I just want to understand you," she whispered.

"You can't understand me. Half the time, I don't understand myself."

She saw the confusion in his eyes, the terrible indecision. And beneath that, she saw the need he tried to hide. "Is it so wrong to need someone?"

"Yes." His voice was implacable. "You shouldn't want me, Shea. And I sure as hell shouldn't want you."

"Why is it wrong?" she asked. She yearned to reach out and touch him, but knew that she couldn't. Not yet.

"Because I don't want to hurt you. And if I touch you tonight, I'm going to end up hurting you."

"You would never hurt me, Jesse." She deliberately misunderstood him. "I've seen how gentle you are with anyone who's weaker than you, and with the animals. You couldn't hurt me."

"I don't mean I'd physically hurt you. My God, Shea! I meant I'd hurt you when I leave."

His eyes were bleak and shadowed with pain, and she ached to take it away. "You wouldn't have to leave."

"Yes, I would. I always leave."

"Everything changes," she said. "You don't know what's going to happen tomorrow, let alone next week or next month. So why live your life according to maybes?"

"There's no 'maybe' about my leaving. It's going to happen."

Her head told her to back away. Jesse was telling her in no uncertain terms that he wasn't going to be there for her in the long run. But her heart refused to take no for an answer. And she had never yet backed away from a challenge.

She lifted her chin. "The only reason I could turn around and walk out of this barn is if I thought you weren't interested in me. Is that the case, Jesse?"

His eyes darkened with desire and need, but all he said was, "Leave, Shea. Turn around and don't look back."

Slowly she shook her head. "I don't think I can," she whispered. She reached out and put her hand on his chest. His heart pounded much too quickly beneath her fingers. "No one's ever made me feel the way you do."

"Hasn't anyone ever told you that your mouth is going to get you into trouble?" he said harshly. But he captured her hand beneath his, holding it in place over his heart.

"I hear that every day." She forced herself to smile, although blood roared in her ears and her heart thundered in her chest. "That's not news to me."

His eyes darkened as desire raged in their depths. "I don't want you to regret anything, Shea," he said, his voice urgent. "I don't want you to hate me, or yourself." He turned her hand in his and twined their fingers together.

"I could never do that," she said. Her heart sang his name and she had to hold herself still. She wanted to throw herself into his arms, but she knew she needed to wait for him to make the next move.

Slowly he let her hand go, then he cupped her face with both of his palms. "I need you, Shea. I don't think I've ever needed anyone more. But that's all I can give you. I can't give you permanence, I can't give you a commitment. And I know you're the kind of woman who needs those things."

"You have no idea what I need," she said fiercely. She wouldn't think about the future right now. The future would take care of itself.

He smiled. It was a slow, hot smile that held intimate promises. The look in his eyes made her throb inside. "I think I have a pretty good idea of what you need." His voice was rough velvet that caressed all the nerves in her body, making her tingle.

She was appalled to feel the heat sweep up her neck and face. His smile faded and his hands slid down to grip her shoulders. Someone was trembling, and she wasn't sure if it was her or Jesse.

"Do you blush all over?" he whispered. He let one hand trail down her chest, between her breasts, and settle on her stomach. Her skin jumped beneath his hand, and deep inside her, a huge, aching hole opened up. "Will you do it again when you're lying naked next to me, when I tell you what I want to do with you?"

Sudden fear gripped her. Would she know what to do? Would Jesse be disappointed with her?

He must have seen the fear on her face, because his hands shifted again. This time he gently gripped her upper arms. "Are you a virgin, Shea?"

She could answer that truthfully. "Of course not."

He stared at her, his eyes narrowed as if he didn't believe her. Then he pulled her against him. "But you're not very experienced, are you?"

With her head pressed against his chest, safe in the shelter of his arms, she could tell him the truth. "No." She thought of the few hurried, fumbling encounters she'd had with the boy she'd been madly in love with as a teenager. "Does it matter?"

"Hell, yes, it matters. Get out of here now. Run away from me as fast as you can." But his arms tightened around her. "If we make love, I may not be taking your virginity, but I'd sure as hell be taking your innocence."

"Maybe I don't want to be innocent anymore."

"You don't know what you're saying, Shea. You don't know what you're giving me." There was desperation in his voice. "You're picking the wrong man."

"You're exactly the right man, Jesse." She raised her head from his chest and looked up at him. "I'm not experienced because no one ever made me feel the way you make me feel."

He stared down at her for a long time. Finally he closed his eyes. "Then God help me, because I can't walk away from you. I've tried to do that since the first day I saw you, and I can't do it. I know I'm the wrong person for you, I know I should be stronger, but I can't do it." He opened his eyes and looked at her again, and she saw the desire that burned there.

"I need you, Shea."

It was a hard thing for him to admit, she knew. And she was sure that he hadn't said it often, or to very many other women. For now, that was enough.

"I need you, too, Jesse."

He pulled her close, and when she wrapped her arms around him, she felt him tremble. The knowledge that he was nervous, that it mattered to him, too, gave her courage. Raising her head, she whispered, "Please kiss me."

But instead of kissing her, he said, "You could have anyone, you know. You're a remarkable woman, Shea."

"I don't want anyone," she said, her voice fierce. "I want you, Jesse."

His eyes turned to green fire. "I'll make your body sing, Shea. I'll take you places you've never been before. I'll give you more pleasure than you've ever had in your life."

"I know you will." She lifted her face to his.

And then he was kissing her. He didn't kiss her gently, or give her time to change her mind. His mouth took hers with a roar of need, a rush of desire. And she felt an answering fire spring to life inside her.

She clung to him while the fire raged inside her, singeing her nerves, burning away everything but Jesse. When he pulled her closer, her body welcomed him. And when he pressed her against the boards of an empty stall, she gloried in his weight against her.

His hands roamed up and down her sides, her back, her hips. He reached around and cupped her buttocks, pulling her closer. When she felt the hot, heavy weight of his arousal burning into her abdomen, she tilted instinctively, wanting him closer.

For a moment he strained against her, then he moved away. "I need to see you again," he said, his voice hoarse in her ear. Letting her go, he began to unbutton her blouse. She felt his hands shake as they pushed each tiny button through the even tinier hole. Watching him undress her made her blood pool deep in her abdomen, until she felt every beat of her heart in a deep, secret place inside her.

When the last button was opened, he brushed her shirt aside, then stared at the lacy bra she wore. His eyes were hot with desire when he looked up at her. "It's a good thing I didn't know you were wearing this earlier. I wouldn't have been able to stop."

"I didn't want you to stop."

He reached out and traced the lace with one finger, brushing closer and closer to her aching peak without actually touching it. When he lifted his hand and moved to her other breast, she clenched her hands in the cloth of his shirt to keep from crying out.

"Jesse, please," she panted.

"What do you want, Shea?" His fingers teased her, straying so close but never touching the place that ached for him.

"Touch me."

"That's what I'm doing," he whispered as he nuzzled her neck.

"No, you're not!"

At that he lifted his head. His eyes glittered with passion and his hands trembled, but he took her hands and kissed her palms. "This isn't going to be a slam, bam, thank you ma'am kind of night, Shea. I'm going to go as slowly as I can. I may not be able to give you much, but I can give you that, at least."

He kissed her again, and he tasted of need and desire and a struggle for control. Her breasts flattened against his chest, and she felt his heart beating against hers. His heat was a contrast to the cool night air, and suddenly she wanted to feel his skin against hers.

But when she started to unbutton his shirt, he covered her hands with his. "Not yet, Shea."

"I want to touch you," she whispered. "I want to feel your skin against mine."

He shuddered against her, and his hands tightened against hers. "I guess I'm going to have to distract you, then."

He lowered his head and pressed his mouth against the top of her breast. The thin lace was no barrier against the hot wetness of his tongue, and she moaned his name as heat shot through her.

When he touched her nipple with his tongue, through the lace, the spasm of pleasure was so strong she nearly cried out. Jesse shuddered, then touched her other nipple with his thumb. If he hadn't been holding her, she would have slid to the floor.

She felt his hands shaking as he fumbled with the clasp of her bra, then the cool night air brushed over her wet nipple, making her gasp. When his mouth followed, suckling gently on her nipple, she shook with the waves of desire and pleasure that crashed over her.

She had to touch him. Her hands trembled as she slid them under his shirt, letting her fingers trace the hard outline of his muscles. His skin twitched and jumped as she touched him, and when she reached his small, hard male nipples, she brushed over them lightly.

He arched into her, pressing closer, and she gloried in his response. When she touched him again, he swirled his tongue around her nipple, making her gasp, "Jesse!"

Suddenly his hands fumbled frantically at the waistband of her jeans. When the button was loosened and the zipper lowered, he shoved the denim down her hips and cupped her in his hand. His heat burned through the skimpy lace panties that matched her bra, burned all the way inside her. She needed him to fill the ache, to fill the empty spot that yearned for him.

But when she tried to unbutton his jeans, he stilled. Slowly he took his hand away from her, then brushed her hair out of her face. When she opened her eyes and looked at him, she saw the fierce desire on his face. But she also saw determination.

"Not here, Shea. I'm not going to take you in the straw, on the floor of a barn. I let this go too far, but we're not going any farther here. You deserve a bed, and some privacy."

As he spoke, he buttoned her shirt, then her jeans. Finally, he took her hand and led her out of the barn. "Will you come to my bed?"

She shook her head. "We'll have more privacy in my room. There's no one even close." She urged him toward the house.

"What about Maria?"

"She has her own apartment on the first floor. And she's a very sound sleeper."

"All right."

Shea led him into the empty, dark house and up the stairs. Her body still throbbed and ached, but she didn't touch Jesse. Finally they stopped in front of an open door. "Here we are."

Moonlight dappled the room and covered the bed, outlining everything in a ghostly white, but Jesse never even looked around. All his attention was focused on her.

"You're beautiful, Shea. Inside and out." He traced her cheek, her mouth, her neck. "And for now, you're mine. I'm not sure how much longer I can wait."

"I don't want to wait," she said, moving closer to him. "I've waited far too long as it is."

When she reached for the first button on his shirt, he stilled. Her hands shook as she moved down his shirt, but finally she drew his shirt off his shoulders and tossed it on the floor. Dark hair covered his chest, and she touched him once, marveling at how soft and silky it felt. Then she touched the waistband of his jeans.

He was hard and throbbing beneath the rough denim, and when her fingers brushed the hot length of him, he sucked in his breath. But he didn't move. When she peeled his jeans down his legs, he bent to remove them, and then he straightened.

He was magnificent. His body was all hard angles and hard muscle, gleaming in the moonlight. And he was fully aroused. A twinge of doubt crept over her.

Then he was kissing her again, and his hands flew through the buttons on her blouse. He swept it off her shoulders, and her bra followed. In a few moments, her jeans and panties joined them on the floor.

They stood naked in front of each other, but she wasn't nervous anymore. All her nerves had vanished in the barn, when she'd felt his struggle for control. Jesse wanted her as much as she wanted him. And while he looked at her, she looked back at him.

"Don't move." Without taking his eyes off her, Jesse bent and pulled his wallet from his pocket. When he stood again, he held a foil packet in his hand.

Shea felt her face getting warm. "I didn't even think about protection."

"I did. I haven't thought of much besides you since the first time I saw you," he said, his voice heavy with desire.

He set the packet on her nightstand and took her hand, leading her to the bed. He touched her face. "I want you, Shea. But I saw the hesitation in your eyes. It's not too late to say no."

"I don't want to say no," she said, but something inside her melted at his words, something sweet that welled up and filled her heart. He might say he wouldn't stay, he might say he didn't want to get involved, but his words told a different story. And so did his eyes.

"Then come to me," he said, and he held out his hand.

She took it without hesitation. When he pressed her down onto the bed, she opened her arms and her heart and welcomed him, holding him close. And when he covered her mouth with his, she tried to tell him everything her words couldn't say.

She felt his muscles tremble with desire, felt him struggle for control. But he kept his promise. His hands were everywhere, touching and caressing. When she moaned his name, he kissed her and touched her again.

Finally, when she felt like she would explode if he didn't fill the empty place inside her, he moved over her. "I can't wait another moment," he said.

"Neither can I."

When he slid inside her, she closed her eyes and said, "Jesse."

Then he was moving and she couldn't say anything at all. Pleasure wound more and more tightly inside her, spiraling out of control. "Jesse," she gasped, and he reached down and touched her where their bodies were joined.

Waves of light exploded inside her, filling her, making her cry out again. He fused his mouth to hers, then shuddered as he joined her.

When the waves of pleasure finally receded and the roaring need inside him was temporarily satisfied, Jesse realized that he was sprawled bonelessly on top of Shea. Shifting so that she wasn't bearing his weight, he pulled her close to him and wrapped his arms around her. Just for a moment, he could pretend they had a future. Just for a moment, he could pretend that this was the first of an infinite number of nights together.

Finally she opened her eyes and smiled at him. The look of stunned delight in her eyes made him lean over and kiss her again.

"I never knew," she whispered, and he felt a small piece of his heart break off and tumble into her hands.

She'd given him everything tonight—her body, her trust, and, he was afraid, her heart. He'd do his best to guard it until he had to hand it back to her, broken into pieces.

"That was just the first lesson," he whispered back. "Are you ready to move on to part two?"

"There's more?"

"It appears that there is." He slid over her, and her eyes widened as she felt the heavy weight of his arousal against her thigh.

"I didn't know that could happen so fast again, either."

He pressed her down into the bed with his kiss. "Neither did I, sweetheart."

He woke fully aroused again to find that Shea was nibbling on his chest. But when he reached for her, she rolled away and sat up. She held the sheet to her chest and said, "I don't mind if Maria finds out you were here with me last night. But if you'd rather not, we'd better get up now. Maria's an early riser.''

For a long moment he hesitated. He wanted nothing more right now than to sink into Shea again, to feel her welcoming warmth, to feel whole again as they made love.

But instead he rolled out of bed. "I'll go shower in my cabin. I'm not sure I want to face Maria just yet.''

Shea watched him dress, and the disappointment on her face was almost enough to make him stay. Almost, but not quite. With one more kiss he slipped out of her room and crept down the stairs. He heard activity from the back of the house, from what he assumed was Maria's apartment, but there were no lights on in the house yet. He could hear Shea's dog Buster snoring in the kitchen as he stepped out into the darkness.

A half hour later he was back, sharing a cup of coffee and breakfast with Shea in the dining room. Maria gave them both a sharp look when she removed the remains of their pancakes, but she didn't say anything. Finally, after another cup of coffee, they both rose from the table and headed for the barn.

As soon as the door closed behind them, he grabbed her and pressed her to the wall, kissing her as if he needed her taste as much as he needed to breathe. She wrapped her arms around him and kissed him back.

"Good morning to you, too,'' she said breathlessly when he lifted his head.

He didn't want to let her go. She fit perfectly against him, and his arms ached to fold her closer. But he dropped a kiss on her head and stepped away.

"Is this where I ask you if you slept well?'' he said, keeping his voice light.

She grinned at him as she grabbed a pitchfork. "I had a great night. How about you?''

"The best.''

Her grin faded, and she looked as if she was going to throw herself into his arms again. So he picked up a shovel and headed for the closest stall. "What's on the schedule for today?"

She didn't answer for the space of a heartbeat. Then she slipped into another stall and began cleaning it out. "I'd like to start moving some of the steers to the pastures we checked yesterday. We'll keep the pregnant cows down here and move them closer to the house. Since the weather is cooperating, I'd like to get started. It's going to take most of the week to get all the cattle moved and sorted."

So it was back to business as usual. Why was he surprised? That's what he wanted, wasn't it? He'd asked her, and she'd told him. He tossed a shovel full of used straw and manure into the wheelbarrow with a violent flick of his wrist. He'd turned away when he thought Shea might start mooning around him. So why was he angry that she wasn't?

Because he was an ass, he told himself harshly. That was the only explanation. Finishing one stall, he moved on to the next. When he was almost finished with that stall, he noticed Shea standing at the door, watching him.

"You're shoveling so fast that your hands are a blur. This isn't the Olympics of stall cleaning," she said, her voice gentle. "What's wrong?"

"Why does there have to be something wrong? I'm just trying to get the job done."

"You look like you could eat nails and spit out rust."

Jesse saw the uncertainty in her eyes, and he set his shovel against the side of the stall and reached for her. But before he could touch her, he realized that his hands were filthy. Letting them drop to his sides, he clenched his hands into fists to keep from touching her anyway.

"I'm sorry, Shea." He hesitated, fumbling for the right words. "I guess I'm not sure how to handle all this. I've never been in this situation before. I've always made sure there wasn't even a morning after, let alone having to work with my lover."

The uncertainty faded slowly from her face, replaced by a smile that warmed her eyes to a brilliant blue. "This is new to me, too," she said. "I don't know what to do, either."

"Then why don't we keep it business during business hours?" he said. "That'll make it easier for you. And for me."

"All right." She picked up her pitchfork again and flashed him a grin, the one that always seemed to land in his heart. "But I reserve the right to fool around once in a while."

"Anytime you like." He watched her turn back to her chore and battled the need that rose inside him.

He'd thought that after they'd made love, the hunger would ease. But it was worse than ever. Now, he knew what they had together. Now, he knew exactly what it would be like. He closed his eyes until he could turn away from her, then began shoveling the stall again. He didn't dare look over at Shea.

When they had finished cleaning the barn, Shea glanced at her watch, then headed for the house. "I'm ready for another cup of coffee. Let's go sit down with Levi and Joe and Dusty and figure out a plan for today."

The other three cowboys were finishing their breakfast when he and Shea walked into the dining room. Pouring herself a cup of coffee, Shea sat down with them and started talking. In fifteen minutes, they'd agreed on a plan to separate the pregnant cows from the steers in the first pasture. She glanced over at him.

"Does that sound okay to you, Jesse?"

He shrugged, moved that she would ask him but determined not to show it. "You four know best. You've been doing this for a lot longer than I have."

She nodded. "Okay. Let's get rolling."

Ten hours later they rode back into the barn, tired and dusty. Shea beamed at Dusty, who'd been given the task of counting the cattle, and Joe, who'd been responsible for opening and closing the gate. "I'm sure glad you two were back on your feet. I'm not sure how we would have done it without you."

They would have done just fine, but Jesse saw how both men seemed to sit straighter in their saddles. Once again, a small piece of his heart broke off and flew in Shea's direction. Not many people would have seen how important it was to two old men to be included.

As Joe, Dusty and Levi swung off their horses and led them away, she turned to him. "I'd like to get away from the ranch for a while. How would you feel about going into Cameron for dinner?"

"And miss one of Maria's meals?" he said lightly.

"Janie Murphy does a pretty good job at her restaurant, Heaven on Seventh." She let her gaze linger on him for a moment. "And I don't feel like having four sets of eyes watching me tonight."

Need stirred in him again at her words. He'd been careful all day, aware of the presence of the other men and reluctant to do anything that might embarrass Shea. Now he wanted nothing more than to be alone with her.

"That sounds okay to me," he said cautiously.

"Great. I'll meet you on the porch in a half hour, then."

Chapter 11

Shea sat beside Jesse in the cab of his truck and looked over at him. His jaw was set and his face was hard. He'd barely said two words to her since they pulled out of the driveway of the Red Rock.

"Is something wrong?"

He glanced over at her, startled. "No. Should there be?"

"You look so...grim."

He smiled at her then, and his whole face softened. Once again, he was her lover of the night before, the gentle, loving man she'd discovered beneath his hard exterior. "I was thinking about the town of Cameron."

"Most people don't look as if they're going to a public execution when they think about Cameron."

"Most of them aren't going out to dinner in public with a woman who knows everyone in town," he retorted.

"Are you worried about that?" She was astounded. She didn't think Jesse cared what anyone thought of him.

"I don't want anyone gossiping about you." His eyes flashed. "Some of the people in town know who I am, know that I'm working for you. I don't want to see anyone snickering at you."

A wave of tenderness washed over her. "No one's going to snicker at me, or at you, either, for that matter. Why should anyone care who I'm with?"

"I know how small towns are," he said. "They thrive on gossip, on who's seeing whom."

"I guess the people in Cameron enjoy good gossip as much as anyone else. But I like to think we judge people by who they are, not what they do."

He glanced over at her again. "I've eaten at Heaven on Seventh. It's not like there's a lot of privacy there."

"We'll see a lot of people I know. Is that going to bother you?"

"Not if it doesn't bother you."

"Why should it?"

He reached over and took her hand. "I'd like to take you to a fancy restaurant, where no one knows us, where we can sit close together and order something exotic for dinner."

She leaned back against the seat, bringing his hand to her mouth. "I didn't know you were so romantic, Jesse."

He scowled. "I'm not. All I meant was, I'd like to eat somewhere that we could be alone."

She felt her mouth curve up in a smile. "I would, too. Maybe later in the week we can take a picnic into the mountains."

Heat flared in his eyes. "I'd like that."

They were approaching the outskirts of Cameron, and Shea sat up straight in the seat. But she didn't let go of Jesse's hand. Pointing with her other hand, she said, "If you take that street there, you'll avoid the rush hour."

He smiled again, and her heart turned over in her chest. "I didn't realize that Cameron had a rush hour."

"We always have four or five vehicles lined up at the stop sign at this time of night," she said with dignity. "That's a rush hour as far as I'm concerned."

He actually grinned. "Then let's take the detour. I hate getting mixed up in traffic backups."

A few minutes later they walked into Heaven on Seventh. Mandy, the waitress, smiled at Shea, and her eyes got bigger when she saw Jesse. "Hi, Shea." She glanced at Jesse again. "Table for two?"

"Please, Mandy."

Before they could sit down, the door opened again and Ben Jackson walked in. His dark gaze flickered from her to Jesse and back again. For just a moment, Shea saw speculation in their depths, then his face was impassive again.

"Hi, Shea." He nodded to Jesse. "Coulton."

"How are you, Ben?" she replied.

"Just fine. I hear Dev is settling things up in New York. He said they might be home for good in a couple of weeks."

"That's what he said last time he called." Anxiety clutched at Shea's chest again, as it had every time she'd thought about her brother coming home. Determined not to let Ben see, she smiled brightly. "I'm looking forward to seeing both him and Carly again."

"It'll be good to have him back at the office," Ben agreed. "And speaking of people coming to Cameron, I understand you're going to have a new neighbor."

"Has someone bought the Hilbert ranch?" she asked eagerly. It had been left vacant when the previous owner, Phil Hilbert, was sent to prison for the murder of her sister-in-law Carly's brother.

"That's what I heard. A man named Whittaker. Cole, I think it was." Ben gave her a half smile. "Should be moving in next month. That'll give you plenty of time to plan your welcoming party."

"Does he have a family?" she asked.

Ben shook his head. "According to Minnie over at the realty office, he's single."

"I'm glad someone will be taking over the Tall T Ranch. I've hated seeing it sit vacant."

"It won't be vacant much longer." Then his face tightened for a moment, and Shea felt him tense. When she turned around, she saw that Janie, the restaurant's owner, was heading toward the front of the store. She stopped abruptly, as if she'd forgotten something, and turned to disappear once more into the kitchen.

Ben turned away. "I'll talk to you later, Shea." He said something in a low voice to the cashier, then walked out of the restaurant.

"What was that all about?" Jesse asked in a low voice.

"I'll tell you later," she murmured.

Mandy stood waiting to escort them to their table. As soon as they were seated, Jesse leaned across and said, "What's going on with Jackson? Didn't he come in here for dinner? Why did he walk out like that?"

Shea sighed. "It's Janie Murphy, the owner of the restaurant. She and Ben are like the same sides of two magnets. Every time they see each other, one of them runs in the opposite direction."

Jesse leaned his elbows on the table. "Maybe I'm catching the gossip habit from Cameron, but do they have some kind of history?"

"I don't think so. That's what's so strange. As far as anyone knows, they've hardly spoken two words to each other."

"And someone in town would know if they had, right?"

She laughed. "You understand perfectly."

They picked up their menus and ordered, then Shea leaned across the table. "I'm glad we came here, Jesse. I hope you don't mind too much, but I had to get away from the ranch for a while."

"I thought you loved the ranch."

"I do. More than anything, but I didn't want to sit and talk to Maria or Joe or Dusty or Levi tonight. I just wanted to be with you."

She saw desire flare in his eyes, and felt an answering curl of passion inside her. "I have a feeling this dinner is going to take too damn long," he growled.

Anticipation swelled inside her, and she reached across the table to touch his hand. "Me, too," she whispered.

He looked like he wanted to take her hand, but he slowly pulled away from her. "I can't touch you in here," he said, his voice low. "I wouldn't be able to stop with just one touch. It's been too long already since I held you."

Shea shifted on the seat, his words arousing her, making her restless and edgy. "Maybe this wasn't a good idea," she said softly.

Jesse smiled at her, his eyes glittering. "I think it was a great idea. Don't they always say that anticipation is half the pleasure?"

"Not in this case." Her voice was so soft that she wasn't sure if he heard her. But when his eyes flashed in response, she knew that he'd heard.

"Shea!"

A delighted voice spoke next to her, and she looked up with a start to see her friend. "Abby!"

Shea leapt out of the booth to hug the woman who stood next to her, then hugged the man behind her. "Damien. How are you doing?"

"We're great." Abby stepped back and reached for the baby carrier her husband held. "And this is Sarah."

Shea looked down at the tiny baby who slept in the carrier. Her face was red and scrunched, and her hands were tightly closed into fists. "She's beautiful," she said with awe. "I got your note, but I never thought I would get to meet her so soon."

"We figured two-weeks-old was old enough to pay her first visit to Cameron. And we wanted to spend some time here." Abby turned to her husband and they exchanged an intimate look. "Back to where it all started, you might say."

Shea turned to Jesse. "I'd like you to meet two friends of mine," she said. "This is Abby and Damien Kane, and their daughter Sarah. Abby and Damien, this is Jesse Coulton."

Shea glanced back at Jesse, and was shocked to see the flash of recognition in his eyes. When she looked at Abby, the other woman was smiling politely at Jesse. But Damien had tensed slightly, and for a moment Shea thought she saw an unspoken message flash between the two men.

Damien relaxed the next moment and nodded to Jesse. "Nice to meet you, Coulton."

Jesse stood up and extended his hand. "Same goes, Kane." He shook Abby's hand, too. "Beautiful baby you have there, ma'am."

Abby melted in another smile, and for a few moments they talked about Sarah. But when Abby and Damien moved away to a booth on the other side of the restaurant, Shea saw Jesse's eyes follow them for a moment.

"Do you know the Kanes?" she asked casually.

His startled gaze flew to her face. "Of course not. Why would you think so?"

"You looked surprised to see them. Almost as if you knew them."

"I've never seen them before in my life." He shrugged. "Kane reminded me of someone I knew once, but I was mistaken."

An uneasy, unsettled feeling swirled in Shea's stomach. "He's an FBI agent."

His gaze flickered toward the Kanes again. "What's the FBI doing in Cameron?"

She wondered if he realized how he'd tensed when he glanced at Damien and Abby. "Damien has a house here. He met Abby when he was protecting her and her nieces on a case. They fell in love and got married afterward."

He glanced over his shoulder again at the other couple. Shea saw how rigid his muscles were, and confusion swirled inside her.

"That sounds like a good story." Jesse's voice was without inflection.

"It is. I'll tell you about it sometime."

Their food arrived then, and neither of them said anything while they ate. Jesse didn't turn to look at Damien and Abby again, but Shea could feel the tightness in the air between them. The intimate, private bubble that had surrounded them earlier had shattered, and now she wanted nothing more than to return to the ranch. At the ranch, at least, nothing from the outside world could affect what she and Jesse had together.

As soon as he'd finished eating, she said brightly, "Ready to go?"

Jesse leaned back in the booth. "You sound like you're in a big hurry. I thought the whole idea was to get away from the ranch for a while."

"We've gotten away, and now I'm ready to go back."

Mandy had left the check on the table, and Jesse pulled out his wallet and placed some money on top of it. "Why don't we take a walk around Cameron before we head back? You can show me the sights."

"All right." Anything would be better that sitting here in Heaven on Seventh, feeling the tension swirling in the air around her and wondering why. "Believe me, it won't take long."

As they walked out of the restaurant, Shea watched to see what Jesse would do. But he didn't look behind him, didn't give Damien Kane another look. It was as if the other man didn't exist.

Once they were on the sidewalk in front of the restaurant, she felt the tightness in his muscles ease. The atmosphere lightened, and Jesse moved closer to her as they headed toward Main Street. But she noticed that his attention wasn't focused completely on her. He was alert, looking around at the buildings and cars they passed. It was almost as if he was cataloging everything he saw.

"I like Cameron," he finally said as they turned a corner and started down Main Street. "I can see why you're so attached to it."

"It looks like you're memorizing everything about the town," she said lightly.

He shot her a startled look. "What's that supposed to mean?"

"I've never seen anyone look a place over so carefully. I'll bet you could tell me every car and building we've walked past."

He shrugged. "It's like the bird-watching, I guess. I like to know as much about my surroundings as I can. I want to know where I am."

She felt him relaxing, and as they moved down the street, he edged closer to her until their arms were almost brushing. His heat chased away the chill from the air, and she pushed her concerns out of her head. Maybe Jesse had had a run-in with the law when he was younger. Maybe that's why he was nervous around Damien. It didn't matter, she told herself fiercely. She knew what kind of person he was.

But a kernel of doubt nibbled at her peace of mind, leaving her confidence slightly shaky.

Jesse slowed down and touched her arm. "Is the newspaper office still open?"

She glanced across the street and saw the lights on. "It looks like it is. With Carly away, their hours aren't always regular, but if the lights are on, someone must be there."

"I'd like to get a copy of the town paper," he said. "Do you mind?"

"Of course not."

Just as they started across the street, the door to the sheriff's office opened and Ben appeared in the door. "Hey, Shea. I was going to give you a call later. Do you have a minute?"

She looked at Jesse. "Why don't you meet me back here?"

He nodded. "Fine."

Shea turned and walked into the office with Ben. "What's up?" she asked.

Ben led her to her brother's office in the back of the building, then shut the door. "I have some information you might be interested in."

Her heart began to pound, but she said lightly, "Must be top secret."

He smiled, but there was no humor in his eyes. "I just didn't want anything to get around Cameron. You know how the walls have ears in this town."

It had to be about Jesse. A fist-sized lump of fear swelled in her throat. "What's going on, Ben?"

"I wanted you to know that I ran a police check on your new employee."

She wanted desperately to ask him what he'd found, but instead she glared at him. "I told you that wasn't necessary."

Ben was unmoved. "I think it was. And if your brother was here, he'd do the same thing."

She scowled, trying to hide her fear. "All right. Since you went ahead and treated Jesse like a criminal, you might as well tell me what you found."

"Absolutely nothing," Ben said slowly.

For a moment Shea didn't understand. Then a wave of relief crashed over her. She gave Ben a cocky grin and said, "You mean he's not a serial killer who's going to murder all of us in our beds?"

"This isn't a joke, Shea," Ben said sharply. "You're isolated out there on the ranch with him, and there's no one to protect you. What if he did have a criminal record? What if he wasn't as innocent as his references make him appear?"

"I've always thought of myself as a pretty good judge of character," she said lightly. "Now you'll have to believe me."

Ben looked down at the papers on his desk, and his mouth thinned into a narrow line. "I'll save this for Devlin. He'll want to see it when he gets back in town."

"Thanks, Ben. I do appreciate the trouble you went to." She smiled at him again, generous in her relief. The meeting with Damien Kane had disturbed her, but now she could brush her fears away. "You're a good friend."

Ben watched her with dark, somber eyes. "I hope you know what you're doing, Shea."

She opened the door to her brother's office, then turned to look at him. "Don't worry, Ben. I know exactly what I'm doing."

"That's what I'm afraid of," he muttered.

She laughed and headed for the door of the office. Before she could open it, Jesse walked in, a folded-up newspaper under his arm.

"I see you found a paper," she said, moving toward him.

"Yeah. Are you finished here?"

"All set." She moved past him onto the sidewalk, then said, "Are you ready to head home?"

"I'm ready." His eyes gleamed down at her, sending her an unmistakable message. "Let's go."

She moved closer to him as they hurried back to the truck her earlier fears erased. "You won't believe what Ben wanted."

"What was that?" he asked. He stayed as close as he could without actually touching her. Shea felt her skin heat and her blood begin to pound.

"He wanted to tell me that he'd run a police check on you."

"Good for him. I'd do the same thing if I was in his shoes."

Surprised, she swiveled around to face him. "Aren't you angry that he invaded your privacy?"

"Hell, no. I told you before, you're a woman living essentially alone. You can't be too careful. I'm grateful someone is thinking."

She tucked her hand into the crook of his arm. "I told Ben that I'm a good judge of character, and this proves it. He told me your record was spotless, by the way."

Jesse felt her hand slide against his skin, curling into his arm, and tried to fight the rush of need that swept through him. He had to keep his head, at least until they were out of Cameron.

"What would you have done if it hadn't been spotless?"

Her hand tightened on his arm for a moment, then she relaxed. He could feel her smile next to him. "I know who you are today, Jesse, and that's all that matters."

She was too damn trusting for her own good. A shame he'd never felt before swept over him as he thought of how he was deceiving her. "You scare me sometimes, Shea."

Her low laugh rippled over him, making his heart flutter in his chest, turning the semidarkness of dusk into a screen of privacy. He wanted to wrap his arms around her and dive into her goodness, her trust. He wanted to forget why he was at her ranch, forget about his job and the way he was betraying her, forget about everything but Shea.

But he couldn't. So he gently detached her hand from his arm and put a step between them.

"Now you're scaring me," she said. "What's wrong?"

"I don't want you to be the subject of the town gossip," he said. "That's what's wrong."

"I don't care if everyone knows how I feel about you," she said, and her voice was fierce.

He wanted to shake her. He was doing his best to protect her from the talk that would erupt after he left, when the people of Cameron found out who he was, but she wouldn't cooperate. Finally he sighed and took her hand. "You're going to age me at least ten years," he said.

She was going to do more than that. If he wasn't very careful, he was going to leave a piece of himself behind when he left Cameron, Utah. But he couldn't step back from Shea now. It was already too late. All he could do was hope that she wasn't doing anything illegal, hope that he could get out of town before he stole her heart as well as her trust.

As they drove home down the dark road, the silence in the truck hummed with tension. Shea had reached across the seat to take his hand, and their fingers clung together on the rough upholstery. He felt her need in her trembling touch, and he was certain she could feel his.

He didn't know how much longer they had together. Seeing Damien Kane in Cameron had shaken him. He'd been afraid that Shea would spot his discomfort. She was too sharp not to notice the signs. But she hadn't said anything, so gradually he'd relaxed. And he sure as hell wouldn't go back to Cameron until Kane was gone. He'd never worked with the other FBI agent, but he'd met him a couple of times. He didn't want to take any chances with Shea's intuition if they ran into the Kanes again. And he intended to savor every minute he had with Shea. Because he never knew which moment would be the last.

Neither of them spoke on the drive home. Their joined hands said everything that needed to be said. When he parked his truck, he turned to her in the darkness. "What do we do now? Do I kiss you good-night at the door?"

"If that's what you want."

Even in the dim light he saw the uncertainty in her face, and cursed himself. He wanted her so badly, and she responded to him so fiercely, that he'd forgotten Shea's essential inexperience. And since she never played games, it was a good bet she didn't know how the sexual ones were played.

He reached over and pulled her close. "You know that's not what I want. What I want is to spend the night with you, in your bed, and sleep is the last thing on my mind. I was trying to be a gentleman and give you a choice."

Her face relaxed and she curled her arms around his neck. "Then I guess I must not be much of a lady. I would have followed you to your cabin if I had to."

His arms tightened around her for a moment, and as they clung together in the cab of the truck, he knew he needed to leave. He'd lost all his objectivity about this case and about Shea McAllister, and he should take himself off the case.

But he couldn't do it. Tomorrow, he promised himself. Tomorrow he'd start looking for more evidence. And if he couldn't find any, he'd tell his boss that there was no case. But tonight was his and Shea's.

He kissed her gently, trying to control the fire that raged through him. Her mouth was eager on his, open and trusting, and a spasm of tenderness moved through his heart. He didn't deserve anything from Shea, but he wanted her desperately.

"Why don't we go into the house? This truck isn't what I had in mind as a final destination for the night," he whispered.

She drew back to look at him, her mouth curving into a smile. "What exactly did you have in mind?"

"I thought you had figured that out already," he said, his hands pulling her close again. "But it looks like I'm going to have to explain it to you."

He nuzzled her ear, telling her exactly what he wanted to do to her. He felt heat flooding her face, but she didn't move away. Instead, she turned and fused her mouth to his.

When he pulled away he was shaking. Taking her hand, he slid across the seat and opened the door on her side of the truck. "I won't be responsible for my actions if we stay in this truck a minute longer." His voice was thick in his throat, and desire was a fire raging uncontrollably through his blood. "Let's go."

She slid out of the truck before him, still holding his hand. Her face was stark in the moonlight, and he saw the need in her eyes. What kind of miracle was Shea? For some reason, she wanted him as much as he wanted her.

The ranch was dark and quiet as he hurried her into the house. There was a light on in Joe, Dusty and Levi's cabin, but only the porch light and a light in the hall burned in the house. Not even Buster greeted them when they slipped through the door.

He led the way up the stairs to her room. When he stepped through the door, he felt like he'd come home. A part of him whispered that he belonged here, belonged with Shea, but he refused to listen. He couldn't let himself be seduced by his own needs. When she found out who he was and what he wanted from her, she would be the first to tell him to go.

So he'd take tonight, and as many other nights as they had together. And he'd show her how special she was, how beautiful. His mind veered away from the other things he wanted to tell her.

Their clothes slipped away noiselessly, falling into a heap on the moonlight-dappled floor. He was already hard and aching for her, but when she turned to him in the moonlight, her skin gleaming like satin, her face eager for him, he almost lost control.

"Do you have any idea what you're doing to me?" he muttered, reaching out to skim his hand down her cheek.

"I hope it's the same thing you're doing to me." She covered her hand with his, then turned her head and kissed his palm.

He couldn't wait any longer. Covering the distance between them, he pulled her close and fused his mouth with hers. He felt her skin heat, her heart pound next to his, and her arms came around him and held him with a fierce possessiveness.

She wasn't going to make it easy for him to go slow tonight. And suddenly he didn't want to go slow. He wanted to take her in a rush of heat and passion, to make her his, and only his. He wanted her to remember him, and remember this, for the rest of her life.

Sweeping her up into his arms, he dragged the quilt off the bed, then laid her down. Her breasts brushed against his chest, making him tighten with a need that was almost painful. Ignoring the rhythm that pounded in his blood, that demanded release, he bent to kiss her. When he took one nipple in his mouth, she strained up to meet him, tangling her legs with his. And when he touched her other nipple, she moaned his name, tightening her hands on his back until her nails dug into him.

Desire was a beast with sharp talons that clawed at him, filling his mind with one driving need. But he clamped down on it, forcing it back into hiding. Tonight was for Shea, and he was determined to give her as much pleasure as possible. Trailing kisses down her stomach, he gloried in the way her muscles jumped under his mouth. And when he slid between her legs and swirled his tongue over her, he listened to her moan his name with fierce satisfaction.

"Jesse! What are you doing?" She tangled her hands in his hair as she drew her breath in sharply.

"I'm loving you." He suckled her gently, then watched as she peaked and came apart in his arms.

He couldn't wait any longer. Twining his fingers with hers, he slid inside her, then started to move. He felt her body clench tightly around him, felt the shudders of another climax as he finally loosened his hold on his own control. And as his body convulsed in a mind-emptying release, he felt the spasms sweep over her again.

When the haze of numb satisfaction began clearing from his mind, he realized he was still lying on top of her, crushing her down into the bed. Shea's arms were wrapped tightly around him, as if she were afraid he was going to sneak away from her. Even when he rolled over, she didn't let go. She sprawled on top of him, her wavy hair almost white in the moonlight, and he never wanted to let her go.

But he would, because he had to. Brushing the hair out of her eyes, he murmured, "That wouldn't have been nearly as much fun in the cab of my truck."

"Mmm," she said. "I'm not sure I'm able to speak yet."

"That must be a first."

Her sleepy chuckle wormed its way right into his heart. The intimacy, the closeness should have scared him, but instead he found himself storing it up in his memory. This is how it would be if there was no deception between them. This is how it would be if they had an endless number of nights in front of them, nights to spend loving each other, then falling asleep together. Nights knowing that they could do the same thing all over again tomorrow.

But since they didn't, he'd make do with what they did have. Tightening his arms around her, he said, "You're not falling asleep, are you?"

"I think so."

He turned his head and kissed her thoroughly, and he felt desire stir to life in her again. "I have plans for you, and they don't include sleep."

He found no evidence of smuggling the next day, or the day after that. He even managed to get to the cabin near the lake again, and found it just as deserted as it had been the previous time he'd been there.

He spent the week watching her during the day and holding her at night, but was no closer to resolving his questions. He was ready to call his supervisor, tell him that there was no evidence of any wrongdoing on the Red Rock Ranch, when he came back to the house unexpectedly one day at the end of the week.

When he walked in the front door, he heard the murmur of voices from the back of the house. They were hushed and hummed with urgency, and his stomach clenched into a knot.

Making his footsteps as quiet as possible, he crept toward

the kitchen. The door between the kitchen and the dining room stood open, and he stopped in the doorway. Shea and Maria were huddled together at the far counter, looking at a list.

He didn't say a thing, but Shea must have heard something. She whirled around. When she saw him standing in front of her, a look of shock filled her eyes. Followed by guilt.

Chapter 12

"Jesse!" Surprised shock swept over Shea, and she grabbed onto the edge of the counter to steady herself. "I didn't expect you back at the house this morning."

His eyes were impossible to read as he studied her, then Maria. Finally he said, "I finished moving those pregnant cows more quickly than I'd expected. I was looking for a cup of coffee."

"Help yourself." She tried to slip the list she'd been working on underneath another sheet of paper, but her hands fumbled and the list floated to the floor. She bent to pick it up, damning her shaking hands. "There's still some in the pot in the dining room, I think."

But instead of turning around and going back into the dining room, he walked over to the counter where she stood with Maria. "What are you working on?"

Her hand tightened on the paper she still held. "A shopping list," she said, trying to sound casual. "Maria and I were just trying to figure out what we need for the next week."

This time the expression in his eyes was impossible to

miss. It was suspicion. "I didn't know you had to do that, too. I thought Maria did all the shopping for the ranch."

"I have to go into Cameron later today," she improvised. "I thought I'd save Maria a trip."

He studied her for what seemed like a long time. "You're a real hands-on manager, aren't you?" he finally said.

"I do what needs to be done." She watched him, uneasy about the expression in his eyes. "What's wrong, Jesse? Did you need my help with something this afternoon?"

Slowly he shook his head. "I'm fine for the afternoon. In fact, why don't I come into Cameron with you and give you a hand? What else did you need, anyway?"

She scrambled frantically in her mind to find some chore in town. "I was going to talk to Becca about Demon," she finally said. That was vague enough. "I want to make sure we're doing everything we can for his foot." She tried to smile brightly. "Thanks for the offer, but I don't need help to talk to Becca."

"Isn't she due out here soon, anyway?"

"I'm trying to save her a trip." Shea swallowed past a swelling lump of fear in her throat. "Her baby is due in a few months, and it's getting harder for her to get around."

He smiled, but it didn't reach his eyes. They were filled with a hard edge of suspicion. "Then I guess I'll see you later this afternoon. I know Levi has all sorts of things to keep me busy here on the ranch."

Shea watched him turn and walk into the dining room, listened as he poured himself a cup of coffee. She didn't say a word to Maria until she'd heard the front door shut behind Jesse.

"He knows," she whispered.

Maria took her hand. "He knows only that you acted strange. There is no way he could know anything about the children in the cabin. The last group was gone before he'd been here a week. And how could he know of the children that just arrived last night?"

Shea shook her head, her instincts telling her that Jesse was a threat to her children. "I don't know. But he looked suspicious. He looked like he knew I was trying to hide something.''

"Why would he think that?'' Maria's voice was patient.

Shea knew Maria was trying to be logical, but she shook her head. "I don't know. But I know Jesse well enough to realize when something is wrong.''

"I thought you were going to tell him about the children, anyway.''

Shea ran her hand through her hair. "I was, but I wanted to pick the time. I wasn't expecting another group so soon.''

"Miguel said there are some in this group who were in danger in San Rafael. That's why he moved so quickly.''

"I know." Shea pushed aside her fears. "That's why I'm going to try and get them all settled as soon as possible. Those children need to be in a place where they don't have to be afraid.'' She smoothed the list she still held onto the counter. It was names and phone numbers of the children's relatives in this country. "I'll start calling these people today.''

"Are you still going into Cameron?'' Maria asked.

"I have to, now. If I don't go, Jesse will be even more suspicious.''

"Well, you can stop at the grocery, like you told him you would. I don't have enough groceries to feed the children.''

Shea forced herself to smile. "That's good. When he sees me pulling up with a truck full of groceries, he'll realize I was telling him the truth.''

Maria's eyes were cautious. "He is going to find out, you know.''

"I'll be careful. After this group is gone, I'll tell him what I'm doing. That way, he'll have time to get used to the idea before the next group comes.''

"Is there going to be a next group? Your brother will be home soon.''

"I know." Shea felt the stress and worry expand in her chest. "I'm not sure what I'm going to do, Maria. But now that I know I'm needed, I can't just abandon children in danger down in San Rafael. I couldn't live with myself if I did.''

Maria looked somber. ''Then I pray your brother sees it the same way you do, cara.''

''He will.'' But she was far from certain. As she slipped into her office to start calling the relatives of the children waiting up at the cabin, she prayed she could get all these children settled before she had to face Devlin with what she was doing. And Jesse.

Jesse was leaning against the fence when she drove back into the yard late that afternoon, almost as if he was waiting for her. As she slowed the truck, he strolled over to her.

''What did Becca have to say about Demon's foot?'' he asked as she swung out of the truck.

She'd had plenty of time to think about what she would say to Jesse. And since she didn't want to tell him about the children yet, she'd already formulated an answer. ''She gave me something else to use to soak his foot, and she's going to check on him again later in the week.''

''Too bad you had to go all the way into town to find that out,'' he said, his voice light. But the hardness in his eyes bored into her chest.

She gestured to the back of the truck. ''Besides the new medicine, I got some things for Maria, too. So it wasn't a wasted trip.''

Jesse walked around and opened the door of the truck cap. ''Maria needed a lot of food.'' His voice was flat.

''We go through a lot of food.'' She pulled out two bags and nestled them in her arms. ''We've been working hard.''

''Hmm.'' Jesse's answer was noncommittal, and neither of them said anything else as they carried the groceries into the house. After their final trip, Shea walked back outside, then turned to Jesse. She'd never believed in hiding from a problem.

''I could take a knife and cut the tension in the air into several pieces. What's wrong?''

Instead of backing down, of telling her that nothing was

wrong, Jesse fixed his gaze on her. "You tell me, Shea. You've been acting odd all day. You're evasive and nervous. In all the time I've been here on the ranch, you've never been nervous about anything."

He was right. And she'd better have a darned good answer for him. Lifting her chin, she said, "I'm sorry, Jesse. I've been a little nervous about my brother." That was the truth, she thought grimly. She just wouldn't tell Jesse exactly why she was worried about Devlin.

"Your brother?" She saw the disbelief in Jesse's eyes. "What does he have to do with anything?"

"For starters, he owns half this ranch," she said, and she heard the grimness in her voice. Trying to lighten it, she added, "When he gets back to Cameron, he's going to need an accounting of what I've done while he's been gone."

"And you're worried about that?" The honest amazement in his voice warmed her temporarily, took away some of the fear that had lodged beneath her breastbone.

"Of course I'm worried about that. I make most of the decisions for the Red Rock, but Dev's always been here to talk them over with me. He's been gone, off and on, for most of the winter, and I've been on my own. Now he's going to come home soon, and I'm a little nervous."

That was the truth, although it wasn't her management of the Red Rock that made her nervous. Jesse studied her for a moment, and she wasn't sure if he believed her or not. Finally he shook his head.

"I never thought I'd see the day." Some of the coldness in his eyes thawed. "Shea McAllister unsure about something. Mark this one down in the history books."

"Everyone's allowed one weakness," she said lightly.

He gave her a sharp look, then his face softened in a smile. It was a controlled smile, but she pushed her misgivings away. Draping one arm over her shoulders, Jesse said, "I didn't think that applied to you. And I never would have guessed that I'd discover your weakness so soon."

"That's not my only weakness," she murmured, stepping closer to him.

She felt him tense, felt the heat from his body rising. "Is that so?"

They moved toward the barn together, and she slanted a look in his direction. "Do you want me to tell you about my other weakness?"

They walked into the cool dimness of the barn, and he turned and backed her into the wall. "I'd rather you show me your other weakness."

Twining her arms around his neck, she fitted herself against him, feeling the now-familiar tide of desire sweep over her. Jesse was the only one who could make her forget her responsibilities, who could make her throw caution to the wind. When she was with him, she didn't care about anything but Jesse. And although she knew that was dangerous, she reached up and kissed him, anyway.

His response was instantaneous. She felt the need that surged through him, matching her own. His hands shifted on her, holding her more tightly, pressing her closer with what felt like desperation. But she also felt a reserve, a watchfulness, that she'd never felt before.

Slowly she opened her eyes and looked up at him. His eyes were dark with passion, but something else lingered in their depths. Something she didn't want to examine too closely. "Is something wrong?"

He bent and kissed her again, then set her away from him. "Only the timing. Joe is just around the corner."

"Are you still worried that Joe, Dusty and Levi are going to find out about us?"

"I suspect they already know," he said, and his voice was dry. "They all have eyes in their heads. But I don't particularly care to provide a sideshow for them. And we both have work to do."

She grinned at him, forgetting the earlier wariness in his eyes, forgetting that she had a secret she wanted to hide from him, forgetting everything but Jesse. "You're right. This isn't the time or the place. But hold that thought for," she glanced at her watch, "about six more hours."

His eyes heated, and she felt his gaze on her back as she

headed into the tack room to grab the medication for Demon's foot. Everything would work out, she told herself.
These children had arrived before she'd had a chance to pre-
pare Jesse for her secret. Now she had to concentrate on the
children, but after they were all placed in their new homes,
she'd tell Jesse what she was doing.

He'd help her, she told herself. He'd believe she was right,
he'd see the need for it. And then she wouldn't have to see
that hard edge of suspicion in his eyes again.

She was good, Jesse conceded as he watched her stroll
into the tack room. So good that he was almost willing to
believe her. Almost, but not quite. Because he'd seen the fear
in her eyes in the kitchen, when he'd walked in on her. And
he'd seen the defensiveness there when she'd arrived back
home from Cameron. Shea had a secret, and he was afraid
he knew what that secret was.

He'd have to get back to the cabin sometime in the next
day to see if it was occupied. But his money said that it
would be. He watched Shea grimly as she filled a bucket
with water and poured in the "new" medication from Becca
Farrell. His money also said that her trip into Cameron today
was a sham, connected in some way with the criminals she
was smuggling into the country.

What a fool he'd been. Disgust at his willing embrace of
Shea's deception filled his mouth with a bitter taste. He'd
allowed a pretty face and an alluring body to make him forget
why he was at the Red Rock Ranch. Dreams he should never
have been dreaming in the first place had derailed his investigation. But not anymore.

A part of him protested, telling him that Shea was much
more than a pretty face and a nicely packaged body. But he
ignored that traitorous voice. Shea was cunning, clever and
charismatic. All the qualities that a good criminal needed.
The fact that she'd managed to deceive him, as well as a lot
of other people, only illustrated her strength.

He wouldn't underestimate her again.

"When I'm finished here, I'm going to check on the herd

we put in that back pasture yesterday,'' she called from Demon's stall. "I could use a hand.''

"No problem. Should I get the horses saddled?'' he answered.

"That would be great. I'll take Bluebell.''

As he gathered the tack they would need and began to
saddle the first horse, he heard her humming in Demon's
stall. She could afford to be cheery, he thought savagely. The
pasture she wanted to check was the farthest point on the
ranch from the cabin by the lake. She figured she could control him, keep him away from the cabin again, but this time
she was mistaken.

This time he'd find a way to get there, and he'd see what
was going on for himself. This time, he'd catch her in the
act. And he would expose her for the criminal she was.

His heart contracted in his chest at the thought, but he
pushed away the pain. It was no more than he deserved, after
allowing her to outfox him. The pain would be a reminder
of what happened if he allowed his hormones to rule his
mind.

Because that was all it was, hormones. How could he ever
care about someone who didn't believe in law and justice?
What kind of life could he make with a woman who didn't
have any honor?

None at all.

When Shea swung into Bluebell's saddle and trotted out
of the barn, he followed her, his chest aching and his heart
heavy. But he welcomed the pain. It would teach him never
to make this kind of mistake again.

She had blinded him with her smile, charmed him into
forgetting why he was at the Red Rock. His own need for
her had made it easy to ignore the telltale signs. He'd been
ready to call his supervisor and tell him there was no evidence of illegal activity here.

Not anymore.

Determination burned inside him like a cauterizing acid,
eating away at all he'd felt for her. She'd played him for a

fool, and she had almost won.

He was going to win the next round.

Shea was at her laughing, teasing best at dinner, and Joe, Dusty and Levi all responded to her. If Jesse hadn't seen it himself, he wouldn't have believed the fear that had filled her eyes earlier, or the deception. But it had been there. Just as there were secrets that now stood between him and Shea, as solid and impenetrable as the steel door of a vault.

"What do you say, Jesse? You up for a round of poker after dinner?" Joe asked.

He'd known the men played cards after dinner, but it was the first time they'd asked him to join them. Forcing himself to smile, he said, "I'd love to." He was pretty sure they knew what Shea was doing. Maybe one of them would let something slip during the course of the poker game.

He glanced over at Shea and saw a shadow of disappointment in her eyes. And in spite of his earlier vows, his body responded, remembering how she felt and how she tasted. Then she glanced at him and smiled.

"You should be honored," she said, and her voice was light. "The poker game is sacred. Very few get asked to join."

"I am honored," he answered, equally lightly. "But that doesn't mean I won't take every penny they have."

The three cowboys erupted in talk at his words, promising with delight that they'd separate him from everything he owned, including his skivvies. Jesse's heart felt like a lump of lead in his chest. Clearly, Joe, Dusty and Levi had accepted him and now considered him one of them. He was deceiving them, too. They wouldn't have asked him to play poker if they knew who he really was. And why he was on the Red Rock Ranch.

"Am I going to need to drive into Cameron and make a withdrawal from my bank account?" he asked, leaning his chair back.

Levi studied him for a moment, then a grin split his face. "Nah," he cackled. "We trust you. Your credit is good with us."

Jesse let the chair crash down to the floor. "Then let the games begin," he said, glancing over at Shea.

She gave him a half smile. "Have a good time. And don't let these three con you."

"I can handle myself," he said.

Her gaze lingered on him for a moment. "I'll see you in the morning, Jesse."

He saw regret and frustration in the blue depths of her eyes, and for a moment felt an answering surge of desire. He still wanted her, damn it. Even though he knew he shouldn't, his body still hadn't gotten the message.

Thank goodness for the poker invitation. It was the easy way out of an awkward situation, a situation he didn't even want to think about. "Bright and early," he answered easily.

By this time tomorrow, he doubted he'd have to worry about invitations to Shea's bed. By this time tomorrow, Shea might well be sitting in a jail cell.

He crushed the protests of his heart without a second thought. This was his job. It was why he'd come to the Red Rock Ranch in the first place. He should be happy, he told himself. He'd always believed that justice was more important than anything. Now he had a chance to prove it.

Shea watched Jesse leave with Joe, Dusty and Levi. As soon as the door banged shut behind them, she missed him. She wanted him close to her. And she wasn't going to enjoy sleeping alone tonight, either. She'd gotten used to Jesse sleeping beside her, holding her through the night, waking her with a kiss in the morning.

But it was good that the men had asked him to play poker with them, she told herself. It meant that they had accepted Jesse, that they thought of him as one of them. It was one more thin strand in a web that she hoped would bind Jesse to the Red Rock.

Maria appeared out of the kitchen. "Have you contacted any of the families yet?"

"I've gotten hold of three of them, and we've made arrangements already. I'm going to call the other three now.

With any luck, all these children should be in their new homes in a couple of days.''

Maria's face relaxed. ''That is good. I have a bad feeling about this group, cara. Something is going to go wrong.''

Shea tried to ignore the frisson of fear that skittered down her spine at Maria's words. There were far too many things that could go wrong. ''Don't be silly, Maria. What could go wrong? We've done this enough times that by now it's routine.''

''You've never done it with a stranger on the ranch,'' Maria said grimly.

''Don't worry about Jesse. Even the men have accepted him.''

Maria's mouth thinned. ''Never underestimate people, cara. That's when you have problems.''

''I'm not underestimating Jesse,'' Shea protested.

Maria's eyes bored into hers. ''And don't think that because he shares your bed, you can lead him around by the nose. That one doesn't allow anyone to lead him.''

Shea felt her face heating. ''What are you talking about?''

The housekeeper sniffed and turned back to the kitchen. ''You think I don't know everything that goes on in my house? I thought you were smarter than that, missy.''

Shea watched Maria leave, a reluctant smile on her lips. She should have known better than to think she was fooling the housekeeper. Maria didn't miss much. And it didn't take a rocket scientist to figure out that she was crazy about Jesse, she admitted.

She had to forget about Jesse, she told herself firmly. At least for tonight. She had work to do, and Jesse was busy playing cards with the men. Trying to put him out of her mind, she headed into her office to make more phone calls.

Shea was already at the dining room table, sipping on a cup of coffee, when Jesse walked into the house the next morning. Her heart leapt when she saw him, and she was certain there was an answering flare of heat in his eyes. Then he shuttered his face.

"Good morning," she murmured.

He grunted in return, and she raised her eyebrows.

"Late night?"

Finally, reluctantly, he smiled. "Why didn't you tell me those three were cardsharps?"

Shea swallowed the bubble of laughter that wanted to escape. "I couldn't spoil the fun for the boys. And I figured you'd give them a run for their money."

"I sent them running to the bank to deposit their winnings. That's about all the running I made them do."

She studied him, her heart lighter than it had been since the day before. "You didn't let them win, did you?"

"Hell, no!" He looked shocked at the suggestion. "Why would you think that?"

"You've gone out of your way to make them feel good since you've gotten here."

"That's different. This was a card game. This was a matter of honor." He scowled at her. "They won, fair and square."

She couldn't hold the laughter in any longer. "Maybe not exactly fair and square. They've been playing poker every night for years. They're not exactly the innocent old men you thought they were."

He scowled again. "You might have warned me."

She studied him, the smile still on her lips. Her heart turned over in her chest. "I have a feeling you didn't need a warning at all. I have a feeling you knew exactly what you were getting into."

His eyes softened, involuntarily, she thought, and he immediately turned to the buffet that stood against the wall and poured himself a cup of coffee. "You think I would go into a poker game, knowing I was going to lose? What kind of idiot do you think I am?"

"You're not an idiot at all, and I think that's exactly what you did." Her smile deepened, and warmth flowed through her veins. "Thank you, Jesse. Thank you for letting Joe and Dusty and Levi feel good about themselves."

His coffee cup clattered onto the table. "I'm no hero,

Shea.'' His voice was grim. "Don't get all rosy-eyed about me, because you're going to be disappointed.''

"You could never disappoint me,'' she said. "I know what kind of person you are.''

"You don't know squat about me.''

She leaned back in her chair and took another sip of coffee, watching him over the rim of the cup. "I learn more about you every day.''

"What's going to happen when you learn things about me that you'd rather not know?'' He leaned forward to challenge her, the hardness back in his eyes.

"I can't imagine anything about you that I wouldn't want to know.''

He slammed his chair away from the table and went to look out the window. "You're too naive, Shea. You take too much on trust. You need to harden yourself.''

"Are you telling me that I need to harden myself against you?'' Her heart began to pound, but she watched him steadily.

"Yes, damn it! You've been too trusting from the beginning.''

"You've never given me any reason not to trust you.''

He took a deep breath and slowly turned around. "What if I do?''

Panic fluttered inside her, but she pushed it away. "Are you trying to tell me something, Jesse?''

He watched her for a long moment, then he shrugged and shuttered his eyes. She couldn't read his expression. "I just don't want to build up unrealistic expectations.''

Shea stood up. "Maybe we need to talk about those expectations. But this isn't the time. We both have work to do today.'' She hesitated. "Do you want to have that picnic tonight? The one we talked about the evening we went into Cameron?''

"Sure.'' His gaze bored into her with an unsettling intensity. "Where did you want to go?''

"There's a spot on the border of our land and the Hilbert's place that would be great for a picnic.'' She grinned at him.

"And it has the added advantage of letting me spy on the Hilbert ranch and see what our new neighbor has been doing there."

The hard edge was back in his eyes. "That's at the opposite edge of the ranch from that little lake we saw the other day, isn't it?"

"Yes." A trickle of fear chased down her back. "Did you want to go to the lake?"

He held her gaze for a long moment. "What if I said yes?"

"Then we'd go to the lake," she said lightly. *Dear God, don't let him choose the lake.*

Finally he shrugged. "It doesn't matter to me. We'll go wherever you want to go."

"Great." She forced a smile on her face. "I'll see you around lunchtime, then."

Instead of leaving the room, he sat back in the chair. "What are you doing this morning?"

"I have some bookkeeping to take care of. Then I'll see what else needs to be done." She couldn't meet his eyes. Jesse would know she was lying.

"I'll see you later, then." His chair scraped against the floor, and he was gone. She didn't let out her breath until the front door eased shut. Then she closed her eyes and thanked God that he hadn't asked her any more questions.

An hour later she reined in her horse as she approached the cabin. There was no sign of life inside, and she breathed a little easier. Miguel was keeping the children out of sight, just as she'd asked him to.

When he'd appeared at the door of the house yesterday afternoon, handing her the papers with the information about the children's relatives, she'd been surprised to see him so soon. She hadn't expected him back for another couple of weeks. But he'd agreed to keep the children quiet and inside, and her heart clenched when she thought about how easy it would be. She knew from past experience that the children in the cabin would be frightened and quiet, both from the trip and from their experiences in San Rafael. They wouldn't go out of their way to make any disturbances.

Tying Bluebell's reins to a tree, she knocked on the cabin door, then waited for Miguel to answer. She slipped inside to see several children freeze, staring at her.

After talking for a moment to Miguel, she sat down on the floor close to several of the children and began speaking to them in Spanish. It took a while, but slowly all but one of them relaxed and began to smile at her. They didn't speak, but she had learned not to expect them to talk to her, not at first. As long as they responded to her, they would eventually speak to her.

All but one boy. He stood in the distance, watching her carefully, his face devoid of any expression. After a while, she turned to Miguel.

"Who is that?"

The older man shrugged. "He hardly speaks. He wouldn't even give us his name. The other children call him Rafael, because all he would say was he needed to leave San Rafael. So I call him that, too." He shrugged again. "He gave us a paper with a name and phone number on it, and I could see for myself that he was in danger. So he came with us. But more than that, I do not know."

Shea moved closer to the boy Miguel had called Rafael. "We'll find your family, Rafael," she said, her voice low. "We'll make sure you're safe here. You don't have to worry anymore."

The boy didn't answer, but there was a tiny flicker in his eyes. Shea prayed that it was hope. She smiled at him and turned back to Miguel. "I've talked to all the others, but I haven't been able to reach his relatives yet. I'll keep working on it, though. And Maria will bring the rest of the food up later."

"That one, she has a sharp tongue," he grumbled. "But she knows how to cook."

Shea smiled at all the children again, then began speaking to Miguel again, asking about the details of the trip.

Jesse backed away from the window, anger raging through him and a sick feeling gathering in his stomach. He hadn't wanted to believe that she'd do something so wrong, hadn't

Chapter 13

Jesse hurried away from the cabin to the horse he'd left tied to a tree. Anger and pain swirled through him, tangling together and swelling until there was room for nothing else in his mind. Betrayal was a sharp knife, slicing cleanly through him to pierce his soul.

As he distanced himself from the cabin, and Shea, he forced the pain from his heart and tried to remember the exact words he'd heard from the cabin. There was no mistake. He'd heard enough of the details to know that a border crossing had been involved. And it had been illegal.

His heart clenched painfully in his chest as he remembered the sound of Shea's low voice coming through the window. He'd almost begun to believe that he was in love with her. He'd tried to ignore the evidence, tried to give her the benefit of the doubt, but there was no doubt about what he'd just heard. Their informant had been right. Shea was smuggling people into the country from San Rafael, and probably getting paid very well for it.

There would be plenty of people who would pay to get out of the war-torn South American country, he thought grimly. Criminals who had escaped capture in the chaos that was San Rafael, or members of the rebel army who saw that the tide was turning against them, would be especially desperate to get out of the country. Shea would have no trouble finding people willing to pay whatever she asked.

Ignoring the pain in his chest, forcing the image of Shea out of his mind, he planned what he had to do. He couldn't think about Shea now, couldn't think about the woman he'd held in his arms at night. He couldn't think about the magic that had spun its web between them, the magic that had bound them together so tightly.

Because it was all a lie. His heart contracted again as he forced himself to face the brutal truth. Everything he'd believed about Shea was wrong. Her innocence, her sweetness, the goodness that shone out of her eyes like a beacon, was nothing more than a mask she wore.

The woman ought to be on stage, he thought bitterly. Because if she could fool him, she could fool anyone. He'd been played for a sucker before, but never with his willing cooperation. He'd always been able to see through the slickest of facades, the craftiest of scams.

But he hadn't been able to see through Shea McAllister.

He should have called for another agent the minute his hormones had made their presence known, he told himself harshly. There was a reason agents were instructed not to get involved with a suspect. And now he, who had always prided himself on being a professional, had almost gotten caught in the biggest scam of them all.

Almost, but not quite. Ignoring the doubt in his heart, ignoring the pain that wanted to overwhelm him, he tuned out his feelings and focused only on the facts. And when he confronted Shea, he'd condemn her with the facts. He wouldn't allow his aching heart and his wounded pride into the discussion. Because they shouldn't have been there in the first place.

He turned into the barn and unsaddled his horse, working methodically as he rubbed the animal down. Demon nickered softly as he walked past the box stall, and he couldn't bear looking at the large black horse. It reminded him too much of Shea.

Before heading to the house, he detoured to his cabin. Rummaging in the bottom of his duffel bag, he found his shoulder holster and strapped it on. Its familiar weight nestled below his left arm, reminding him that he had a job to do. From now on, Shea wasn't his lover. Shea was the woman he had come here to stop.

But he hesitated before slipping his gun into the holster. He wouldn't need a gun to arrest Shea. She might be a criminal, but she wasn't a violent criminal. He stared at the gun for a long time, unable to imagine pointing it at Shea and pulling the trigger. Finally, he laid it back into the drawer where he'd hidden it. He would need it later, when he arrested the men in the cabin, but he wouldn't need it when he talked to Shea.

He stepped out of his cabin into the sunshine of a warm spring day. No one else was around. The rest of the men were out doing chores, and Shea would still be up at the cabin. The scenery was still magnificent, the air carried the perfume of pine and sage, and the only sounds were the far-off trills of birds and the distant calls of cattle. The Red Rock was still a beautiful, peaceful place.

He was about to shatter that peace forever.

It didn't matter, he told himself as he opened the door to the house. It had been Shea's choice to destroy that peace. It had been her choice to commit a crime. And now she was going to have to pay the price.

He settled himself at the dining room table to wait for her.

Shea walked through the kitchen door half an hour later and smiled at Maria. "How's everything going?"

"You tell me," she answered in a quiet voice.

"We're doing fine. I told Miguel you'd be up later with the groceries."

Maria stared at her, dark eyes somber. "Jesse is in the dining room."

"What's he doing here?" She drew her eyebrows together,

puzzled. "I thought he and the rest of the men would be busy all morning."

"Maybe you should ask him."

"I will."

Pushing through the door into the dining room, she spotted him sitting at the table. "Hey, Jesse. What's going on?"

He looked at her, his face expressionless. "I was just going to ask you the same thing."

A tiny lump of apprehension lodged in her chest. "What do you mean?"

He stared at her for a long time. Finally he said, "Why did you do it, Shea?" The words sounded as if they'd been torn from his throat. "Did you need money that badly? Had something gone wrong, something you didn't want to tell your brother? Is that why you did it?"

"Did what?" she whispered, grabbing the edge of the table to support herself. The anger and distaste in his face made a slippery sickness gather in her stomach. "What are you talking about?"

His face filled with a weary disgust. "The innocent act won't work anymore. I'll admit you do it very well, but it's too late. I know."

"You know what?"

A flash of rage crossed his face. "You want to play the game? All right. I'll play it with you. I was at the cabin this morning. I know all about what you're doing."

She felt the blood drain from her face. "What were you doing up at the cabin?" she whispered. "I thought you and Joe were going into Cameron to pick up parts for the truck."

"I sent Joe into town alone. You've been acting so strange that I wanted to see what you were up to. I followed you to the cabin."

"Why would you do that?" She stared at him, confused. "And why are you so angry? Is it because I didn't tell you about it? I thought you would agree with what I'm doing."

"Agree with you?" An incredulous look crossed his face. "Did you think I needed money so badly?"

"What does money have to do with it?"

He made a sound of disgust and jumped to his feet. "I figure it has everything to do with it. Why else would you have gotten involved?"

Jesse stood before her, but he was a total stranger. His eyes were harder than she'd ever seen them. His mouth was tight with anger and disgust. And strapped to his shoulder was an empty holster.

For the first time, real fear shivered through her. "What's going on? Who are you, Jesse? And why are you wearing a gun holster?"

Instead of answering her, he pulled out his wallet and flipped it open. Inside was a gleaming badge and an identification card. She sank into a chair, her legs suddenly trembling.

"That says FBI," she whispered. "What does that mean?"

"It means I'm an FBI agent." His voice was cold and distant. "I came here because of a tip from an informant that you were smuggling illegal aliens into the country, men who were wanted criminals in their own country. And now I know that it's true."

"Kyle Diggett." She stared at Jesse, wondering where the pain and fear had gone. "That's who your informant was. I should have known he'd try to get even with me."

"I'm not at liberty to reveal that information." His voice sounded stiff.

She didn't understand why she didn't feel anything. Staring at Jesse, at the stranger who stared back at her, she felt nothing but a huge emptiness that seemed to swell and grow inside her. The pain would come, but now there was only numbness.

"Why didn't you just ask me what I was doing?" she finally said, staring at the empty holster.

He laughed, but there was no humor in the sound. "And you would have told me exactly what was going on, right?"

"I was going to tell you." She swallowed, feeling the first shards of pain stabbing into her at the sound of his laugh. "Next week, after this group was gone."

"How convenient." His mouth curled into a sneer. "I can't tell you how many criminals tell me the same thing, after they're caught. 'I was going to tell you. I was going to become an informant.' It's amazing how many people get religion when there's no other alternative."

Only the width of the table stood between them, but it might as well have been an ocean. This wasn't the man she'd given her body to, the man she'd trusted, the man who'd taken her heart. This was a stranger, a cold, unforgiving stranger who mocked her with eyes as hard as granite.

"It's not like that at all."

"That's what everyone says when they get caught."

The contempt in his eyes broke down the last of her defenses. The pain came quickly, overwhelming her. It squeezed her heart and stole her breath, leaving her reeling from the agony. "What happens now?" she managed to ask.

"Everyone in the cabin will be sent back to San Rafael. And you'll be taken into custody." For the first time, a flicker of emotion crossed his face. "If you cooperate with the investigation, I'll try to make sure you get a lighter sentence."

"A lighter sentence?" she whispered. The pain inside her grew and grew, until there was room for nothing else.

"You can make this easier for both of us. I cared about you, Shea," he said, his voice gruff. "And I'd like to think you genuinely cared about me."

His words were like a slap across the face. Then, thankfully, a red mist of anger filled her mind, masking the pain. "What are you saying, Jesse?" She stood up to face him, her fingers gripping the edge of the table. "Are you saying that I came on to you, seduced you, so you would go easy on me when you eventually caught me in the act? Is that what you think this last week was about?"

He had the grace to flush. "That's not what I meant, and you know it. I thought I knew you, Shea. I thought I knew what kind of person you are. And now I find I didn't know anything about you, after all."

"I'm the same, exact person I was yesterday, but you've been deceiving me all along," she cried, feeling her heart crumble into little bits. "You lied from the very beginning. You came to my home and made me think you were someone else, someone I could care about. You betrayed me from the first day you stepped onto the Red Rock."

"I was doing my job," he said, his face hard and closed again.

"Your job. Is seducing your suspects part of your job, too?" she asked, her voice hot and scathing.

"I told you I didn't want to get involved with you."

"And I was supposed to believe you when you were kissing me?" He opened his mouth to answer, and she cut him off with a knifelike motion of her hand. "I'm a big girl, Jesse. I went into our affair with my eyes open. I wasn't expecting hearts and flowers and forever after." But deep down inside, she had been, and her heart shriveled a little more. "But I was expecting the truth from you."

"And I couldn't give it to you. That's part of my job, too. I didn't want to hurt you, Shea. And after I got to know you, I didn't want to believe that you were doing anything wrong. But my job comes first."

"Is your job that important to you? More important than what we had?" she whispered.

She thought she saw a flash of pain across his face for a moment, but then he was cold and impersonal again. "It's all I have."

"Then I feel sorry for you, Jesse." She drew herself up and stared at him, trying to keep her pain out of her eyes. Her heart felt exposed and raw, bleeding from the wound he'd struck. But she wouldn't beg, wouldn't shame herself in front of him. "Or is your name a lie, too?"

His lips tightened. "It's my own name."

"No wonder you acted strange in Cameron the other night when we ran into Damien and Abby. You and Damien are probably old buddies."

"I know Kane slightly. And he knows better than to compromise me or an undercover operation."

"That's all it was for you, wasn't it, Jesse?" she whispered. "An 'undercover operation.' That's all it will ever be.

I thought there was some warmth in you, some feeling. But the only feelings you have are for your job.''

''What's more important than justice?'' he demanded.

''Love and caring. That's more important than justice,'' she answered swiftly.

''Without justice, love doesn't have a chance.''

''Without love, justice is harsh and uncaring. There can't be true justice without love.''

''You can't justify what you've done, Shea. And all the talk in the world won't change a thing. You were wrong, and I'm going to do what needs to be done to make it right.''

He was not sending those children back to San Rafael. She thought of little Rafael, so frightened by what had happened there that he wouldn't even give them his real name. And she thought of the others, their relatives already on the way to pick them up.

''You can do whatever you want to do to me. But I won't let you harm the innocent ones in my care.''

''Who said anything about harming them? I'm going to send them back where they belong.''

''They belong right where they are.''

She spun around from the table and ran into the kitchen, grabbing her car keys from the counter. She heard Jesse behind her, scrambling to catch up, and as she ran out the back door, she saw Maria move into place in front of the door.

Jesse watched Shea's truck disappear into the distance, and called himself every foul name he could think of. He should have realized that she'd do something crazy. He should have realized that Shea would never meekly give in to him.

He should have realized how much he'd hurt her.

It would be a scar on his soul for a long time, but he couldn't think about it now. He had to catch up with Shea before she disappeared with the illegal immigrants she was harboring. Turning, he headed back into the house.

''Maria,'' he called, ''I need the keys for Devlin's truck.'' It was the only vehicle still in the yard, and he knew they kept the keys in the kitchen. Dev's truck didn't get used often enough to leave the keys in the ignition.

The housekeeper stood in the dining room with the keys in her hand. She glared at him out of stone-cold eyes, then dropped the keys down the front of her blouse and into her ample bosom. "If you want them, you're going to have to take them from me, FBI agent."

"Maria, you're not helping Shea." He tried to be patient.

He was afraid that Shea would be gone by the time he reached the cabin, but her truck was still parked next to it. "Thank God," he whispered. If she had managed to get away with the illegals that were in the cabin, he wouldn't have had any bargaining power with his bosses. Now at least he had a chance of making things a little easier for her.

As he edged toward the door, preparing to step inside, he heard Shea speak.

"No!" she said, and he heard the frantic note in her voice. "I won't let you do that. I won't allow it!"

Jesse heard the rumble of a man's voice, but he couldn't hear the words. Then he heard Shea again, her words sharp and tinged with fear.

"I don't care, Miguel. He's staying."

Jesse had heard enough. It sounded as if Shea was in danger, and he wouldn't stand here and build his case at the expense of her safety. Pulling his gun out of the holster, he pushed the door open and stepped into the little cabin.

Shea and an old man turned to face him, and behind the two of them, he saw a group of children, none of them more than eight or nine years old. Fear and terror filled their young faces at the sight of his gun, and they cringed away from him.

Slowly he replaced the gun in his holster. A sick feeling gathered in his stomach as Shea pushed the children behind her. One child, a boy with a pale face and huge, dark eyes, clung to her for a moment before she gently shielded him with her body.

"Are you happy, Jesse?" Shea asked. "Are you proud of

how you've terrorized these children?'' She stared at him, her eyes fierce. ''Do you know what these children have gone through, what they've seen in San Rafael? And now you've just brought it all back to them.''

''Why are there children here? Where are the men you're smuggling?'' he asked, but the sick feeling in his gut only grew as he watched the children behind Shea.

''There are no men,'' she said, her voice full of scorn. ''There's only these children. There's always only been the children.''

''I don't understand.''

Shea turned to the old man and said something in Spanish, then she turned and crouched down to face the children. Gathering them close, she murmured something to them, her Spanish too rapid and too low-pitched for him to understand. Finally, after a while, she stood up and faced him again.

''It would be better if we went outside. The children are frightened of your gun.''

He turned and exited the cabin without another word. Shea led him to a group of trees a few feet away from the door, then stopped.

''If you try to touch one of those children, I'll kill you myself,'' she said, and he didn't doubt her for a moment.

''I'm not going to hurt them. My God, Shea, what kind of man do you think I am?''

''I don't know, Jesse.'' She watched him with somber eyes, and her expression was unreadable. ''I have no idea what kind of man you are.''

''I thought you were hiding men in this cabin.''

''I know what you thought. You took the word of a thief about what I was doing, didn't you?''

''We had no idea he was a thief when he came to us. And he had lots of details. We had to take him seriously.'' He reached out for her, but stopped and let his hand drop to his side when she flinched away from him. ''Why don't you tell me what's going on?''

She stared at him for what seemed like a long time, then she sighed. ''I suppose it doesn't matter if you know the details. We'll have to figure out another method anyway, now.''

''Are you telling me you're not going to stop?'' he asked, incredulous.

She tilted her chin in a familiar gesture that made his heart ache. ''There are children who need homes, and they have relatives in this country who want to provide homes for them. Of course I'm not going to stop.''

''What are you doing, Shea?'' He wanted to reach out for her, but he kept his hands at his sides. She wouldn't welcome any kind of touch from him.

''The children are from San Rafael.'' She lifted her chin in defiance. ''They're all orphans who've lost their families in the fighting. They have relatives in this country who want to provide homes for them, but because of the war in San Rafael, they're having a hard time getting visas into this country.''

''So you bring them into the country illegally, then reunite them with their family members.''

''That's right.''

''How do they get across the border?''

She gave him a smug smile. ''In a car, with Miguel driving them, at night. He has a legitimate visa issued for a family with six children. When he crosses the border, the guard only sees that the visa is for a family of six. He doesn't bother to count the children, or wake them to ask them to verify what's on the visa.''

''Very clever. What happens after they get here?''

''I call their relatives, they come get them, and they live happily ever after.''

''How can they live happily ever after if they're in the country illegally? They need documentation.''

Shea shrugged. ''Most of them have birth certificates. Parents sent a lot of documents out of the country after the war started. Everything else they need, they'll get it after the war in San Rafael is over. Until then, it's hard to get anything out of the country.''

''Why are you doing this, Shea?'' he demanded.

Her face softened, and for a moment she was the Shea he'd known before he shattered her world. "Isn't it obvious? They're children, and they were all alone. They need families, and there were families here that wanted them. It seemed pretty obvious to me."

"How did you get started?"

She slanted him a look. "It started with Maria. She's from San Rafael. I don't think you need to know anything more than that." Her face hardened again. "You haven't given me my Miranda warning. You can't ask me any questions."

"I just have one more for now. I heard you arguing with the old man, and you sounded upset. That's why I came barreling in with my gun drawn. I thought something was wrong."

"There was something wrong." Her face filled with anguish. "One of the boys doesn't have any family in this country. He lied to Miguel to get out of San Rafael. Miguel isn't sure what happened to him, but it had to be awful. The boy wouldn't even tell us his real name. Anyway, Miguel said he has to take the boy back to San Rafael. He's afraid that the child will jeopardize the whole operation if there is no one to take him."

"And you were telling Miguel that you wouldn't stand for it."

"That's right."

"What are you going to do with the boy if he doesn't have any family here?"

She gave him a fierce look. "I'll think of something. But that's another thing I'm not going to tell you."

"I'm not your enemy here, Shea."

"Oh, yes, you are. You want to take those children back to San Rafael."

"That was before I knew they were children."

He saw the hope spring into her eyes. "Does that mean you've changed your mind?"

"That means I have to think about what to do next."

She looked at him, the hope gone. "In that case, you can do your thinking back at the ranch. It's going to take me a

while to make the children comfortable again.'' She turned
to go back into the cabin.

''I'm not going to leave, Shea.''

She rounded on him. ''Yes, you are, Jesse. Haven't you
scared those children enough? What do you think is going to
happen if they see you again?''

''I'll wait out here.''

''They know you're here. How can I make them believe
they're safe if they know the man with the gun is waiting for
them just outside the door? Go back to the ranch, Jesse. I'll
meet you there.''

''Do I have your word on that?''

She watched him steadily. ''You have my word.''

Before he could say anything else, she spun around and
disappeared into the cabin. He waited for a moment, then
turned and walked over to the truck. Shea was right. He
would never forget the look of fear and terror on the little
faces inside that cabin when he'd burst in with his gun drawn.

Sick at heart, he headed back down to the house. Everything had changed. He felt as if his world had been tipped
on its side. He had to regroup and think this out before he
could act. And he didn't want to do anything in front of the
children.

Levi and Maria sat in the dining room, drinking coffee,
when he walked in the door. They stood when they saw him,
accusation in their eyes, and walked into the kitchen without
a word.

He followed them. ''Why didn't you tell me when I chased
after her?'' he asked Maria.

''It wasn't my place to tell you, if Shea didn't want you
to know.'' Her face was hard and her eyes cold.

''You're all keeping her secret for her, aren't you?'' he
asked.

Levi glared at him. ''And why wouldn't we?''

''Maybe because what she's doing is wrong.''

''It may be illegal, but it's not wrong.'' Maria spoke up.
''You saw those children. Can you tell me it is wrong to
rescue them from the hell that San Rafael has become?'' she

demanded. "Since the rebels took over, there has been constant fighting, no food, complete lawlessness. God only knows what atrocities those children have seen. Can you tell me it's wrong to give them a future?"

Jesse looked at the two stony faces staring back at him and felt his heart shrivel a little more. He turned and headed for the front door. "When Shea gets back, I'll be in my cabin."

Chapter 14

It was nearly dark by the time Jesse heard Shea's truck pulling into the yard. Slamming out of his cabin, he met her as she was sliding out of her truck.

"You said you would meet me back here." He tried to control the anger that roiled inside him.

She glanced over at him, then turned away. "Here I am. And there you are. I'd say we met back here."

"You knew I thought you'd be coming right back."

"I knew no such thing." She finally swung around to face him again. "I didn't tell you when I'd meet you back here. I only said I would." For a moment, the fatigue and fear she tried so hard to hide was carved into new lines on her face. Then she closed her eyes, and when she opened them again, there was only scorn. "You're going to have to learn to be more precise. I would have thought they'd teach you that at FBI school."

"What's wrong, Shea?" he said, his anger washed away by the weariness and worry he saw on her face. He reached out to touch her face, but she knocked his hand away.

"You mean besides the fact that you're going to arrest me?"

"Something happened after I left you up there. I can tell. What is it?"

For a moment he was sure she wasn't going to answer him. Then her face crumbled. "It's Rafael, the boy who doesn't have any relatives here. While I was talking to you and then Miguel, he ran away, and we can't find him."

Without thinking, he pulled her into his arms and folded her close. She stiffened against him and tried to push away, but he held on. After a while she collapsed against him. Her shoulders shuddered with her sobs, and her tears soaked into his shirt. Her hands dug into his back as she clung to him.

Overwhelming tenderness swept over him for the complicated woman he held in his arms. How could he have ever thought she'd commit a crime for the sake of money? Everything he'd learned about Shea since he came to the Red Rock contradicted that. But he had been afraid to trust himself, or his judgment. And now Shea was sobbing against his chest and a boy was lost in the mountains.

"We'll find him, Shea," he murmured. "We'll go up and search for him until we find him."

She pushed away from him. "You don't know a thing about our mountains," she said, wiping her face with her sleeve. "How can you imagine that you would be any help at all?"

Her voice was withering, and the sting of her rejection reverberated in his chest. He knew he deserved it. "I'll help you search."

"We don't have time to look for you, too." She turned away from him, and at the same time he heard a truck pulling into the yard. It skidded to a halt, and Ben Jackson, the deputy from Cameron, jumped out of the truck.

"I got your message, Shea," he said, hurrying over to her. "What's wrong?"

"There's a boy lost in the mountains," she said, her voice catching on the words. "We need a tracker to help find him."

"You've got one." He loped around to the back of his

truck and pulled out a backpack. "I keep the things I need with me all the time."

"Can you get started right away?" Shea asked.

Ben frowned. "Of course, but I might not make a lot of progress until the morning. The moon will be almost full tonight, but if it clouds up, I'll have to wait. I don't want to take the chance on missing or destroying any signs."

Jackson looked around the yard, as if looking for answers. "Who is the boy? Someone from one of the ranches?"

Shea hesitated, then the entire story spilled out of her. Jackson watched her as she spoke, but didn't try to interrupt. When she finished, he asked, "Does Dev know about this?"

"No. But he will now." She shot a bitter glance over at Jesse, and Jackson's gaze followed.

"What do you mean?" Jackson had gone very still.

"He's an FBI agent." Jesse heard the loathing in Shea's voice. "He came here specifically to stop me. This was an undercover operation."

Jesse saw the speculation sharpen Jackson's eyes, followed by grim satisfaction. "That would explain it, then."

"Explain what?" Shea asked.

"His references. I knew there was something wrong, but I hadn't been able to get to the bottom of it."

"Those references were perfect," Jesse said.

Jackson looked over at him, and the dislike in his eyes told him exactly whose side the lawman was on. "That was the problem. They were too perfect. You'd never even had a parking ticket, and that made me suspicious. I figured Jesse Coulton wasn't your real name. But I hadn't been able to pin anything down yet."

Jesse knew his smile was without humor. "I'm glad to hear the FBI stayed one step ahead of you."

"I would have figured it out eventually," Jackson said, and there was no inflection in his voice.

Jesse watched as the deputy turned back to Shea, ignoring him, and realized he'd been dismissed. If he was smart, he would have accepted the dismissal. He would have walked back to his cabin and figured out what to do next.

But he hadn't been smart since the first day he'd arrived at the Red Rock Ranch. In spite of the fact that Shea was furious with him, that she had expressed her opinion of him in the most scathing way, he couldn't leave her alone with her fear and her guilt.

She felt it was her fault that Rafael ran away. She felt she hadn't done a good job protecting him, and now he was gone. He couldn't let her bear that burden alone.

He stepped closer to Shea and Jackson in time to hear Ben say, "No, Shea, you can't come with me. You're not a trained tracker, and you'd only get in my way and slow me down."

"I won't just sit here and wait," she said, her voice passionate.

"You and I can search together," Jesse said.

Both of them turned to look at him. Shea narrowed her eyes and said, "I don't want you anywhere near my children."

"What's more important, your pride or the lost boy?" he shot back, then regretted his words when he saw her stricken look.

"Are you a trained tracker?" Jackson stared at him, hard-faced.

"No, I'm not," he admitted. "But I know enough about tracking to be some help. Enough to make sure we don't mess up the signs for you."

"It would be best for everyone to wait here." Jackson's voice was resigned, as if he knew he was destined to lose the battle against Shea.

"I can't wait here, Ben," Shea said. She shot a sidelong look at Jesse. "And he says he knows something about tracking. Surely that's better than nothing."

"All right." Jackson's gaze measured them. "Get a pack together, and a couple of flashlights. I want to leave in ten minutes."

Shea immediately ran toward the house, and Jackson fixed his harsh gaze on Jesse.

"If her brother was here, he'd beat the hell out of you.

ut Dev's gone, and I'm standing in for him.'' His gaze
ouched briefly on the house again. ''I have other things to
vorry about at the moment, but I won't forget about you.''

''I understand.'' And he did. ''And just for the record, I
idn't intend to hurt her.''

''But you did anyway.'' Jackson's dark eyes were unread-
ble. ''Right now we need your help. That boy is more im-
ortant than you. But once we find him, all bets are off.''

Jesse nodded once, shortly. Ben couldn't make him feel
ny worse about what he had done to Shea. ''Tell me what
ou want us to do, and we'll do it.''

After a moment, Ben's face relaxed slightly. ''Once we
et to the cabin and I've looked around, I'll tell you exactly
vhere I want you to go and what I want you to do. I expect
ou to follow my instructions to the letter.'' His gaze traveled
o the house again. ''Can you keep her with you and out of
ny way?''

''Yes. I'll keep her out of your way if I have to handcuff
er to my arm.''

Jackson's closed face became even darker. ''That wasn't
he best choice of words, Coulton.''

''I don't think it'll come to that.''

The look Jackson gave him held a grim promise. ''It better
ot, Coulton.''

Jesse hurried into his cabin and threw a few essentials into
. pack. When he emerged, Shea and Ben were standing by
ackson's truck, talking in a low voice.

''Are we ready to go?'' Jesse asked as he approached
hem.

Jackson nodded. ''The moon won't be up for another half
our or so, but we can leave for the cabin now so we're
eady to begin searching as soon as there's enough light.''

A few minutes later, Jesse sat in the back of Jackson's
3lazer and watched Shea in the front seat as they bumped
p the road toward the cabin. He could have reached out his
and and touched her, but she was miles away from him.
'hat was the way it had to be, he reminded himself. He was

here to do a job, and he couldn't let his feelings for Shea interfere.

Except that now he wasn't sure what his job was supposed to be. Realizing that Shea was smuggling children into the country changed everything. His job was no longer as simple as finding the refugees and arresting both Shea and the criminals she was bringing into the country. But right now he couldn't afford to worry about it. Because now there was a lost child who had to be found.

Jesse leaned forward on his seat. "What's the plan, Jackson?"

Ben spared him a quick look out of the corner of his eye. "We'll figure it out when I get to the PLS and take a look around."

PLS, Jesse knew, was shorthand for point last seen, the place from which the boy had disappeared. "Do we know what kind of shoes he was wearing?" he asked Shea.

"Sandals. I'm pretty sure the sole was made out of an old tire. That's what most of the kids seem to wear."

"That should make it easier to track him," Jesse said.

Jackson made a cautious sound in his throat. "Assuming there's enough light to follow any tracks."

"If we don't see anything tonight, we'll just wait until first light."

"Do you know how scared he must be, out on the mountain by himself?" Shea's voice was so quiet that Jesse wondered if she'd meant to speak out loud.

"We'll find him, Shea." He wanted to reassure her, to make her feel better. But he knew Shea well enough to realize she wasn't going to be reassured until she was reunited with the child.

She didn't turn around to look at him. "With three of us, we should be able to cover a lot of ground."

"You and Coulton have to stay together." The deputy's voice was unwavering. "Too many inexperienced people going in different directions is only going to make it more difficult to find the boy. I agreed to let you come if you took orders from me, and I'm telling you to stay with Coulton."

"I'll do that if it helps to find Rafael more quickly."

Her voice was low-pitched and passionate, reverberating with the fear Jesse knew she was feeling. He ached to reach across the seat, to clasp her hand. But he didn't move. He'd forfeited all his chances to comfort Shea.

After what seemed like hours on the road, they pulled up to the cabin and stopped the truck. Lights streamed out of all the windows, and he imagined the old man and the other children inside, wondering what was happening.

But when they entered the cabin, it was empty. All of the children and the old man were gone. And from the evidence in the cabin, they'd left in a hurry.

"Where are the other kids, Shea?" he asked in a low voice.

She ignored him as she pulled a pitifully small pack from one of the bedrooms. "These are Rafael's belongings," she told the deputy.

He slowly pulled a tattered lace shawl, a silver comb, a chipped white mug and a small square of multi-colored cloth out of the bag. "Is this it?" he asked.

"Apparently so. Miguel said that Rafael always kept this pack close to him, and he never took anything out of it."

"It's not much, is it?" Jackson stared at the objects laid out in front of him.

"My children often come here with nothing," she said softly. "Rafael actually has more than some of them."

My children, Shea had said. Jesse looked at the meager collection of possessions that defined one child's life, and a profound sadness moved through him. He was responsible for destroying what she had built here, destroying the security of the children she so obviously loved. And he was responsible for forcing one of them to flee into the mountains.

"Why don't we get started with the search?" he asked in a harsh voice.

Jackson looked over at him, and a ghost of understanding passed over the deputy's face. "You're right. There's nothing here that will help us understand where he might have gone."

He carefully replaced the boy's belongings into the pack,

then laid it gently on one of the beds. "Let's take a look outside."

The moon had just risen above the edges of the cliffs surrounding the cabin, and a milky white light spilled on the ground. "Both of you stay on the porch," Jackson instructed as he switched on a flashlight. Training it on the ground in front of the cabin, he crouched on the porch stairs as he examined the area.

After what seemed like a long time, he stood up. "All the footprints here stay together. I don't think he came out the front door."

Shea shook her head. "Miguel would have seen him. We think he climbed out one of the windows."

"Stay here," Jackson instructed. "Don't step off that porch until I tell you it's all right."

The deputy disappeared into the darkness, and only the beam of his flashlight was visible, bouncing off the trees next to the cabin. Shea stood rigid on the porch, her arms wrapped around herself, and stared off into the night.

"Are you cold?" Jesse finally asked.

She turned to him as if in a trance. "What?"

"I asked if you were cold."

She shook her head. "I'm fine."

But he saw her shiver, saw the goose bumps on her arms. Shrugging out of the flannel shirt he wore, he draped it over her shoulders.

Immediately she handed it back to him. "I don't want your shirt," she said. He saw her gaze slide over his chest, saw the momentary heat in her eyes, then she looked away.

For a moment he couldn't speak. Desire rushed through him in a wave of need, and he wanted nothing more than to feel Shea wrapped around him one more time. Then he forced himself to look away from her. "Take it," he said, pulling the shirt around her shoulders, being careful not to touch her. "I have another one in my pack."

"I have warmer clothes in my pack, too," she muttered.

"But we can't get to our packs right now," he said patiently. "So take the shirt."

He thought she was going to rip it off and throw it back at him, but finally she slipped her arms into the sleeves and buttoned the shirt. "Thank you," she said, and he knew that she hated taking anything from him. He knew she was only doing it for the sake of the lost boy, and pain twisted inside him again.

Neither of them spoke again until Jackson rejoined them on the porch. "I've found his tracks," he said without preamble. "He went out one of the windows and headed around the lake." He waved in the opposite direction. "You were right about the tire tread on his sandals. So far, the trail is a good one."

Jackson looked at the lake, placid and peaceful in the moonlight. "You know this area much better than I do, Shea. Where would he likely head?"

"There isn't anywhere to go up here." Jesse heard the despair in her voice. "This little valley is surrounded by cliffs. I don't think a boy his size could climb over them."

"You'd be surprised what desperation will allow a person to do. Even a child," Jackson replied, and Jesse wondered sharply what desperation had driven the deputy to do. Because he clearly spoke from experience.

"What are we going to do?" Shea's voice rose, and Jesse realized she was terrified.

He took her upper arms and drew her around to face him. "We'll find him, Shea. Jackson knows what he's doing, and we'll help him. We're three adults, and we can move a lot more quickly than a small child. We'll find him."

She nodded once, jerkily, but he felt the tremors in her muscles that told him of her fear. Jesse looked over to Jackson. "Tell us what to do."

"I'm going to follow his trail. I want you to follow the other side of the lake, and when you get to the other end, head over toward the cliffs." He hesitated. "Keep an eye on the ground, and if you see his footprints, stop and call me." He looked over at Shea. "You have your phone, don't you?"

She nodded. "I always carry it. After I started hiding the

children in the cabin, it seemed like a good idea for everyone on the ranch to be accessible all the time.''

"Why don't you show us the footprints before we leave, so we know exactly what they look like?" Jesse asked.

Jackson glanced over at him with grudging approval. "Good idea."

The footprint looked appallingly small, Jesse thought moments later as he stared down into the red dust. Way too small to belong to a child alone in the wilderness at night.

Guilt stabbed at him again, and he grabbed Shea's hand. "Let's go," he said brusquely.

Shea pulled her hand away from him, but she saw the determination on Jesse's face and noticed the guilt that lingered in his eyes. *Good,* she thought grimly to herself. She was glad he felt responsible for the fact that Rafael had run away.

But her conscience wouldn't get away with blaming Jesse for the loss of Rafael. She knew it was far more likely that he'd run away because he'd heard her and Miguel fighting about whether or not to send him back to San Rafael.

They stopped at the truck to pick up their packs and hadn't yet reached the lake when she said in a low voice, "It's not your fault, you know."

He shot her a startled glance. "What's not my fault?"

"Rafael running away. I can see that you're blaming yourself. Don't."

"It is my fault," he said, and she heard the bitterness in his voice. "You don't have to sugarcoat it for me."

"I don't think it is. I think he ran away because he heard Miguel and I fighting about him. I think he realized that Miguel wanted to take him back and I wanted him to stay, and that's why he ran."

Jesse didn't say anything for a while. Finally he said in an odd voice, "Why are you trying to protect me, Shea? That's the last thing you should want to do."

"I'm not trying to protect you. You have plenty of things to feel guilty about." Her anger flashed again, and she tried to smother it. Anger at Jesse wouldn't help find Rafael any more quickly. "Rafael just isn't one of them."

"We have no idea why the boy ran away," he said quietly. "There's probably plenty of blame to go around. If I promise not to feel guilty, will you do the same?"

"I'm so scared," she whispered. "He's so small, and so alone. And this is not a forgiving place to be lost."

He wrapped his arm around her shoulder, and in spite of the pain in her heart, she couldn't move away from the warmth of his embrace. As they walked along, she told herself that Jesse's touch didn't move her anymore. He was only offering impersonal comfort, and that's all she was accepting.

But her body clearly didn't understand the difference. A wave of heat grew inside her, sweeping over her until she no longer needed his shirt to stay warm. She didn't give it up, though. She burrowed into the soft flannel and luxuriated in the scent of Jesse that surrounded her.

"Do you want to call for him? He might not answer to me," Jesse asked in a low voice, jerking her out of the bubble of sensuality that had surrounded her for a moment.

Shea felt like he'd tossed a bucket of cold water over her. She'd almost forgotten why they were here. And she'd almost forgotten what Jesse had done to her.

Almost, but not quite.

"Let's stop for a moment." She moved away from him, refusing to allow herself to feel bereft without the weight of his arm on her shoulder and the warmth of his body burning into her.

She waited until there was no sound, until even their breathing was muffled. Then she called, "Rafael? If you can hear me, please say so."

Nothing.

The night remained silent. She called again, just to be sure, but there was no answer.

"He's not here," Jesse said quietly.

"No, he's not." A ball of fear grew in her throat again. For a while, she'd forgotten about Rafael, forgotten about everything but her own need. Need for a man who'd betrayed her, she reminded herself harshly.

Moving two steps away from Jesse, she said, "I'm sure he got farther away from the cabin than this. It'll probably be a while until we find him." She tried to make her voice sound positive.

"Probably," Jesse answered, his voice objective. "If he was scared, he'd probably run for a long time. So he's not going to be close to the cabin."

"You're right," she said, grateful for his steadiness.

"I still think you should call for him, though." She could feel Jesse's gaze on her in the darkness. "I don't want to take a chance on passing him up."

So she called Rafael's name every minute or so, but there was no answer. They curled around the lake, reaching the other end, and she looked back at the cabin on the other side. The lights in the windows were beacons, and she desperately hoped they would lead Rafael back to safety.

"He's not here," Jesse said gently, after a minute.

"I know." Furiously she blinked back the tears. "I was just hoping that he sees the lights in the windows of the cabin and is able to get back there."

"I hope so, too," he answered, but from the lack of inflection in his voice, she knew Jesse didn't think he would.

"Jackson wanted us to head over toward the cliffs," he said. "Are there places a kid could hide?"

"There are about a million of them." She scanned the irregular faces of the cliffs, dark and mysterious at night. "The whole area is riddled with caves hidden in the rock. Maybe he's found shelter there."

"Let's take a look, then." She could feel Jesse's gaze on her again. "Do you want me to carry that pack for you?"

"I'm all right." Once again, her voice was too brusque, but she refused to let Jesse see how his consideration affected her. She still cared about him, even after what he'd done to her, and she called herself a fool. But she couldn't stop her heart from yearning for him.

By the time they reached the cliffs, the moon was high in

the sky and they hardly needed the flashlight to study the rocks in front of them. But they stopped regularly so Jesse could turn on the flashlight and study the ground. Each time he shook his head and stood up again.

Finally her curiosity couldn't be contained. Even after telling herself that she didn't want to hear any details of Jesse's real job, she asked, "How much training do you have in tracking?"

"Not much," he answered, still looking at the ground. "Just enough to know to leave it to the experts. But I do know what to look for on the ground. And there are no signs that Rafael has been this way."

"Should we go back toward the other side of the lake?"

"No." His answer was sharp. "That's probably where Jackson will find him. And the last thing he needs is for us to mess up his prints and add more of our own. That'll just make his job ten times harder." He glanced over at Shea, and she could see the wry set to his mouth. "Your buddy sent us over here to keep you out of his way, Shea. He doesn't expect us to find anything. And if we do find any evidence that Rafael came this way, we need to stop and let Jackson know."

"You're both treating me like a child," she said, her voice hot. She welcomed the anger that swept over her. It was far better that the guilt and fear that coiled inside her.

Jesse stopped and turned to face her. He reached out slowly for her, and she told herself to move away. But she didn't. When he pulled her into his arms, she couldn't stop the surge of pleasure that made her heart begin to pound.

"We're not trying to treat you like a child," he said, his voice muffled against her hair. "Jackson knew you had to help, and so did I. But the deputy is the expert. He knows what he's doing, and you and I both would only be in his way. He knew you couldn't just sit and wait, and that's why he suggested we look over here."

"I'm not even sure Rafael would answer me if he heard me," she whispered. It was her deepest fear, the dread that had been growing inside her since they set off from the cabin.

"Of course he would." His answer was instantaneous. "I saw you with him. He trusts you, Shea."

He moved his hand up and down her back, in what she was sure was supposed to be a soothing gesture. Instead of soothing her, his touch made hot sparks of need flare to life inside her.

When she realized she was pressing closer to Jesse she jumped away from him. He stepped back immediately, but she saw his eyes glittering in the moonlight and knew that he was as aroused as she.

"Let's take a look at those cliffs," she said, turning away from him, confused by her response to him. Jesse had betrayed her in the most despicable way possible. How could she still want him?

After they'd walked for a few more minutes, he turned on the flashlight once more and studied the ground. "Nothing," he said, looking up at her. She saw the sympathy in his gaze and looked away. She didn't want anything from Jesse, she told herself fiercely. Not even his sympathy.

Hours later Jesse finally stopped and put his flashlight into his pack. "You're exhausted," he said. "We need to stop."

"I can't stop now," she cried. "He might be around the next corner."

"Shea, you can hardly put one foot in front of the other," he said, but his voice was gentle. "You're not going to be much help to Rafael if you get hurt because you were too tired to pay attention."

"What if he comes this way, but we're gone because we went back to the house to sleep? We might miss him in the morning."

"I doubt that's going to happen," Jesse said patiently. "But our search will go more quickly in the morning. If he's been this way, we'll be able to see his tracks in the daylight. We can't see anything now. And the moon is going to set behind the cliffs in a few minutes. Then we won't have any light."

"I can't just abandon him out here," she whispered.

Jesse took her arms and swung her around to face him.

"Shea, I saw you stumble over that rock a few minutes ago. And I saw the time you stumbled before that, and the time before that. You can't go on. You have to rest."

"I don't want to go back to the house," she insisted. A part of her knew Jesse was right, knew she was being irrational, but her fear for Rafael couldn't be submerged.

"All right," he said after a moment. "We won't go back to the house. We'll spend the night out here. Then at first light, we'll be ready to go again."

"How can we spend the night up here? I already drank all my water and we don't have shelter."

"I do." Jesse gave her a grim smile. "I'm prepared for anything. I'm an FBI agent, remember?"

Chapter 15

"I haven't forgotten anything," she retorted. "So what do you have in that pack of yours, FBI agent?"

He dropped it on the ground and pulled out two bottles of water. He handed one to her, and opened the second himself.

The water wasn't cold, but it felt wonderful sliding down her throat. "I hadn't realized how thirsty I was," she admitted.

"I know. You were too focused on our search to think about it." He replaced the top on his bottle of water and put it into his pack. "Let's look around for a place to spend the night." He glanced over at her. "There aren't any more cabins up here that you haven't told me about, are there?"

"No." She looked at the cliffs above her with uncertainty. "We could try and find a cave."

"I'd rather stay at ground level. That way, if Rafael does come this way, we have a better chance of hearing him."

"You're right." She couldn't suppress a shiver. "It's going to be a chilly night, though. It gets cold this high in the mountains."

"We'll keep each other warm."

He bent down to retrieve his flashlight, and she narrowed her eyes at him. "What exactly is that supposed to mean?"

"It means that we're going to have to share our body heat." He straightened up, but didn't look at her. He was too busy scanning the rocks at the base of the cliffs. "It's simple, Shea. We can either shiver separately, or stay warm together. Which is it going to be?"

"Together, I suppose," she said after a long silence.

"Think of it as survival training," he said. "It'll be completely impersonal."

Sleeping next to Jesse would never be impersonal, she thought with a flash of heat. But she would die before she let him see that. "There's a spot that's protected from the wind," she said, aiming her flashlight at a small depression in the rock partially sheltered by a boulder. "How about that?"

"Looks good." Jesse tossed his pack behind the boulder, then picked hers up. "Did you bring any extra clothes?"

"Just a shirt and long johns. I wasn't thinking about spending the night up here when I packed it."

"I know." He glanced over at her, and she thought his face softened for a moment. "I have a survival blanket. If we stay close, it should be enough to keep both of us warm."

He pulled out a fist-sized packet from his pack and opened it to reveal a shiny, metallic piece of what looked like plastic. "Come on over," he said as he slid into the basin in the rock. "Make yourself at home."

Her heart pounded as she climbed into the hollow next to him. At this rate, she wouldn't need the survival blanket, she thought, scowling. The blood pounding through her veins was doing a fine job keeping her warm.

Jesse had set their backpacks at head level to act as pillows. When Shea eased herself down onto the rock, he curled his arm behind her and pulled her against him.

"There's no reason both of us have to sleep on the rocks," he said gruffly. "You can use me for a cushion."

She wanted to relax against him far too much. She fit perfectly into the curve of his arm, and her body moved instinctively to meld with his. A sense of rightness crept over her, a feeling she thought had vanished forever earlier that day in the dining room of her house. She couldn't allow herself to feel that way, she thought frantically. Pulling away and turning her back to him, she lay stiffly against the cold ground, feeling his heat surrounding her, unable to relax.

"I won't bite, Shea," he finally said.

"I hope not." Her voice was tart. "I haven't had my shots this year."

His chuckle rippled over her, sounding more relaxed than he had any right to be. "I was beginning to worry about you. But it sounds like you've recovered. You're back to my smart-mouthed Shea."

"I'm not 'your' anything, Jesse." Her chin trembled, and she tucked it furiously into the stiff, crackly blanket. The last thing she would ever do is let Jesse catch her crying.

He pulled her against him. She tried to resist, but he was too strong for her. When she was tucked against him, spoonstyle, he wrapped his arm around her and held her close.

"You'll always be a part of me," he said, his voice so low that she wondered if she'd really heard him, or just imagined the words.

She wanted to argue, to tell him that there was no connection between them, but she was afraid that if she spoke, her voice would break. So she took a deep, trembling breath and tried to wipe her mind clean. She couldn't bear to think about Jesse, not while she was blanketed against him, not while his scent filled her head, not while she ached to feel his hands on her.

The night was a clear one, and millions of stars covered the sky. The glow from the moon filled the sky to the west of them, but above them there was nothing but tiny points of light. She stared at the sky and tried to pretend that she was out here by herself.

It didn't work. Jesse was a warm, reassuring presence beside her, and she knew she wouldn't have felt nearly as safe without his arm curled around her. Far off, a coyote howled, and Jesse tightened his hold on her. "He sounds too far away to be a problem."

"The coyotes won't hurt us," she replied. "They're more interested in rabbits and mice."

The low rumble of his laugh vibrated against her. "I thought I needed to reassure you." The laughing stopped, and after a moment he said, "But you don't need me at all, do you, Shea?"

Oh, yes I do, she cried to herself. *You don't know how much I need you.* But she said instead, "I'm the one who grew up around here. I know the Red Rock like other people know their backyards. A pack of coyotes isn't going to scare me."

"I guess I should have realized by now that nothing scares you. You're the most fearless person I know."

There was plenty that scared her, and most of it involved her feelings for him. "Not finding Rafael. That scares me."

"We'll find him. Or Jackson will. He struck me as a man who knows what he's doing." He skimmed his hand along her arm, and she knew it was supposed to be a reassuring gesture. But his touch made her burn with need.

"Ben is a great tracker," she said, and her voice was low and strained. She hoped he assumed it was anxiety about Rafael. "When my sister-in-law, Carly, was kidnapped, he's the one who found her tracks."

"And he'll find Rafael, too." His arm tightened around her. "Now go to sleep, Shea. It'll be daylight before we know it, and we've got a lot of walking ahead of us tomorrow."

She didn't want to fall asleep in his arms. She refused to be that vulnerable to him. Stubbornly, she tried to keep her eyes open, but she felt safe and secure and warm, and finally her eyes drifted shut. Just before she fell asleep, she turned her head so that her cheek rested on his arm.

She awoke the next morning to the sound of birds twittering above her and a gentle breeze ruffling her hair. Jesse's heart beat steadily below her cheek, and his arms were wrapped tightly around her. Her face was tucked into his chest.

Smiling, she burrowed against him and his arms tightened around her. But when she shifted to get closer to him, something hard and sharp gouged into her hip.

When she reached down to pull it out of her mattress, her hand encountered rock. With her fingers splayed against the cold, grainy surface of the rock, the day before came flooding back, and she remembered everything that had happened. Jesse's betrayal. The confrontation in the cabin. And Rafael running away.

Abruptly she realized how intimately she was entwined with Jesse. Sometime during the night she'd turned around, and now not only was her face buried in his chest, but one of her legs was wedged between his thighs. Her hand rested against his chest, and his hand cupped her buttocks.

Maybe he wasn't awake yet, she thought frantically. Maybe she could extricate herself from him, and when he woke up, she would be sitting on a rock twenty feet away.

But then he shifted, and the hard length of his arousal burning into her thigh told her that he was awake, too.

Tensing, she tried to pull away from him. His arms tightened around her for a moment, and she felt his lips brush her hair. Then he rolled to one side and sat up.

"Good morning, Shea." His voice was low and gravelly, as it always was the first thing in the morning.

Swallowing hard, she tried to banish the other early-morning memories of Jesse that filled her mind and aroused her senses. "Good morning. It looks like we overslept."

"I've been awake for a while," he said easily as he swung to his feet. "I didn't want to wake you, so I didn't move."

She sat up and brushed her hair out of her eyes, then stood up and stretched. It was a clear morning without a cloud in the sky, but there was still a bite of early spring cold in the air.

"I'm going to call Ben and see if he's had any luck," she said, reaching into her backpack for the cell phone.

A moment later she was talking to the deputy. "I've got

"im, Shea," Ben said, and she closed her eyes as relief washed over her.

"Is he all right?"

"He's fine." There was an odd note in the deputy's voice, and Shea gripped the phone more tightly.

"Tell me the truth, Ben," she demanded. "Is he hurt?"

"There's nothing wrong with him, Shea." Ben turned away to speak to Rafael, then came back to her. "I think he could use a good meal, but other than that, he's in good shape."

"You sound funny," she said.

There was a long pause. "I'm all right, too," he finally said. "We'll meet you back at the cabin."

Shea closed the cell phone and looked over at Jesse. "I guess you could tell that Ben found him."

"You don't sound too happy about it."

She forced herself to smile. "I'm thrilled. I'm just worried."

"Did something happen to Rafael?" Jesse asked sharply.

"Ben says no. He said he's hungry, but otherwise okay."

"Then what are you worried about?"

"Ben sounded funny. Different than I've ever heard him sound before. Almost as if he was scared."

"He's probably just tired," Jesse said, shouldering his pack and handing the other one to her. "My guess is that he didn't sleep last night."

"You're probably right." Shea slid the backpack onto her shoulders and took a drink of water. "But I'm still worried."

"Then let's go meet them at the cabin, and you can see for yourself that Rafael and Jackson are both all right."

They hiked in silence for a while, taking the shortest route to the cabin. Finally Jesse said, "What happens after this, Shea?"

"I imagine we'll find Rafael something to eat," she said lightly.

He scowled. "That's not what I meant, and you know it. What happens with Rafael and the rest of the children?"

"That's none of your concern." She kept her voice cool.

"They're safely hidden and out of your reach. As I think pointed out yesterday, I don't have to answer any of you questions. I know enough to realize that, even though yo didn't read me my rights."

"I'm not your enemy here, Shea."

She whirled around to face him. "You're not? Then wha would you call it? You tricked me into hiring you, you mad me fall in l…" She clamped her lips together, feeling the ho tears trembling beneath her anger. "You seduced me, and al the time you were planning to arrest me. You betrayed me Jesse. How else would you describe an enemy?"

"I didn't know what you were doing. I didn't know it wa children you were bringing into the country. That change everything."

"Is that so? Does that mean you're not going to tell you boss what you found? Does that mean you're going to forge all about my children, forget you ever saw anyone at th cabin?"

"I can't do that. I've sworn to uphold the law." His voic was low, and he didn't look at her.

A wave of pain and despair rolled over her. The sweetnes of waking up in his arms, the tenderness she'd felt from hin as they'd huddled together the night before, all faded slowl away.

"So you're on one side of the fence and I'm on the other."

"It doesn't have to be that way, Shea."

"Tell me how it can be any different." Her voice rose int the thin desert air. "I'm not about to hand my children ove to you to send back to San Rafael. And you can't turn you back on your job." She swallowed once. "I know what kin of person you are, Jesse. Your job is important to you, an you're very good at what you do. Ignoring what I'm doin; would be wrong. It's your job to turn me in. I understan that."

"Do you think I want to put you in prison, Shea?" Hi voice trembled with emotion. "I'm not sure I can do that. can't bear to think of you, with your vitality and your lov of life, locked into a cage. Why are you making me do this

Tell me where the children are. Maybe they won't have to go back to San Rafael.''

"Can you promise that? Can you tell me, without any hesitation or doubt, that they'll be safe?" she demanded. "Can you assure me that they won't have to face the horrors they left behind in San Rafael?"

"You know I can't promise anything." He didn't look at her. "All I can promise is that I'll do my best."

"I'm sure you would do your best, Jesse." Her voice softened. "I know that you don't want to hurt those children any more than I do. But I can't put those children's lives at stake. If there's even the slightest chance that they have to go back to San Rafael, I can't let you have them."

"Even if it means you end up in prison?"

"Yes." Her voice rang out passionately, echoing off the cliffs. "What would happen to Rafael if he had to go back to San Rafael? I don't think he'd survive. And I don't know about the others. All I know is that they were desperate enough to go with a man they don't know, away from everything that was familiar to them. How can you expect me to send them back?"

"I don't." He glanced over at her. "I know you, too, Shea. I didn't expect you to agree. But I needed to give you a chance."

"So we're back to square one."

"Not quite. Jackson found Rafael. That's one good thing that's happened."

Shea glanced over at Jesse as they walked. More than one good thing had happened on the Red Rock in the last few weeks, she thought. Jesse had made her feel things she hadn't thought possible, things she didn't even know existed. And she had almost slipped and told him the truth. She'd fallen in love with him. He'd betrayed her and thrown that gift back in her face, but she couldn't regret it.

She and Jesse didn't have a future, but she would have the memories of these few weeks to nourish her. He had betrayed her, but she couldn't banish him completely from her life.

He would always occupy a secret place in her heart, a corner that would never belong to anyone but Jesse.

"We must be close to the cabin," Jesse said.

She wanted to slow down, to tell him to stop. She wasn't ready yet to rejoin Ben and Rafael, she wasn't ready to resume the fight with Jesse. She wanted more time. She wanted to try and find a way to compromise with him.

But she knew there was no compromise possible. She wouldn't have loved him if he'd been the kind of man who easily compromised his principles. And she couldn't have loved him if he'd been the kind of man who expected her to back down from what she believed.

She'd always looked trouble in the eye and faced it down.

So she said, "Let's hurry. I'm anxious to see Rafael."

He glanced over at her, but he didn't say anything. She wondered what he was thinking. She wondered if he, too, wished that the cabin was miles away. She wondered if he wanted to turn back time, the way she longed to do.

Jesse watched the expressions flit across Shea's face and wondered what she was thinking. He wondered, with a stab of pain, if she was memorizing what she thought was her last sight of the mountains. Was she thinking about him at all, or had she already put him out of her mind?

He had no right to ask her. Hell, he had no right to even wonder.

He ached to touch her one last time, to pull her close and hold her like he never had to let her go. But they hiked up a small rise, and the cabin came into view below them. His last chance was gone.

Shea didn't look back as she began to run toward the tiny cabin. "Hold on a minute," he called to her, and she paused and looked over her shoulder.

"Why?"

"The air is too thin to be running up here," he said. "You'll tire yourself out."

She narrowed her eyes at him. "This is where I live. This thin air is a part of me. And even if I do tire myself out, it's no concern of yours."

Without waiting for an answer, she turned and headed toward the cabin again. By the time she was fifty feet away, she was going at a dead run. Jesse ran behind her, but he wasn't able to catch up until after she'd disappeared into the cabin.

When he pulled open the door, he saw Shea down on her knees, her arms wrapped around the boy. Jackson stood above them, his expression impossible to read.

Finally the child pulled away from her. Far from the frightened child he'd expected, Rafael was smiling and happy. His eyes shone with excitement.

"Do you know what Señor Ben found?" he demanded in accented English.

"What did Ben find?" Shea asked. Jesse watched as she curled her arm around the boy, pulling him closer.

Rafael didn't seem to notice. He looked up at Ben, adoration shining out of his eyes. "He found a cave for us to sleep in. I think there might have been bears," he said, his voice dropping. "But we scared them away. Then he found water for me to drink." He looked back at Shea. "I was very thirsty," he confided. "But Señor Ben knew just where the water was."

"Ben is good at things like that."

Shea glanced up at Ben, and Jesse saw her eyes soften. For a moment, an icy hot spear of jealousy stabbed through him. Then he caught himself. He had no right to be jealous of anyone. He'd forfeited those rights when he'd pulled his badge on Shea.

Jackson cleared his throat and looked uncomfortable. "Rafael is a real trouper," he finally said. "We had an adventure, didn't we, buddy?"

Rafael nodded vigorously. "Señor Ben said we could go hiking in the mountains again sometime, but that I had to come back now." He looked at Shea, and his mouth trembled. "He said I have to tell you I'm sorry that I scared you."

Shea hugged him again, then stood up. "You're forgiven, Rafael. I know you were frightened and confused. Later, we'll talk about what we need to do when we're scared, but right now, I'm getting kind of hungry. How about you?''

The boy nodded solemnly. ''Me, too.''

''Then what do you say we head back to the house?''

Jesse watched her with the child and felt his heart break all over again. She was so gentle with the boy, so kind. And so thoughtful. He knew Shea would talk to him about running away, but she wouldn't do it in front of an audience. Rafael would get his scolding in private.

He bent to pick up the pack she'd dropped as she rushed in the door, and she glanced over at him. Almost, he thought with a pang, as if she'd forgotten his existence in her concern for the boy.

''Thank you, Jesse,'' she murmured, and he felt his gut tighten.

''I'm glad I could help.'' He was glad he'd had one last night with her, even if she'd been angry and hurt. He'd have one more memory to cherish.

No one said much on the trip back to the house. Rafael sat in the front seat with Jackson and stared out the window, wide-eyed. Jesse realized it was probably the first glimpse the boy had had of the ranch in daylight. Shea sat in the back seat with him, but she might as well have been miles away.

Just before they reached the house, she roused herself and gave him a brief smile. ''Thanks again for helping us search, Jesse.''

Her words were polite and distant, as if he'd been a neighbor or acquaintance who'd volunteered to help her out. There was no passion in her voice, no warmth in her eyes. There was nothing left of the heat he used to see every time he caught her gaze.

And it was exactly what he deserved, he told himself harshly. She was right. He had betrayed her.

But he'd been doing his job. And his job often required that he betray people who'd thought he was their friend. It was the essence of undercover work. It had never bothered him until now.

Now, looking at Shea sitting so close to him, but in reality so far away, he felt dirty inside, as if his soul was stained. It was his own fault, for getting involved with a suspect. But he didn't think the ache in his heart was part of his job description.

As the house came into view, he saw a tall man with golden brown hair step out onto the porch. He stood staring at them, and Jesse felt Shea stiffen next to him.

"What's wrong?" he asked sharply.

For a moment she didn't answer. Then she sighed. "Just what I needed today. That's my brother."

Before the truck had completely stopped, Shea's brother strode toward it and wrenched open the door. His mouth a thin line, he glared at his sister and said, "What the hell have you been doing, Shea?"

"It's good to see you, too," she retorted.

His mouth softened and the tall man dragged her out of the car and into his arms for a hug. Then he stepped back. "Maria and Levi have been talking," he said without preamble. "I've been getting some wild story about an FBI agent working here undercover." His eyes narrowed. "In more ways than one. And now they claim that this guy is ready to haul you off to prison for smuggling illegal aliens. What the hell happened here while I was gone? And where the hell is this FBI agent?"

"That would be me." Jesse slid out of the car and stood next to Shea. "I'm Jesse Coulton." He didn't offer his hand, and neither did the other man.

Her brother's mouth thinned. "I'm Devlin McAllister, and I'm the sheriff of Cameron. Why was the FBI running an undercover operation on my territory without informing me?"

"First of all, you weren't here when I arrived. And secondly, we didn't inform you because we were investigating your ranch." He gave Devlin a thin smile. "As a law enforcement officer, I'm sure you understand my dilemma."

Devlin scowled at him, but before he could say anything, a tall, striking woman with dark red hair walked out of the house.

"Shea!" she called. "I thought I heard a truck pull up." Hurrying down the steps, she reached for Shea and hugged her. Then she stepped back and searched Shea's face. "It's good to see you," she said softly.

"You too, Carly." Shea turned to Jesse. "This is my sister-in-law, Carly," she said. "Carly, this is Jesse Coulton. I'm sure Maria and Levi have told you about him."

Jesse shook the other woman's hand, taken aback by the cool appraisal in her eyes. "Nice to meet you, Mr. Coulton."

Jesse watched as Devlin and Carly turned back to Shea. No one noticed that Ben and Rafael got out of the truck and headed toward the house. The deputy's hand hovered over the boy's shoulder, but he didn't actually touch Rafael. When the child looked up at Jackson, adoration in his eyes, Jesse saw Ben wince.

Jesse watched thoughtfully as the pair disappeared into the house. At least Jackson had the foresight to remove the boy from the discussion, which was bound to get ugly. Jesse wondered what would happen to the boy, then told himself that wasn't part of his job.

But as he turned back to Shea and the others, he wanted to break down the rigid barriers of his job. He wanted to be a part of the group that stood next to him. He listened to the rise and fall of voices as Shea and her brother and sister-in-law all tried to talk at once. Levi and Joe came out of the barn and added their voices to the din.

Suddenly Jesse spun around and headed for his small bunkhouse. He didn't belong here. In spite of his feelings about Shea, he was still an outsider. And because of what he'd done, he'd always be an outsider at the Red Rock Ranch.

It was time to leave. He had a job to do, and decisions to make. He'd always defined himself by his job, and nothing had changed. It was time to move on.

It only took a moment to replace his clothes and belongings into his duffel bag. Just as he was ready to close it up, he found the radiator cap he'd taken from the truck. It had only been a few weeks, but it seemed like a different lifetime.

"Was everything a lie, Jesse?"

Shea's voice came from the doorway behind him, and he spun around to face her, the radiator cap in his hand. He heard sadness in her voice, and loss. She was staring at the round metal cap he held.

"I was going to give this back to you."

"I didn't want to believe that everything was planned, everything was staged," she whispered. "But even then, you were lying to me. Even then, that day I caught you up near the cabin, you were working the angles, weren't you? You took the cap so you would have a story ready for me if I caught you up there."

Jesse set the radiator cap gently onto the table. Suddenly it seemed like a symbol of all the ugliness and lies that stood between them. "I wish it could have been another way, Shea. I wish I hadn't come here like this."

"But you did, and it's too late to change anything." She gestured to his packed bag. "Where are you going? Or should I ask, where are *we* going? Am I supposed to be packing a bag, too?"

"You're not going anywhere, as far as I know. At least, you're not going anywhere with me. I'm going back to Washington." He hesitated. "Have you thought about what we talked about earlier? About telling me where the children are hidden?"

She raised her chin. "What do you think?"

"I think you're the most stubborn woman I know," he said, sighing. "I should have known you wouldn't be swayed by logic."

"I made a very logical decision. It would hurt the children if I told you where they were. Therefore, I can't tell you."

"Shea, I don't want to leave like this." The words felt like they'd been torn from his heart.

For a moment, he saw the pain in her eyes, and the sorrow. Then she looked away. "Does this mean you're not coming back?"

"I have to come back, and you know that. One way or

another, I have to resolve this case. I can't pretend that non-
of it happened."

"I know," she whispered. "I know you can't."

He took two steps toward her, then pulled her close. "
care about you, Shea," he said into her hair. "I didn't wan
to hurt you."

Instead of pulling away from him, as he expected, she
wrapped her arms around him and held him fiercely. Ther
she backed away. Her eyes glittered as she stared at him.

"When are you coming back?" she asked, her voice
barely more than a whisper.

"I don't know. It depends on a lot of things."

She nodded. "I'll be waiting. I'm not going anywhere
Jesse. You know where to find me."

Without saying anything more, she turned and slipped ou
of the cabin. As he stared after her, his heart seemed to crack
open in his chest and tumble onto the floor.

She would be waiting for him to come back to the Rec
Rock and arrest her.

He hoped to God it wouldn't come to that.

Chapter 16

Jesse stopped his truck on the driveway that led to the Red Rock Ranch and let the engine idle. It looked the same as it had a week ago. Cattle grazed in the pastures, the mountains standing guard over them. The barn was open, meaning someone was working inside, and two trucks stood in the yard. On the surface, nothing had changed.

But he knew better. Everything had changed at the Red Rock. Shea was waiting for him to return and arrest her. If he knew her, and he did, she had worked day and night during the past week to get the ranch ready to function on its own.

He was the last person on earth she would want to see.

Setting his jaw, he shifted the truck into gear again and slowly drove toward the house. She deserved to know what had happened in Washington, and he was selfish enough to want to see her again.

Before his truck had stopped in the yard, he saw her. She was in the corral with Demon, working the big black horse around the barrels. She hadn't noticed his truck yet, so he sat and watched her for a while.

Shea bent low over Demon's neck, urging him to go faster. The horse didn't need much urging, Jesse thought, as he raced from one barrel to the next. There was no sign of the injury that had hobbled him after his last race, and Shea must have realized it. After she made the turn around the last barrel, she pulled him up. Jesse could see the smile on her face as she patted Demon's neck and murmured something to him.

As she was swinging off the horse's back, she looked up and saw his truck. She froze for a second, then continued her easy descent from Demon. Jesse got out of the truck and walked over to the corral.

"Hello, Jesse." Her voice was even and her normally expressive face was carefully blank.

"Hi, Shea." He nodded at Demon. "I'm glad to see he's feeling better."

Shea glanced down at his leg. "Becca gave me the go ahead to start working him a couple of days ago. I thought we'd better get in as much training as possible before…"

Her voice trailed off, and Jesse saw her hand tighten on the reins she held. "Anyway, he's doing well."

"Good."

Shea wrapped the reins around the top rail of the corral and then looked directly at Jesse. "I don't like games, Jesse. Tell me why you're here."

Another piece of his heart broke off at her words and her familiar directness. He knew he would always remember her as she looked right now, her wavy blonde hair streaming in the breeze, her chin lifted in defiance, and her bright blue eyes staring a hole through him.

"I thought you would want to know what happened when I talked to my bosses in Washington."

"I assume it's not good news, because you're here in person."

His heart clenched into a fist. "Isn't it possible that I would come back because I wanted to see you, too?"

Her direct gaze never wavered. "I don't know, Jesse. There's a lot I don't know about you, including how you really feel. For all I know, I was just a means to an end here at the Red Rock.''

He didn't like being put on the defensive. And no one did it better than Shea. ''You weren't just a means to an end, Shea. Surely you know that. What I felt for you was real.''

''It couldn't have been real, because it was based on a lie,'' she shot back. ''Everything you told me was part of your plan.''

''Not everything. I never planned on my feelings for you.''

This time he let his gaze lock with hers, and finally she looked away. ''Go ahead and tell me what happened in Washington.''

''Why don't we put Demon away first? I'll help you.''

They worked together silently, their rhythms just as much in sync as they had been before he left. In a few minutes, Demon had been rubbed down and his lower leg had been wrapped to protect it while his foot continued to heal. Finally Shea walked out of his stall and leaned against the wall. ''Shoot.''

''Don't you want to go into the house?''

''Do you want everyone on the ranch to hear what you have to say?'' She raised one eyebrow.

He didn't want to talk to her in the barn. There were too many memories there, memories of the times he'd kissed her, the times they'd worked together, laughing and comfortable. But she was right. The house would be worse.

''I talked to a lot of people at the Bureau and at Immigration,'' he said without preamble. ''No one wants to send those children back to San Rafael, and no one wants to arrest you.''

''But,'' she said as he hesitated.

''But we're dealing with a politically sensitive issue here. San Rafael isn't the only country in the middle of a civil war. It's not the only country where there are children at risk. And bureaucrats don't like to be caught pulling strings and breaking the rules.'' His mouth thinned as he remembered some of the conversations he'd had in the past week.

''What does that mean?'' Her voice was even.

"It means that no one is willing to say that the children can stay. But I was promised that heaven and earth would be moved to get them back here as soon as possible. Visas would be issued very quickly for any child sent back to San Rafael."

Shea pushed away from the wall and bent to pick up Demon's bridle. "In other words, nothing has changed."

"No."

When she straightened, Shea's eyes were carefully blanked. "What happens now, Jesse?"

"Where are the children?"

Her jaw clenched. "They're gone. They've all been reunited with their family members, and I won't tell you where they are. So don't even ask."

"What about Rafael?"

"What about him?" Her jaw jutted forward.

"He didn't have any family to sweep him away. Where did he go?"

She studied him for a moment, as if appraising what she could tell him. Her assessing look made his heart ache.

"Rafael is with Ben Jackson," she finally said. "And that's where he's staying."

Jesse frowned. "He's actually living with Jackson?"

"What's wrong with that?"

Jesse shrugged. "Nothing, I guess. I just got the impression that Jackson was uncomfortable around him."

Shea hesitated, then she nodded. He saw the uncertainty in her eyes. "I think he is. It's almost like he won't allow himself to get close to Rafael. But Rafael adores him." She smiled at the memory. "And I think Ben is finding Rafael hard to resist."

"What's going to happen to Rafael?"

"I was hoping that Ben would adopt him." Her smile dimmed. "But I suppose you'll have some say in that."

"Do you think I'm going to snatch the boy away from Jackson?" he demanded.

Slowly, reluctantly, she shook her head. "I don't think you'd do that, Jesse. I'd like to think so, but I can't."

"Why would you want to think something like that?"

She gave him a humorless smile. "It's much easier to hate someone capable of doing evil."

"I don't want you to hate me, Shea," he whispered.

"Don't worry about it. I don't hate you."

He couldn't stop himself. "Then what do you feel for me?"

"It doesn't matter anymore, does it?" For an instant, he saw the pain in her eyes, a deep, soul-searing pain. Then she stepped past him into the tack room to put the bridle away.

When she stepped out of the tack room, her eyes were carefully blank again. "What happens now, Jesse?"

"Nothing, yet."

"I thought there were only two things you could do— either bring the children in, or bring me in. Since the children aren't available, that leaves me. When do we have to leave?"

"Neither of us is going anywhere just yet." He'd known Shea wouldn't give up the children, so he'd come up with a plan. Now he'd have to see if his plan would work. "I have an idea, but it's going to take time."

He saw hope flare in her eyes, along with a light that made his heart leap. He wanted to reach out to her, to pull her close and tell her that everything would be fine, but he didn't have the right. So he clenched his hands into fists and shoved them into the back pockets of his jeans. The light in her eyes died.

"Will you trust me, Shea?"

"I don't have much choice, do I? I'd say you were calling all the shots right now."

"Will you at least believe that I don't want to hurt you?"

"I've never believed you wanted to hurt me. But your job, who you are, is completely opposed to who I am and what I'm doing." She shrugged. "And your job obviously comes first."

Her words were another tiny tear in his soul. She was right. When he'd come to the Red Rock, his job *had* been all he cared about. But everything had changed. And it had changed because of Shea.

He ached to tell her so, but knew that he couldn't. Not yet, anyway. It was time for actions, not words. He didn't deserve a future with Shea if he couldn't fix what he'd done.

"I'm going to head back to Cameron. I have a lot of things to do."

"Where are you staying?" There was only cool inquiry in her eyes.

"Is there anywhere to stay besides Melba Corboy's?" His voice was dry.

A faint smile flickered across her face, and then was gone. "Stupid question."

He didn't want to go. He didn't want to leave her here, alone, worried about what would happen.

But if he didn't go, nothing would change. "Can you trust me, Shea?" he asked again. "Trust me to make everything all right?"

"I want to, Jesse," she whispered.

But she couldn't. The words were unspoken, but he understood. He'd betrayed her once, and it was hard to trust after that.

He nodded, his heart aching for what he'd done to her. "I'll see you soon, Shea."

She started to say something, then closed her mouth and nodded. "Take care."

"You, too."

He climbed into his truck and drove out of the yard without looking back. He was afraid that if he looked at Shea, he would stop the truck and beg her to forgive him. And he refused to do that. He refused to ask for forgiveness until he had something concrete to offer her.

He prayed it would be soon.

It didn't take long to stop at Melba Corboy's house and ask for a room. The older woman stared at him suspiciously for a moment, and he was afraid she'd heard what happened out at the Red Rock, afraid she'd refuse to let him stay. But finally she opened the door and motioned him in. When he told her he didn't want meals, she actually smiled at him.

When he walked in the door of the *Cameron Weekly Sen-*

tinel office a while later, Carly McAllister was sitting at a desk, scowling at a computer. He watched her for a moment. She was so absorbed in what she was doing she hadn't even noticed him. When he cleared his throat, she jumped and spun around.

"You startled me!"

"Sorry. I didn't know how else to get your attention."

To his surprise, she grinned at him. "I do tend to be focused." Her gaze sharpened and her smile faded. "You're that FBI agent who was working at the ranch."

"That's me." He hesitated, unsure how to approach her, then decided to dive in. "I have a problem, and I think you can help me."

Her eyes narrowed. "Why would I want to do that?"

He pulled up a chair and told her.

It had been five days since Jesse returned to Cameron. He'd driven away from the ranch without looking back, and Shea hadn't seen him since that first day.

He was still in Cameron. Levi had reported just yesterday that he'd seen Jesse eating lunch at Heaven on Seventh. She had acted unconcerned, but the ball of anxiety that had lodged in her chest grew a little bigger.

Jesse had asked her to trust him. She wanted to, desperately, but it was hard to hold onto her faith with so little substance to sustain her. As far as she could tell, Jesse was staying at Melba's, eating at Heaven on Seventh, and just waiting.

Was he waiting for her to change her mind and tell him where the children were? She couldn't believe that. Jesse knew her well enough to know she'd never give the children up. Was he waiting for Ben to get tired of Rafael, and agree to turn him over?

Jesse wouldn't do that to Rafael. She wouldn't even allow herself to consider the possibility. Her thoughts raced around in her mind, tripping over themselves, keeping her awake at night and making her close to useless for working during the day.

What was Jesse doing?

Fifty times she'd grabbed her keys to head into Cameron to confront him. And fifty times she'd stopped herself, replaced the keys on the hook by the front door, and forced herself to stop.

She was afraid of what would happen if she went to Jesse. She had been appalled by her reaction when he'd driven into the Red Rock five days ago. Her heart had leapt in her chest, and she'd had to stop herself from jumping into his arms.

Because nothing had changed. She knew he'd tried to make a deal with his bosses in Washington, but no deal had been forthcoming. And Jesse wasn't the kind of man who could walk away, leaving his job unfinished. Jesse was going to have to make a choice, and she was afraid she knew which one it would be. As an honorable man, he would do his job.

Throwing herself into the swing on the front porch, she picked up the mail that Maria had left sitting on the table. *Focus* magazine was on the top of the pile, and she idly began thumbing through the pages.

The name Utah in the title of a story caught her eye, and she began reading. Moments later, she shot out of her seat, staring at the magazine with incredulous eyes. Hurriedly she finished reading, then threw the magazine on the floor and raced to her truck.

The truck had barely stopped on Main Street when she leapt out and ran into the *Cameron Weekly Sentinel* office. "Where's Carly?" she asked June Hanson, Carly's office manager.

"She was here until early this morning, getting the paper out. If she has any sense, she's home in bed."

Without answering, Shea dashed out the door and ran across the street to the sheriff's office. When she burst through the door, Marge the dispatcher looked up, startled.

"Where's my brother?" she demanded.

"I think he's at Heaven with that nice FBI agent," Marge said.

Shea ran out the door and around the corner, heading for the restaurant. When she ran through the door she saw that the restaurant was half-full, even though it was the middle of the afternoon. Stopping, she drew in a lungful of air and surveyed the restaurant, looking for Jesse and Dev.

They were sitting in the corner booth with Ben Jackson, and all three men looked like they were getting along just fine. Shea marched over to the booth.

"Well, isn't this cozy?" She glared at her brother. "I'm glad to see you're enjoying yourself with the man who's trying to put me in prison." She stared hard at him, then looked at Jesse. "What's going on?"

Jesse smiled at her, apparently unconcerned. "There's something we'd like you to see."

He pulled out a copy of *Focus* magazine and handed it to her. She waved it away.

"I've already seen it. What I want to know is, why?"

Jesse's face softened. "Sit down, Shea. People are looking." He grabbed her hand and tugged her into the booth next to him. He held onto her hand, and although she told herself to pull away, she couldn't do it. He curled his fingers around hers and held tight, and she began to warm. She'd been cold for so long.

"Did you read the article?" Jesse asked.

"I did. How did you persuade Carly to write it?"

"I didn't have to persuade her. I just told her the facts, and she took it from there."

Shea grabbed the magazine and read the title of the article. "Small Town in Utah the Stage for Big Drama. Will the Government Force Refugee Children to Go Home Again?" She set the article down. "This is a national magazine. Everybody in the country who reads this article is going to be howling about what the big, bad, unfeeling government is doing to these helpless children."

Jesse smiled again. "That was the idea."

She turned to Devlin. "And you agreed?"

He gave her a wry grin. "I don't recall having a vote. But I'm glad Carly wrote the article."

Shea could only stare at him. "For the past six months

I've been terrified of what would happen when you found out what I was doing. Do you mean you're not angry?"

"I've sworn to uphold the law, Shea, and you know I take my job seriously. But there are times when you have to obey a higher law, and this is one of them. What you did with those children was the right thing." He shook his head and cleared his throat. "It took a hell of a lot of guts to do it, and I'm proud of you."

A lump of tears grew and swelled in her throat. "Thank you, Dev," she whispered.

She turned to Jesse. "Why didn't you tell me?"

"I couldn't." He tightened his hand on hers. "I wasn't sure Carly would write the article, and I wasn't sure if *Focus* would run it. Hell, I'm still not sure if it's going to make any difference."

"It will." It had to make a difference. "It has to, Jesse."

He smiled and brought their joined hands to his mouth. After brushing her knuckles with a kiss, he let her go. "I have a meeting in a few minutes," he said. "May I come out to the ranch later?"

"I'll be waiting for you."

Their eyes met and held, and then he nodded. "I'll be there."

Shea watched him leave the restaurant, feeling dazed. "I feel like I've fallen through the rabbit hole."

Devlin laughed. "Serves you right. That's just how you make me feel most of the time."

Instead of responding, she leaned against the cushion in the booth. Finally she looked over at Ben. "What's going to happen with you, Ben?" she asked.

"What do you mean?" he asked cautiously.

"They talk about Rafael in this article. There are going to be all sorts of reporters sniffing around him, wanting to ask him questions."

"They won't get to him." Ben's voice was quiet, but completely confident. "Rafael is too fragile right now to deal with this. As long as everyone in the town understands that, he'll be fine. No one will bother him."

"Carly wrote an article about that for this week's *Sentinel*," Devlin said. "She spelled it all out. No one's going to tell a soul who Rafael is or where to find him."

Shea nodded. "Good. I think Rafael is happy, Ben."

"I intend to make sure he stays that way, for as long as he's with me."

Shea started to ask him what he meant, ask him if he was going to adopt Rafael, but she stopped when Ben stiffened. She didn't have to turn around to see that Janie Murphy was behind them.

Janie hurried away to the kitchen, and Ben stood up. "I'll go back to the office. Someone has to do some work around here."

Shea stood up to leave, too. "It seems I have a date out at the ranch."

Before she could leave, Dev stopped her with a hand on her arm. "I like Coulton, Shea. I didn't think I ever could, after what he did to you, but he's all right."

The lump in her throat grew again. "Thanks, Dev. Thank you for telling me that."

He nodded. "I want you to be happy, Shea."

"I know." Her voice was barely a whisper.

Her brother leaned over and kissed her cheek. "Now see if you can make it back to the ranch without forcing one of my deputies to give you a speeding ticket. I'll talk to you later."

Her mind raced as she drove sedately back to the Red Rock. Who was Jesse meeting? And what was it about?

Her hands grew damp on the steering wheel as she thought about their "date." What would he say to her? And more importantly, what would she say to him?

Chapter 17

Time stretched and dragged for the next three hours. Shea couldn't bear to sit and wait, but she was too distracted to concentrate on the chores she tried to do. For the first time in her memory, the Red Rock wasn't her all-consuming passion. She could think only of Jesse, and what he might say to her.

And what she had to tell him. There had been too many lies between them, and she'd decided on the way home from Cameron that she owed him the truth about how she felt. So she paced in the yard and the barn, trying to find ways to keep her mind and her hands occupied while she watched the drive for a plume of dust.

She was essentially alone on the Red Rock, and Jesse would be here very soon.

Wandering into the house, she saw the copy of *Focus* that she'd dropped on the floor earlier. Picking it up, she settled into the swing on the front porch and reread the article that Carly had written.

In spite of the knot of anxiety that grew in her stomach, she couldn't help but smile at the story. Carly had deliberately made it inflammatory, and Shea imagined she could hear the howl of thousands of voices raised in outrage across the country. Carly had made it sound as if the government was bullying small, helpless children, terrorizing them for no good reason and refusing to let them join their relatives in this country. It was an article designed to stir up an uproar.

As she finished the article, she heard the sound of a truck pulling into the yard. The magazine dropped from her suddenly nerveless fingers as she watched Jesse's familiar form climb out of the truck. Her heart began to pound in slow, deliberate thuds that she was sure he could hear. Hoping her cheeks weren't flushed, she stood up to greet him.

"Hello, Jesse."

"Shea." He stopped at the bottom of the porch steps. "May I join you?"

"Of course." She stepped to the far end of the swing and sat down. Her heart dipped with the swing as Jesse took a seat at the other end. For a moment, they simply looked at each other. Jesse's face looked peaceful, and his eyes had lost the hardness that had filled them when he'd left Cameron a week ago.

"Jesse," she began.

At the same time, he said, "Shea."

They both stopped, and Shea felt stupidly awkward. Determined to keep her cool, she gripped the arm of the swing and said, "There's something I need to tell you, Jesse."

His face tightened, and for a moment he looked vulnerable and uncertain. Then he nodded.

"Fair enough. But first let me tell you why I came out here. I thought you deserved to know what I've been doing."

"All right." She took a deep breath, prepared for anything. Her fear that Jesse would arrest her had eased since she'd seen the article in *Focus,* but she still had no idea what he intended. For all she knew, he could be planning on solving the problem in Cameron and moving on to his next assignment.

"I've been on the phone to my boss in Washington for most of the afternoon," he said without preamble. "He's seen the *Focus* article, and he's furious. He's promising me all kinds of grief the next time he sees me."

"I'm sorry, Jesse." Impulsively, she leaned over and touched his arm. "I know how important your job is to you."

He reached for her hand almost absently and twined their fingers together. Shea told herself to let him go, but Jesse didn't seem to realize that he was holding onto her. "I'm not worried. Sam'll get over it. I'm the best agent he has, and he knows it."

He tightened his hold on her hand and swiveled to face her. "I didn't tell you that to make you feel sorry for me, or because I'm afraid it'll affect my job. I told you because I think it's a good sign."

"What do you mean?"

"I think it means that Sam has been getting pressure from someone higher up the chain of command. Carly's article doesn't make the Bureau look good, Shea. Sam told me that the phone calls from the citizens have already started. And if they're calling us, they're calling their congressmen, too. Before the week is finished, there's going to be a huge stink in Washington about your children."

Shea sat back in the swing, stunned. "What does that mean for the children?"

"It means that if anyone tries to send them back to San Rafael, they're going to be lynched by an angry mob of citizens. The same mob Carly stirred up with her article." He grinned at her. "I never thought I'd say it, but God bless the press. They're going to save us on this one."

"So Rafael's safe? And you won't have to try and round the other children up?"

"No one in Washington will be willing to touch the children. And Rafael is going to have a long and happy life in the U S of A." He shot her a quizzical look. "Aren't you interested in what's going to happen to you?"

"Of course I am. I just needed to know about the children first."

"That's why I told you about the children first. I knew

they were more important to you than whether you were going to be spending the next twenty years in prison.''

His eyes softened until they glowed a gentle green. He brought her hand to his mouth, and let his lips linger there. Need stirred inside her, but she tried to ignore it. There was too much unsettled to allow herself to give in to the passion that coiled inside her.

"So what *is* going to happen to me?" Her voice sounded breathless and unsteady.

"Absolutely nothing. Sam told me that he wouldn't dare recommend we arrest you, after that article in *Focus*."

"How can you be so sure? I committed a crime, Jesse. I smuggled those children into the country."

"It was a crime of the heart, Shea. No one wants to prosecute you for loving too much."

She slumped back into the seat of the swing. "So it's all over?"

"That depends on if you intend to stop bringing in the children."

"I can hardly continue now. I'll be watched more closely than a hawk watches a mouse. It would be too cruel to bring children here, only to have them sent back."

Jesse smiled and leaned toward her. "I also spent part of the afternoon with Damien Kane. I know him slightly, and I know he has connections in Washington. So we had a talk." He brought his other hand up and touched her face. "It seems that you helped his wife, Abby, when she was alone and needed help. And he's a man who doesn't forget that kind of thing. We pooled our contacts and came up with some interesting names. When I left him, he was on the phone, talking to someone at the State Department. I think you'll find it much easier from now on to get visas for the children who need to be reunited with their relatives in this country."

"Are you saying that I don't have to stop bringing the children into the country?" she whispered.

"I'm saying that you don't have to do it on the sly. As soon as Damien and I get the kinks ironed out, the kids can come into the country legally."

Shea stared at Jesse, stunned. He'd just handed her everything she wanted. Or almost everything, she corrected painfully. Because he hadn't offered her the one thing she wanted more than anything.

He hadn't offered himself.

She hadn't expected him to, she reminded herself. Jesse had a job he loved, and it wasn't on the Red Rock Ranch. He had more important things to do than spend the rest of his life on a ranch in Utah.

"Thank you, Jesse," she said, her throat almost closed with emotion. "Thank you for everything."

"I didn't do squat," he said bluntly. "Carly wrote the article, and Damien is the one who made the phone calls to the State Department."

"But you orchestrated all of it. Carly wouldn't have written that article if you hadn't asked her, and Damien wouldn't have thought to work on the visas without you, either."

"It was the least I could do. I owed you."

"You don't owe me anything, Jesse."

He stared at her, a strange light in his eyes. "You don't think so?"

"I know so." Her voice was firm. She didn't want him carrying regrets about her through the rest of his life. "You were doing a job. I understand that now."

"I lied to you."

"I know you did. And your betrayal hurt. I won't deny that. But I was lying to you, too. I hadn't told you what I was doing with the children. We both thought we were doing the right thing." She tore her gaze away from his face and looked at her beloved ranch, the scenery dissolving into a blur. "I can't be angry with you for doing what you thought was right."

"You're more generous than most people would be." His voice sounded heavy, as if he had a hard time forming the words. "Why is that, Shea?"

"I should have trusted you." She didn't trust herself to look at him. "I knew what kind of a man you were. I should have known you would never hurt my children. How can I blame you for not trusting me when I didn't trust you?''

Silence thickened the air between them, and Shea held tightly to the arm of the swing. She didn't dare look over at Jesse. He would see the truth in her eyes, the truth of her love for him, and she wasn't sure how he would respond.

"You wanted to tell me something, too," he finally said.

Her gaze flew involuntarily to his. Hazel eyes watched her with a gentleness she'd never seen on Jesse's face before. Gentleness, and something more. Her heart began its painful thudding again.

"I'm not sure it matters anymore," she whispered.

"Try me and see."

He watched her steadily, and she took a deep, trembling breath. She loved Jesse, but she hadn't trusted him. Now it was time to put her love to the test. Did she have the courage to tell him how he felt, not knowing what his answer would be?

She had no choice. She would never forgive herself if she let him walk away without knowing she loved him. So she took another breath and said, "I wanted to tell you that I loved you. I didn't want you to leave without knowing that."

He closed his eyes, and a wave of panic gripped her heart. Then he opened them, and she couldn't mistake the love that shone on her.

But instead of the words she wanted to hear, he said, "I'm the last person you should love, Shea."

"According to whom?" She lifted her chin and refused to look away.

"According to me. I betrayed you. I used you and lied to you and ended up betraying your trust in me. How could you love me?" The hope in his eyes belied his words.

"I guess I'm just a sucker for a pretty face," she murmured, encouraged by the love she saw in his eyes.

He jumped up from the swing and moved to the rail, staring out at the Red Rock. "Can you ever forgive me, Shea?"

"There's nothing to forgive. I told you, I understand now

that your job was as important to you as saving the children
was to me.''

"You have such a generous heart," he whispered. "I can'
believe you've given it to me.''

"It's yours, Jesse, for as long as you want it.''

He turned around slowly. "How does forever sound?" He
reached for her and pulled her roughly into his arms. "I love
you, Shea," he said against her hair. "I didn't know wha
love was until you showed me. The last week has been nothing but hell for me. I was sure you wouldn't be able to forgive me.''

"I love you, Jesse. How could I not forgive you?''

"It can't be that easy.''

She leaned away from the haven of his arms to look up a
him. "I didn't tell you what I was doing. I didn't trust you
with my secret. Have you forgiven me for that?''

"Of course I have.''

She smiled at him then, feeling the last band around her
heart loosening. "See how easy it is?''

"You make everything easy, Shea," he whispered. "I fel
in love with you before I even realized what was happening
I think I fell in love with you the first time I drove into the
yard and saw you wrestling with that steer.''

Moisture gathered in her eyes, but she grinned at him
"And I fell in love with you when you gave me that cocky
smile and dared me to hire you.''

He bent and kissed her again, and passion rose, hot and
urgent. It had been far too long since they'd touched each
other, far too long since they'd kissed.

Jesse apparently felt the same, because his hands gripped
her tightly and his mouth was hard and demanding on hers.
When she curled her hands into his back, she heard his groan
vibrate through her mouth.

Slowly he pulled his mouth away from hers. "We have to
stop now, or I won't be able to stop." His voice was low
and husky, full of need.

"There's no reason to stop. We're alone here. There isn'
anyone else around.''

"Are you sure?"

She pulled his mouth back down to hers. "I'm positive."

He kissed her again, passion raging wildly between them, then moved away and took her hand. "Let's go upstairs."

They hurried through the door, clinging to each other, and managed to make it to Shea's room before their trembling hands began to pull at each other's clothes. Shea couldn't get the buttons on Jesse's shirt undone, and finally he ripped it over his head. When they were both naked, standing in the golden light pouring through the window, he reached out and touched her cheek. "You're even more beautiful than I remember."

"I've missed you so much, Jesse." She captured his hand in hers and held it to her face.

Then there was no more time for words as they melted together, tumbling to the bed. Jesse's touch trailed fire everywhere, until she burned for him. And she couldn't get enough of touching him. Everywhere her hands lingered, she felt his muscles tense and quiver.

Finally, her heart thundering, her body aching for him, she pulled him to her. "I can't wait any longer, Jesse."

He covered her mouth with his as he joined their bodies together. "I've been waiting forever for you, Shea," he whispered. "And now I've come home."

Pleasure built in waves, until she thought her heart would burst with it. And when she tumbled over the edge and shattered into a million pieces, she felt Jesse fall with her, whispering her name.

It seemed like hours later when they moved again. "I love you, Shea," he said, pulling her close and wrapping his arms around her. "I feel like the luckiest man on earth. I have everything I ever could have hoped for, and some things I didn't even know I wanted."

"I never knew I could feel this way." She closed her eyes and tightened her arms around him again. "I never want to let you go."

"You'll never have to, I promise."

A ragged edge of anxiety fluttered inside her. She hesitated, unwilling to spoil the moment, then blurted out, "What about your job? Aren't you going to be gone for long stretches of time?"

"My job." He caressed her back almost absently, his fingers tracing a pattern down her spine. "Did you know they call me the Renegade?" he asked, pulling her closer. She could feel his heart beating next to her ear, strong and steady.

"The Renegade? Why is that?" She held her breath, afraid of what he was going to say.

"Because I always work alone. I didn't want a partner, I didn't want anyone distracting me from what I had to do. I got the job done by myself, in my own way."

He leaned back so he could look down at her. "I'm retiring my title. I don't want to be a renegade anymore. I don't ever want to work alone again. I have a partner now, a partner I intend to keep for the rest of my life."

The last, frozen ball of fear inside her slowly began to melt. "Does that mean you're quitting the FBI?"

He hesitated for a moment. "Not completely," he finally said. "I have too much expertise to just walk away. I told my boss I would be available for special assignments occasionally. But Cameron is a part of me now, and I want to be a part of it. I made it clear that I intended to live here in Utah, and spend my time helping you on the Red Rock. If you'll have me, that is."

"If I'll 'have' you?" The last of her fears laid to rest, knowing that he wouldn't be leaving her again, she smiled at him. "What exactly is that supposed to mean?"

He looked steadily at her, his gaze unwavering. "Will you marry me, Shea?"

"Yes," she whispered. "Yes, I'll marry you, Jesse. But are you sure you want to give up your career?"

"I'm not giving it up." He cupped her face and kissed her deeply. "I can go back to the Bureau anytime I want to, anytime they need me, and I will. I was getting too cynical and hard, Shea. I needed you to shake me up, make me see that about myself. I needed you to show me that there are more important things in life. And now I want to explore all of them, with you."

She returned his kiss and felt desire explode between them again. She had a feeling it would still be this way fifty years from now. "I love you, Renegade."

"And I love you." He kissed her one more time, then slanted her a grin as he pulled away and swung his feet over the side of the bed. "Let's move it, boss. There are chores waiting to be done."

Her heart melted with love as she returned the grin. "Since when did you get to be such a slave driver?"

"Since I fell in love with a rancher. She taught me everything I know about working hard." He lifted her to her feet and folded her close, kissing her again. "We've got a lot of work to do if we're going to be spending time with the next group of kids Miguel brings in. Especially since, next time, they won't have to hide in the cabin. So we'd better get started."

The sunset painted the cliffs a brilliant red as they walked out of the house a few minutes later. They stopped to watch, and Jesse murmured, "This is what I want for our children, and our children's children. To stand where we're standing right now, and be able to watch the sun setting in the same place. I want forever, Shea."

"It's ours, Jesse."

Shea wrapped her arms around his waist and leaned into him. As the colors darkened into the soft shades of dusk, she knew she was looking at the future. And it was perfect.

Epilogue

She stood in front of the mirror, smoothing one hand down the creamy antique lace and satin that had been her mother's wedding dress, and wondered what Jesse was doing. Was he thinking about her, waiting for her to appear at the top of the stairs? He'd better be, she told herself, grinning at her reflection in her mirror. Suddenly she couldn't wait to go downstairs to the living room, couldn't wait to stand in front of the minister and pledge herself to Jesse.

She picked up the bouquet of flowers that Abby Kane had gathered from her garden and closed her eyes as their fragrance washed over her. They smelled like summer in Cameron, like all that was good in her life. Then, taking a deep breath, she turned to Becca Farrell and said, "Ready to go?"

Becca smiled at her, and opened the door. "Anytime you are. You're the guest of honor, after all."

Becca headed down the stairs, but Shea paused before she followed, listening to the murmur of voices from the room below. All their friends were here, as well as their families. Jesse's mother had flown in from the east coast several days earlier. Her heart swelled with emotion, and she swallowed twice before she slowly started down the stairs.

The murmur of voices stopped abruptly as the first notes of the music she and Jesse had chosen rippled from the piano. Bach's "Jesu, Joy of Man's Desiring" spilled over her as she reached the bottom of the stairs. Her brother Devlin stepped forward to meet her, and she smiled at him as she took his arm.

As they paused in the doorway to the living room, her gaze swept past the minister and found Jesse, standing in front of him. He looked elegant in the dark gray suit and white shirt he wore, and far more handsome than anyone had a right to be. Her mouth went dry as she stared at him.

When their eyes met, Jesse stilled. Then his gaze swept over her with a hot, hungry intensity that made her quiver. She tightened her grip on Devlin's arm, then started down the small aisle to Jesse.

She didn't even look at Dev as he handed her to Jesse. The music faded away, but she hardly noticed. And she could barely tear her gaze away from Jesse when the minister started to speak.

Reluctantly, she turned to face the minister she'd known since she was a child. Jesse held her hand tightly, their fingers twined together. As she repeated the words the minister spoke, she turned to look at the man she loved.

He returned her gaze steadily, his love for her shining out of his face. When it was time to exchange rings, he slipped a plain, wide gold band around her finger, and she did the same for him. Then the minister said, "You may kiss your bride."

Jesse's mouth brushed over hers, a prayer and a promise. And before they could lose themselves in the kiss, he stepped away.

Shea felt her throat swelling as they turned to face their families and friends. She spotted Dev and Carly, grinning at her from the front row, along with her mother and Joe, Dusty and Levi. Becca stood with Grady and their two children right behind them. Cassie was holding three-week-old Tyler, beaming with pride at being the big sister. Abby and Damien Kane stood behind them, Damien holding Sarah as she slept peacefully in his arms.

Then Keara Carmichael began playing the piano again, this time Beethoven's "Ode to Joy," and Shea felt a prickle of tears as the music swelled around her. Swallowing once, she walked with Jesse to the back of the room, then turned and waited for Becca to follow. She embraced her friend with shaky arms, then waited for the rest of her friends and family to close around her.

An hour later, she stood with Jesse as they watched the people they loved gathered around them. Janie Murphy from Heaven on Seventh had insisted on catering the party as her wedding present to them, and she hurried in and out of the kitchen. Keara Carmichael, the music teacher from the elementary school who had asked to play the piano for the wedding, had quietly slipped away from the party, but everyone else had stayed, eating, talking and laughing.

Jesse bent over Shea and murmured, "Are they going to miss us if we leave?"

Shea smiled, but her heart began pounding beneath the lace of her mother's wedding dress. "I doubt it. Everyone's having too much fun. They'll be here for hours."

But instead of heading upstairs so they could change their clothes, Jesse led her to the front door. When they stepped out onto the porch, he closed the door behind them, closing out the sound of the crowd.

"I need to have you to myself for a few minutes," he said, bending to kiss her. "I haven't even had a chance to properly kiss my bride."

"You'll have me to yourself for four days in San Francisco." But she pressed against him, her mouth suddenly as hungry as his. When the kiss threatened to spiral out of control, Jesse broke it off and buried his face in her hair.

"You're my wife."

Shea heard the wonder in his voice, and closed her eyes against the tears that prickled against her eyelids again. Then ne leaned away, and she saw the devil dancing in his eyes. "My bride, the fugitive."

Her mouth curled into a slow, answering smile. "And lon't you forget it, either. Us fugitives are known to do desperate things."

"I can't wait." His eyes flared hot in the summer sun, and ne kissed her again. She felt the passion waiting to burst into ife, and hummed with an answering desire.

Jesse touched her face once more, then drew away. "Let's get one last look before we leave," he whispered, and they turned to watch the sunlight dance over the cliffs and the pastures. They stood for a long moment, savoring the sight, then turned and headed back into the house to begin the rest of their lives.

* * * * *

Be sure to look for
BEN AND JANIE'S LOVE STORY,
coming only to Silhouette Intimate Moments
in September.

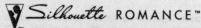

If you enjoyed what you just read,
then we've got an offer you can't resist!

Take 2 bestselling
love stories FREE!

Plus get a FREE surprise gift!

THE MacGREGORS ARE BACK!

#1 *New York Times* bestselling author

NORA ROBERTS

Presents...

THE MacGREGORS:
Daniel ~ Ian
April 1999

This book contains two wonderful stories.
The first features Ian and Alanna, when she
took him *In from the Cold.*
For Now, Forever features
the love story of the
infamous Daniel MacGregor
and his beloved Anna.

Available at your favorite retail
outlet, only from

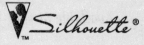

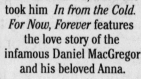

Coming in May 1999

BABY Fever

by
New York Times Bestselling Author

KASEY MICHAELS

When three sisters hear their biological
clocks ticking, they know it's
time for action.

But who will they get to father their babies?

Find out how the road to motherhood
leads to love in this brand-new collection.

Available at your favorite retail outlet.

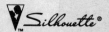

COMING NEXT MONTH

#925 CATTLEMAN'S PROMISE—Marilyn Pappano
Heartbreak Canyon
Guthrie Harris was shocked when Olivia Miles and her twin daughters showed up on his Oklahoma ranch—with a deed!—and claimed it was *their* home. But since they had nowhere else to go, the longtime loner let them stay. And the longer Olivia stuck around, the less Guthrie wanted her to leave—his home *or* his heart.

#926 CLAY YEAGER'S REDEMPTION—Justine Davis
Trinity Street West
Clay Yeager hadn't meant to trespass on Casey Scott's property—but he was glad he had. The emotions this ex-cop had kept buried for so long were back in full force. Then Casey became a stranger's target, and Clay knew the time had come to protect his woman. He was done with moving on—he was ready to move in!

#927 A FOREVER KIND OF COWBOY—Doreen Roberts
Rodeo Men
Runaway heiress Lori Ashford had little experience when it came to men. So when she fell for rugged rodeo rider Cord McVane, what she felt was something she'd never known existed. But would the brooding cowboy ever see that the night she'd discovered passion in his arms was just the beginning—of forever?

#928 THE TOUGH GUY AND THE TODDLER—Diane Pershing
Men in Blue
Detective Dominic D'Annunzio thought nothing could penetrate his hardened heart—until beautiful but haunted Jordan Carlisle needed his assistance. But Jordan wasn't just looking for help, she was looking for miracles. And the closer they came to the truth, the more Dom began wondering what was in charge of this case—his head or his heart?

#929 HER SECOND CHANCE FAMILY—Christine Scott
Families Are Forever
Maggie Conrad and her son were finally on their own—*and* on the run. But the small town of Wyndchester offered the perfect hideaway. Then the new sheriff, Jason Gallagher, moved in next door, and Maggie feared her secret wouldn't stay that way for long. Could Maggie keep her past hidden while learning that love *was* better the second time around?

#930 KNIGHT IN A WHITE STETSON—Claire King
Way Out West
Calla Bishop was desperate to save her family's ranch. And as the soon-to-be-wife of a wealthy businessman, she was about to secure her birthright. Then she hired Henry Beckett, and it wasn't long before this wrangler had roped himself one feisty cowgirl. But would Henry's well-kept secret cause Calla to hand over her beloved ranch—and her guarded heart?